Love on the Dark Side
A collection of paranormal erotica and romance from Black Lace

Look out for other themed Black Lace short-story collections

Already Published: *Sex in the Office, Sex on Holiday, Sex in Uniform, Sex in the Kitchen, Sex on the Move, Sex and Music, Sex and Shopping, Sex in Public, Sex with Strangers*

Love on the Dark Side

A collection of paranormal erotica and romance from Black Lace

Edited by Lindsay Gordon

Black Lace stories contain sexual fantasies.
In real life, always practise safe sex.

This edition published in 2007 by
Black Lace
Thames Wharf Studios
Rainville Road
London W6 9HA

What Witches Want	© Mathilde Madden
The Black Knight	© Olivia Knight
An Earthquake in Leamington Spa	© Kristina Lloyd
Stranger to my Shores	© Sophie Mouette
Lust for Blood	© Madelynne Ellis
Sun Seeking	© Janine Ashbless
Power Play	© Katie Doyce
The Shadow of Matthew	© Gwen Masters
Magic for Beginners	© Sabine Whelan
Sweet Dreams	© A.D.R. Forte
The Girl of his Dreams	© Heather Towne
To Stand between the Wild and the Human	© Teresa Noelle Roberts
Watching the Detective	© Portia Da Costa
All I Want for Christmas	© Mae Nixon
The End of the Pier	© Angel Blake

A catalogue record for this book is available from the British Library.

www.black-lace-books.com

Typeset by SetSystems Limited, Saffron Walden, Essex
Printed in the UK by CPI Bookmarque, Croydon, CR0 4TD

The paper used in this book is a natural, recyclable product made from
wood grown in sustainable forests. The manufacturing process conforms
to the regulations of the country of origin.

ISBN 978 0 352 34132 7

Distributed in the USA by Holtzbrinck Publishers, LLC, 175 Fifth Avenue,
New York, NY 10010, USA

Contents

Newsletter .... *vii*

What Witches Want Mathilde Madden *1*
The Black Knight Olivia Knight *19*
An Earthquake in Leamington Spa
Kristina Lloyd *38*
Stranger to My Shores Sophie Mouette *57*
Lust for Blood Madelynne Ellis *77*
Sun Seeking Janine Ashbless *93*
Power Play Katie Doyce *114*
The Shadow of Matthew Gwen Masters *136*
Magic for Beginners Sabine Whelan *151*
Sweet Dreams A.D.R. Forte *166*
The Girl of His Dreams Heather Towne *183*
To Stand between the Wild and the
Human Teresa Noelle Roberts *198*
Watching the Detective Portia Da Costa *217*
All I Want for Christmas Mae Nixon *235*
The End of the Pier Angel Blake *253*

Newsletter

Want to write short stories for Black Lace?

Please read the following. And keep checking our website or contact us for information on future editions.

- Your short story should be 4,000–6,000 words long and not published anywhere in the world – websites excepted.
- Thematically, it should be written with the Black Lace guidelines in mind.
- Ideally, there should be a 'sting in the tale' and an element of dramatic tension, with oodles of erotic build-up.
- The story should be about more than 'some people having sex' – we want great characterisation too.
- Keep the explicit anatomical stuff to an absolute minimum.

We are obliged to select stories that are technically faultless and vibrant and original – as well as fitting in with the tone of the series: upbeat, dynamic, accent on pleasure, etc. Our anthologies are a flagship for the series. We pride ourselves on selecting only the best-written erotica from the UK and USA. The key words are: diversity, surprises and faultless writing.

Competition rules will apply to short stories: you will hear back from us about your story *only* if it has been successful. We cannot give individual feedback on

short stories as we receive far too many for this to be possible.

For future collections check the Black Lace website.

If you want to find out more about Black Lace, check our website, where you will find our author guidelines and more information about short stories. It's at www.black-lace-books.com

Alternatively, send a large SAE with a first-class British stamp to:

Black Lace Guidelines
Virgin Books Ltd
Thames Wharf Studios
Rainville Road
London W6 9HA

What Witches Want
Mathilde Madden

'You know the worst thing about being a witch?' Lilith said, world-weariness chiming in her voice.

'The clothes? The religious intolerance? The cackling?' Cate didn't really want to be drawn into one of Lilith's circular conversations, but she didn't dare completely bail out either. Not after what had happened during the coven meeting. Lilith was clearly not in any mood to be trifled with. As usual.

'Men,' Lilith said, ignoring Cate's suggestions. 'Men just don't take you seriously if they know you're a witch. In fact, that's not quite right. They *do* take you seriously. *Too* seriously.'

'What?' Cate had always thought that man-troubles of the *Bridget Jones/Cosmo* variety were the least of the average witch's concerns. In fact, she tended to think – rather smugly – that witches had those particular problems solved. 'They take you too seriously? So what? Who cares? You're a witch. You can have any man you desire. You can appear before him as the answer to his heart's most secret prayers. You can charm him away from those he holds most dear.' Cate was starting to feel quite impassioned by the subject, and was only a couple of sentences away from jumping up and whirling around like Maria on a mountain top to emphasise her witches-have-it-all point.

'Yeah, I know. Obviously. I know I can bewitch them into doing my will,' said Lilith, digging her fingers into the earth and screwing up her long elegant nose, 'but that just isn't very *sexy*, is it?'

'Oh, I don't know.' Cate couldn't help smirking at the thought of the last man she'd treated to a week of willing servitude entranced by her latest glamour. Good times.

Lilith looked at Cate condescendingly and smoothed down her skirt. Lilith had a very strange dress sense for a witch. Witch fashion did vary, but mostly around the same floral, floaty, natural fibres axis. Cate had never met another witch who dressed like a businesswoman. Then again, Cate had never met another witch like Lilith.

Once Lilith seemed satisfied that her smartly tailored skirt was wrinkle free, she said, 'OK, maybe you get off on the my-wish-is-your-command-oh-mistress thing. And I'll admit it does have its moments. But sometimes I just want a man who's there of his own free will. Is that too much to ask? A man who's all muscle and grunt. You know a man who's all *man*. Who'll bend me over the kitchen counter and pull my hair back and damn well force his way in because he knows I want it. And who'll be so hard for me. And know that when he yanks my knickers down he'll find that, despite my protests and struggling, I'm soaking wet for him because I'm a filthy little cockteasing bitch and I just need a proper man to show me how to . . .' Lilith stopped and sighed.

Cate squinted and looked at her. 'Are you OK?'

'Fine, fine. It's just . . . it's hot today. Don't you think it's hot today?'

'Yes. Too hot. You want me to turn up the cloud cover?' Cate raised her fingers to the sky, poised to make magic.

Lilith waved her offer away. 'Oh, no, no. Don't bother. I like the heat.' She leant back against the tree behind her and rolled her head on the bark. 'But you know,' she said, 'you just can't get a man to do that if you're a witch.'

'Do what?'

'Do what I was just saying, bend me over the kitchen counter, yanking knickers, soaking wet, "I'll show you what happens to tarts like you, you little cockteasing bitch," etc, etc.'

'Oh, that. Well,' said Cate, 'if you want a man to do that . . . although, do you even have a kitchen counter?'

Lilith paused as if thinking for a second, then snapped her fingers. 'Have now!'

'OK, well, if you want a man to do that, find one, and bewitch him into doing it.'

'No! Not the same. It's not the same if I bewitch him into doing it. I want *him* to do it. I want the loss of control, that eager erection, grunt. I want him to want it. Desperately. I want to be overpowered, manhandled. I want to have no choice but to submit to his domineering macho will.'

Cate narrowed her eyes. Lilith was known for being left-field, talked about politely as being rather 'eccentric', but this was a new one. 'Erm . . . OK.'

'And, you know, I'm a sodding witch, a hugely powerful witch. Mistress of more than seventeen covens. How's he ever going to overpower me?'

Cate looked at Lilith and frowned. 'Um, well, I guess he can't. Not really. But it's just a fantasy, isn't it? Couldn't you pretend? Suspend your disbelief. Make believe.'

'But would he even dare? You know what a reputation witches have for avenging ourselves on men who have wronged us. What kind of a man is going to force his will on a woman as powerful as me?'

Cate laughed. Too easy. 'The kind who doesn't *know* how powerful she really is.'

'Ooh.' Lilith smiled. 'I like that idea. Find a man and

not tell him I'm a witch and wait for him to get masterful with me because he thinks I'm just a weak and powerless normal woman.'

Cate nodded. 'Yeah, just make sure you keep your cool.'

'What do you mean?'

'Well, you know, you'll be walking a dangerous line. Pretending you're not immeasurably powerful. Just don't, you know, lose your temper if it doesn't go just so.'

'What, you think he might spank me the wrong way and I'll turn around and smite him?' Lilith chuckled to herself.

'Well, you and smiting do tend to go hand in hand. I mean, just now, during the coven meeting, you eviscerated those poor people.'

'Well, they were very annoying.'

'They were just tourists. I think they must have wandered over by mistake. The cloaking spell must have had a hitch in it today.' Cate's gaze followed Lilith's to where the bodies of an overweight middle-aged couple were steaming softly in the sun. Cate was still talking. 'I mean who even eviscerates people these days? Talk about a way to start up the awkward questions. It's not like you don't have other options, with all the power you've got at your fingertips. You ever thought of trying something subtler when you get annoyed with people? I mean look at those creatures, we can't leave them like that.'

'Oh,' said Lilith, 'so that's why you're still here. You're waiting for me to leave so you can clean up my mess.'

'If, by "clean up your mess", you mean put that nice couple's vital organs back on the inside again, then yes, I am.'

'Well, if you're having a bit of a Glenda moment, I'll get out of your way,' said Lilith, getting to her spike-heeled feet and brushing the dirt off her manicured hands. 'It's time to put my perfect plan into action and find a man who doesn't know how powerful I really am.' She set off with a spring in her elegantly shod step.

'Just keep your cool,' Cate called after her, before turning her attention to waking the dead.

Lilith's house was wherever she wanted it to be and whatever she wanted it to be. Yesterday she'd lived in a gigantic castle of snow and ice, staffed by creatures that were a cross between male models and polar bears. That had been fun – if somewhat shallow. And cold.

Perhaps that was why she wanted cosy today. She walked a short way through the Botanical Gardens, rounded a clump of trees and found herself clipping up the path of a dear little cottage. Perfect. She walked in through the rose-framed front door and saw a roaring fire, a bubbling cauldron, a cat asleep on the hearth rug. An incongruous kitchen counter was floating in mid-air next to the back door. Lilith frowned and it vanished apologetically. Then she settled herself into a rocking chair by the fire to start planning.

First she needed a man. She flicked through some in her mind. Men her memory had stored and filed. She rejected the first few out of hand. She knew exactly what she wanted. Not necessarily good looking. Looks were nice but they weren't everything. This was mainly about finding someone with the right attitude. Someone with grunt. To put it bluntly, someone who was a bit of a bastard.

When she finally found him, sitting in a corner of her mind, she knew at once. Something in that fine-boned face, that sneering mouth, that unkempt dark hair grazing his collar. She knew just where to find him.

* * *

Lilith had been worried about how to get a man's attention without using magic. But the bar-room pick-up had been easy.

They'd already exchanged names – his was Blake and he hadn't baulked at Lilith – now all she had to do was keep the conversation going until Blake let loose with his barely contained masculine desire and slammed her up against the nearest wall. Her heart beat a little faster at the prospect.

'What do you do?' she said to him.

'You wouldn't believe me if I told you,' he said. Then he leant closer. 'But you don't really need to worry about what I *do*, baby, so much as what I'm going to do *to you.*'

Oh, he was such a good choice. Lilith's mouth got a little drier. She found herself looking at Blake's tie and wondering how easy it would be to persuade him to use it to fasten her wrists to her bedframe. She did some quick mental magic to make sure that she had the right kind of bedframe.

A few minutes of flirting later, Blake said, 'So, baby, your place or mine?'

Lilith bit her lip as coyly as she could and said, 'I'd really like to see you in my new bed.'

Lilith's home was now a second-floor flat in a converted Victorian terrace.

'So,' said Blake, when he was standing in the middle of the modern-but-with-homely-touches sitting room, 'what are you in the mood for, babe?'

Lilith wet her bottom lip with her tongue. 'Well, that depends. What do you want?'

'What do *I* want?'

'Yes,' said Lilith, 'what do you want with me, big boy?'

'Big boy?'

Lilith frowned. Blake wasn't really a big boy at all. He was hard and muscular and masculine with hair like a dark mane and a mouth that seemed to quirk into a sneer all too easily, but he wasn't much taller than Lilith herself. 'Well, OK, perhaps that's not the phrase exactly,' said Lilith, 'but you're still a man. All man. Why don't you just do as men do? Um, you know – for want of a better way of expressing it – take me.' And she spread her arms wide, inviting.

Blake took a step back. 'Do as men do? Take you? Look, babe, OK, couple of things. First of all, what the fuck? And second, and rather more to the point, you, darling, are a bloody witch.'

'Oh. How did you . . . ?'

Blake rolled his eyes. 'It's obvious. You act like a witch and talk like a witch and look like a witch – well, apart from the suit, which is rather a cut above the jumble-sale look that witches wear. Look, you even have a witch's name.'

'Actually, most witches have very ordinary names.'

'Sure, sure, I know that, but even so. Look, babe, you might have fooled a civilian or a non-believer, but I'm in the business, baby. Sorry.'

'In the business?'

'In the paranormal business. I'm a werewolf hunter.'

'Oh,' Lilith said, her heart sinking.

'Hey, don't look like that, babe. I mean we can still have a good time. Have sex. Obviously. If that's what you actually want. But I'm not about to push any of my desires on a witch because that's just fatal. So if it's one of *those* traps, I'm not falling in, sorry.'

'What traps?'

'Those traps for arrogant men. Oh, you must know. Witch pretends to be a normal woman, picks up a guy and then, when he gets too domineering, he ends up living the rest of his life in a pond.'

'Oh, *those* traps.' Lilith smiled slightly. Those traps were amusing. But also annoying if Blake wasn't going to give her what she wanted because he was scared of falling into one. She sat down on the beige sofa. 'It really isn't one of those traps. The whole point of the operation tonight *was* to find a guy who didn't know I was a witch, but not so I could trap him – just so I could have a good time.'

'Don't witches always have a good time?'

'No! Why does no one get this? Look, when did you know I was a witch?'

'About ten seconds after you started talking to me.'

'And if I hadn't been a witch would you still have come home with me?'

Blake looked a little puzzled by the question. 'Of course.'

'Are you sure? As soon as you knew I was a witch, you knew you had to come home with me if I wanted you to, right?'

'Um, well, I guess.'

'Well, that's the thing. I don't want you to be here because you know I'm a witch. I want you to be here because you *want* to be.'

'What? I swear I want to be here. I'm not trying to leave, am I?'

'Yeah, in case I eviscerate you.'

'I don't think you're going to ... Uh, you're not going to eviscerate me, are you?'

Lilith shrugged. Blake looked pale. Lilith said, 'See, that's the problem too. I can't go two minutes without making you afraid of me and if you're afraid of me you're hardly going to put me over your knee and spank me, are you?'

Blake's throat moved as he swallowed hard. 'You want me to spank you? You're a witch!'

Lilith sighed. There was something so appealing

about this taut conundrum of a guy, who was wearing a suit that flowed over his body like it was in love with him and yet appeared not to have brushed his over-exuberant hair for a fortnight. 'What do you do with the werewolves?' she said. 'Do you always kill them or do you ever capture them and keep them?'

'Rarely. Well, I do sometimes capture and keep them, but I'm not meant to. It's not policy.'

'What do you do with the ones you capture?'

Blake's face went cold, like the shutters had come down. 'Extract information.'

'How do you do that?'

'Various methods. And I know where you're going with this, but they're werewolves. Outside full moon they're no more powerful that the average pissed-off human. But it's different with you, Miss Witch. One false move, you'll flay me.'

'Oh, please try not to think like that,' Lilith said. 'So, do you tie them up?'

'Who?'

'The werewolves.'

Blake narrowed his eyes. 'Are you serious? You want me to tie you up?'

Lilith nodded vigorously.

'But, what'd be the point? You're a witch. It's not like I could make you *actually* helpless. If that was what I wanted. If that wasn't a ridiculously stupid thing to try and do. Even,' he added with heavy emphasis, 'if the witch *claims* she wants you to.'

Lilith wet her lips. She'd seen a little chink then. A little bit of something that said he was warming to the idea. But it was only the tiniest thing. She knew she still had a long way to go. She sighed. 'Well, that's just it, isn't it? I want a man to be all, I don't know, mannish with me and the minute he finds out I'm a witch . . .'

'Well, OK, I rumbled you, but you won't be so unlucky

next time. Try again. Find someone else who doesn't know how powerful you really are.'

Lilith stamped her foot. 'I don't want to try again. I chose *you*. I want you. I want you to overpower me and fuck me hard. Right now.'

'Overpower . . . ? What? Bend you over the table and rip your knickers down?'

'Yes! Damn it, yes. Forget about my powers. We'll pretend I don't have them.'

Blake was breathing a little more heavily now. He was still standing in the middle of the room, squarely facing the sofa where Lilith sat. Lilith's eyes flickered to his crotch.

'But what if I get it wrong?' Blake said, with every part of his voice sounding like resignation. 'What if I bend you over and rip your knickers off and spank you and pull you hair and fuck you hard and one of those things is the wrong thing and you turn around and go all black-eyes and uber-powered and give me sodding small pox or something? Witches aren't exactly known for their restraint.'

'I could mind-wipe you,' Lilith said suddenly. 'Make you forget I'm a witch.'

'Won't work. You didn't tell me you were a witch, I worked it out. Take away that knowledge and I'll just work it out again.'

'Unless . . .'

Blake interrupted. 'Well, unless you take away all my knowledge of the paranormal, which would leave me unable to do my job.'

Lilith shrugged. 'Well, I'm sorry about that, but it might just be the only option.'

Blake raised his eyes to the ceiling. 'Great . . .' he said, tailing off as if words failed him. 'Well, that's just great.'

'OK, OK,' Lilith said, 'I have another idea. How about this? What if I remove my powers – temporarily – and place them in a suitable receptacle? Would that make you feel safe enough to bend me over backwards?'

Blake frowned. 'Can witches do that?'

'Witches can do anything. That's kind of the point of witches. I can make the dead walk and the seas boil. I can alter the fabric of the universe. I think I can put my magical powers in that vase without too much trouble.' She pointed at a cheery little pink pot stuffed with white roses.

Blake glanced over his shoulder at the vase and then looked back at her. His eyes were inscrutable. 'How would you get your powers back? With no magic to do the spell?'

Lilith shrugged. 'Break the vase.'

'What if you come after me then? When you're all powered up again.'

'What are you thinking of doing to me?' Lilith laughed. 'I won't. You know I won't. You know I want this. All you're scared of is my temper. The heat of the moment. But this way I won't be able to smite you in anger and, afterwards, when I restore my powers, you know I'm going to be thanking you. Are you really telling me that a man like you – a werewolf hunter, no less – is going to pass up this opportunity to fuck a witch harder than any other mortal man has ever dared to? And then have her thank him for it afterwards?'

One corner of Blake's mouth twitched into a half-smile for a moment. Just up and then down again. But it was enough for Lilith to know she'd cracked it. 'Well, in that case . . .' he said, crossing the room and straddling Lilith's tailored lap. He leant in and kissed her.

When he pulled back from the kiss, he shook his head lightly. 'I don't know quite what it is, baby,' he whispered. 'I still think this is a scary, hair-raisingly-dumb idea, but something about you must appeal to my better nature. You're getting to me. But I think you'd better do your magic trick before you get to me much more and I jump the gun and screw you while you're still a fucking powderkeg.'

Lilith felt herself actually shiver with delight. She slipped out from underneath Blake and went over to the small table where the vase sat. She emptied it of flowers (manually) and water (magically) and then used a little more concentration and care to perform the second, far more complex, magical procedure.

Once it was done she looked over at Blake. 'Gosh, that feels really weird. I'm so *empty*.'

'I'll bet.'

Lilith swayed a little and clutched at the edge of the small table. 'I think I'd better sit down.'

'Perhaps you'd better lie down.'

'Bedroom's through ...' The end of Lilith's sentence disappeared as her legs gently melted away underneath her. But Blake was already zipping across the room to catch her in his strong arms.

Blake threw her down on the bed amongst a patchwork bedspread and heart-shaped pillows. As Lilith woozily took in the froufrou around her, she wondered what her subconscious mind must have been thinking when she created this as her seduction den for a macho brute of a man.

But she stopped caring about that pretty quickly when she looked up at Blake, already on top of her in his dark-blue suit, caging her with his strong wiry body. He pushed his messy dark hair out of the way with one hand as he moved in and kissed her hard, hard and demandingly down into the mattress.

His mouth was hot on hers and devouring. His erection was rubbing against her thigh. She could feel every part of his firm body, heavier, stronger, harder than hers. And the taste of him in her mouth – the cigarettes and whisky from the bar, the last shreds of his fear, the overwhelming swirl of his arrogance. He took her wrists and pinned them up above her head. Then he made it clear that he was kissing her at *his* pace, for *his* pleasure – if what he was doing was also turning her into a breathless, writhing mess, trapped underneath him, that was just coincidence.

Then his mouth found her ear. 'Is this what you wanted, witch? Like this? To know how it feels to have a man controlling you? Using you? Needing you? To feel his hard dick pressing against you and to know that he is going to use your body to get himself off, no matter what you think about it.'

Lilith moaned out loud.

Blake released Lilith's hands and sat up and back, still straddling her. He started to remove his jacket. She watched him idly, boneless with lust. He dropped the jacket on the floor and started on his tie.

'Now,' he said, 'didn't we have an idea about tying you up? I really don't want you to get any ideas about slipping away from me and smashing that vase if I do anything you don't like. I could just pin you down all evening, but I think this would make things more straightforward. And a lot more fun.'

With his tie in his hand, he leant forwards in his shirt sleeves and fastened Lilith's wrists together neatly. Then he hitched them – up and over her head – to the swirly wrought-iron bed-head.

'Something tells me you're not a bondage novice,' Lilith said, twisting her wrists in the slick cool fabric.

'Werewolves, witches, I guess roping up one human-oid paranormal is the same as another.' He dipped his head and ran the tip of his tongue across her cheek. The move ended in a kiss. If it hadn't, Lilith might have said something about witches being *actual* humans not humanoids. But her mouth was suddenly full of the delicious deviant taste of Blake and she didn't – *couldn't* – say a word.

When Blake stopped kissing her and moved to nip at her ear, she still didn't get the chance to speak – not that there was much she wanted to say beyond 'yes' and 'more' and 'please' – because Blake slipped a hand over her mouth before he hissed into her ear, 'I know you'll have left yourself another way into your power base, witch.'

Blake raised his head a little and Lilith looked at him with wide eyes.

'I know you'll have left yourself a way to break that vase without getting off the bed. Thing is,' he added with a low nasty tone, 'I'm almost certain that what you've left yourself is a word, a verbal command, and that's pretty useless if you can't talk.'

With a muffled protest, Lilith tried to pull her head away from the hand over her mouth, but he was too strong, far too strong, even stronger than she had estimated. He clamped his hand more tightly, squeezing the bottom half of her face hard. Leaning down, he licked her cheek just on the edge of where it wasn't covered by his hand, then he ran his tongue down in the crack between two of his fingers and managed to lick her top lip. Lilith moaned.

'Magic words, safe words, whatever you call them, neither is a lot of use to you now are they, witch?'

This added layer of helplessness just made the burn between Lilith's legs intensify. She bucked her hips against Blake and he reached down with his free hand and slid her skirt up her body. Its silky lining skated frictionless against the slick of her stockings. It was up around her waist in moments. Then she was just knickers and lace stocking-tops under his sober suit trousers. Blake clearly liked her dishevelled because he smiled and started to unbutton her shirt one-handed, while she panted against his other palm which was still stopping her mouth.

When her shirt was open so wide she might as well not be wearing it, he started alternating between biting the angles of her neck and shoulder, and sitting back and stroking the skin that covered the top of her breasts. He laughed when he bit her so hard she screamed into his fingers.

Eventually, he said, 'You know, witch, I really can't keep this up. I'm going to have to stop your mouth with something else.'

Lilith squirmed. Blake knelt up astride her and – in a last bit of one-handed expertise – had his trousers and underpants down in moments. Lilith saw his cock jutting out from under the hem of his shirt – bold and hard – as he moved towards her. And then the hand on her mouth was gone and she had enough of a moment to take one big breath before he grabbed a handful of her hair and forced his cock deep into her mouth.

Lilith gasped and struggled again, pulling at the tie holding her wrists, trying not to choke.

'Take it,' Blake grunted. 'Come on, witch, suck my dick.' His voice seemed to crack a little with the words.

Lilith looked up at him looming over her. He grinned down and let go of her hair for a moment to yank his shirt off over his head.

Lilith saw his upper body for the first time then, compact, muscled and hard. There was something nasty about his physique. Something brutal.

'Maybe after I come in your mouth I could find something else to gag you with,' Blake panted as he thrust mercilessly into her throat, bracing himself against the wall behind the headboard. 'Your fancy underwear maybe? Then you'd really be helpless. *Powerless*. I could leave you here for as long as I wanted then. Days. How would you like that? Imagine what they'd say at work if

I told them I had a witch for a prisoner, tied to the bed, just aching for another chance to suck my dick.'

Lilith moaned around the taut flesh filling her mouth. Blake tasted like oceans and dark places, like basements and fear. Blake tasted like a man who had stared at things that even a witch might turn away from. Masculine pride and arrogance, slugs and snails and puppy dog tails.

He sneered down at her. 'I could just take your old magic vase of powers somewhere safe, witch. Far away. Make sure it never got broken. Put it in a vault somewhere.'

Lilith gasped and, in that moment, as she broke the vacuum seal around his cock, he withdrew, and whispered, 'Going to fuck you now, witch.'

He slid down her body, slipped her damp knickers out of the way and drove into her, coasting on her wetness. His hands were gripping her taut bound arms. His mouth now the thing keeping her quiet.

When he began to move – to fuck her as promised – it was hard and nasty. Harder than any man who valued his entrails should ever fuck a witch. Lilith squirmed under him. Desperate.

'God,' Blake said, breaking the kiss, 'you are so fucking wet for me. You love this, don't you? You love me inside you?'

'Uh, yes.'

'Fucking say it, witch.'

'I love you inside me.'

Blake moved his face closer and sneered. 'You love me in control. Say it.'

'I love you in control.'

'You love my hard dick,' he panted.

'I love your hard dick,' Lilith managed, panting so hard now she could barely speak at all. Blake moved down to kiss her again. She wanted more. She wanted to come. Like this. Tied up. With him on her, driving into her, holding her and owning her and making her confess her darkest desires. She moaned into Blake's mouth.

Blake moved his head back and looked at her, still thrusting. 'You going to come for me, witch?'

Lilith nodded.

Blake's right hand was moving then, down, down between their bodies and into place. One expertly crooked finger giving her exactly what she needed.

Another thrust, and another. She was so close. Then Blake said, 'Come on, witch, now. For me. Give it to me.' And she was there. Coming up to meet him.

Blake was winding his way lazily back into his clothes. Shirt, trousers, jacket. His tie was still tight around Lilith's wrists. Lilith knew she was post-orgasm and kind of loved-up hazy, but she couldn't stop staring at his body as he dressed. He really was magnificent on his own small scale.

'Are you going to untie me now?' she said.

Blake stared at her. He was fully dressed now and he let his eyes glide over her stockings and wide-open shirt.

'Blake?'

Blake started. 'Yeah, I guess.' But he didn't move.

'Well, come on, then.'

Blake walked over and took hold of her bindings, then stopped and swallowed hard. 'OK, now you promise that as soon as you've got your powers back you're not going to eviscerate me, or anything, right?'

'Course not. You know, all that vengeful, knee-jerk over-the-top stuff is really out of fashion, anyway. Who really eviscerates people these days? If I wanted to make you miserable, Blake, if I had any reason to, you'd never even know for sure if it was me that had done it.'

'But you don't have any reason to, right?'

'Right.'

Blake still didn't move.

'Oh, for God's sake,' Lilith said.

Lilith cast three spells at once. One to whisk the tie from her wrists to around Blake's neck, one to dress herself and one to put the kettle on. Then she looked at Blake.

Blake looked back at her, his mouth slightly open.

'Oh,' said Lilith, 'yeah, about that thing I told you about putting my powers in the vase. Well, I didn't *actually* do that. It would have been stupid, anyway. And dangerous. I've only just met you.'

Blake was staring at her, his mouth hanging open a little. He closed it. 'You tricked me,' he said.

'Kind of, except I also did just exactly what you told me to do. I just found myself someone who didn't know how powerful I *really* was. Turned out I didn't really have all that far to look.'

Lilith, Blake and Cate also appear in Mathilde Madden's Silver Werewolf trilogy: *The Silver Collar*, *The Silver Crown* and *The Silver Cage*. For more details please visit www.mathildemadden.co.uk

The Black Knight Olivia Knight

Once upon a time, there was a hero of most unusual qualities, known as the Black Knight. He was as beautiful as the night, with long silky hair like the sky spangled with stars. His long limbs were as lithe and swift as a deer's. On the battlefields, his bravery was famous, and every knight would rather fight at his side than anyone else's. His quick eye, fast reflexes and dexterity with both sword and bow had saved many of his countrymen's lives – and ended many of their enemies'.

If all this had made him swagger, the other knights would've hated him. In fact, he was quiet and unassuming when he joined them in the taverns, and uncomfortable when attention was drawn to his daring exploits. The prettiest girls always clustered near his table, and bright eyes darted his way invitingly – but, even then, the other men were content. He had eyes for these beauties, to be sure, but he was wholly faithful to his own true love.

The spurned lovelies were usually happy to salve their pride with the attentions of the other knights, with hair and talk a little coarser, but still powerful men for all that. Later in the night, with muscular hairy thighs scraping hard between their own more delicate legs, pinned down by the heaving sweaty beefy weight, they thought it was just as well – the Black Knight was a shade too womanly, and might not have such a hefty slab of meat as this to offer a girl.

So the years went by, with the other men revelling in the wenches, while the Black Knight's fame continued to spread. Before long, the stories held him to be the most lovely, the most chaste and the most skilful man ever to exist. Though he was much embarrassed by these tales, nothing he did disproved them.

His own love, Lily, lived with her mother in a quiet valley far from the kingdom's castle. There she gathered herbs and made potions, as well as the usual homely tasks: feeding, healing and slaughtering the livestock; curing meat and scraping skins; planting, weeding and harvesting the vegetables; picking and preserving fruits; making bread, soap, candles and cheese; scrubbing and sweeping; spinning, knitting, weaving and dyeing; sewing, cleaning and mending clothes; and so on. She had a lock of her darling knight's black hair, which she treasured, rubbing its softness against her cheek late at night when she longed for him.

Whenever his duties permitted, the Black Knight leapt on to his fast horse and galloped all day and night to visit her. Then Lily laid aside her work and they walked together, dreaming of the day when they could be man and wife. She was still a little too young, he was still a little too poor, the King could not yet spare him, the borders were being challenged again ... For three years, this continued, and it was always to be next spring, next autumn ... until it seemed the day would never come.

Her mother was a wise woman, as well as the wise-woman. She made sure her daughter knew enough of the rhythms of life to avoid being embarrassed before her wedding day by an early guest. The Black Knight and his true love lay down in the forest, in summertime, and he disproved the suspicions of the tavern wenches as he made her wail and screech with his thick staff. One sunny afternoon, they discovered that kisses could be even sweeter when mouths didn't meet. They were elated and shocked by their invention, and she saw all the stars of the universe in the hair on his bowed head. The mother, seeing the cloud of birds frightened into the skies from the treetops, smiled to herself as she rocked and wove her wool on the cottage porch. In winter, whenever the Black Knight visited, the mother would remember an urgent visit to an invalid. Then, by the fireside, on the pile of rag-rugs and warm woollen blankets that the two women had made, in the close smoky air of the little cottage, he would prove his love for Lily again and again. Her mother always paused at the path's summit, to see the steam that billowed from the snowy cottage, and smiled.

Now the king's need of the Black Knight was no invention to keep his best fighter close. The little kingdom was hard pressed by its neighbour, which was ruled by a sorcerous queen. She used her dark arts to impart strength to her fighting men, and her cruelty to ensure they would always fear her more than death. Even her beauty was torture to them: her black dresses always cut low, her talons and lips crimson, her black crown of spikes resting high on her imperious brow.

The sorceress enjoyed the battles. Sometimes she watched from her horse on a hill crest, other times as a screeching crow, discernible from the other carrion-eaters by her crimson beak and claws. She savoured the bloody pitting of man against man, the straining muscles and spraying sweat of their toughened bodies. Less pleasing was how the Black Knight cut down her best knights. He lent courage to his comrades and darted nimbly through the press of bodies, playing both archer and swordsman, bringing death to her forces from far and near.

One spring day, watching from the clifftop, it seemed at last she would win. The Black Knight was hemmed in, unable to help his own side for fear of his life, and the black-armoured men were pushing the king's forces steadily back. Then – the effrontery took her breath away – *in the midst of battle*, he broke off from returning the sword strokes of his adversaries. Dancing and leaping over the cold steel thrusts, he whipped an arrow from his quiver, fitted it to his bow, and pointed it – upwards. At *her*. Before she could even grasp his intent, the arrow was flying through the air and had buried itself in her gown. Flung from her horse, she was knocked out cold and did not see the remainder of the fight. By all accounts (reluctantly and bloodily obtained), her men had believed her dead and fled the field. She was gravely wounded, and any mere mortal would've no doubt died. As it was, she took two months to recover, nursing herself and her hatred in equal proportions.

For the Black Knight, those were months of purest happiness. As soon as possible, he escaped the celebratory banners and drunken feasting at the castle, readied his horse and sped towards his love. In the heavy warmth of Lily's breasts, he drowned out the memories of bloodied flesh. The song of her ecstatic screams replaced the echo of battle in his ears. All her gentle, long, soft body wrapped him in its welcoming embrace. Peace, it seemed, had come at last, and the time of war was over – the time for love had begun. They set a date in midsummer for their marriage and began the preparations for a feast and celebration worthy of the king's greatest knight being wedded to his one true love.

The first day that the sorceress was strong enough to walk on the ramparts, she was consumed with bitterness. The farms were long neglected during her campaigns. Swathes of forest lay scarred and bare. The king's lands were rich and fertile, and she longed for them. It was all the fault of that damnable, beautiful knight! If only he were dead ... But imagining his mangled corpse only made her sigh over the waste. He should be *hers*, not fighting against her, but using all that limber strength to please her. How powerful those slim limbs would be! How pared and graceful his bare body would look, spread on her sheets. That long black hair would curtain her face as he sank into her in quiet worship. His only weapon would be between his legs, leaping up in fat readiness ... She rang her bell wildly. 'Send me Sir Garth,' she ordered. All night long she rode her knight, using him repeatedly while he sweated with fear lest he fail her – whether by weakening or by coming. She bucked and screeched, ordering him into this position and that, all the while imagining the Black Knight.

At dawn, she fell at last into a feverish exhausted sleep. Sir Garth miserably put an end to his longing, his fist working fast and furtively, and crept from the ghastly woman's bed with his shame cupped in his palm.

The Black Knight's wedding present for Lily was to be a silver brooch to hold the lock of his hair, which he would ask her to twine with her own. Then the two would lie curled together, the gold and the black, encased in silver. When he took the king's wedding invitation, he planned to detour past a silversmith, leave instructions and on the way back collect the finished piece.

He set off early in the morning, and Lily came out in her long nightgown to wish him farewell. He clasped her close, feeling the loose weight of her breasts beneath the fabric, and thought with longing how soon they would rest against him every night.

'Ow!' cried Lily at a sharp pain in her scalp, as a black bird flew away, the shining threads of hair caught in its crimson beak. 'That bird pulled out my hair!'

'It's so golden that even the magpies can't resist its lure,' replied her lover, chuckling and kissing the little injury tenderly.

All day he rode, thinking dreamily of his beloved. It occurred to him that he had never yet kissed the soft skin behind her knees, though he'd often admired it when he lifted her legs high and slid back and forth inside her. When he returned, he promised himself, he would amend that oversight. He'd raise her leg, her skirt slipping over her thighs, and brush his lips over the soft crease of skin. Then he'd raise the other leg, and her skirts would tumble further ... The fantasy spun on pleasantly, so that by sundown he hurt with need for her. He lay by his fire, under a thin blanket, and let his hand wander inside his trousers, his mind full of his darling Lily, as he had done so often before. Soon, it would never be necessary again ... He began to plan their wedding night while his hand stroked, but he got no further than undressing her before he came with a long shuddering groan.

The silversmith's village was near the sorceress's lands, and the knight shook his head at the sharp difference between these healthy fields and those neglected stretches. He lodged in the local tavern, where his identity was quickly discovered and many drinks pressed on him. Even one of the women, exceptionally beautiful and forward, insisted on buying him a glass of golden mead. He accepted it, not wanting to embarrass her in public, but said, 'My fiancée will be very grateful to all these good people for their kindness to me.'

If she was disappointed, she didn't show it. Instead, she was coolly charming, entertaining him with her witty cruel humour. He noticed how lovely her dark hair was, how pale her skin. The merciless perfection of her beauty cut the eyes, and her painted smirk suggested she was knowledgeable, too. He glanced at her plump half-naked breasts, and imagined releasing and handling them ... At that, he decided the mead had gone to his head, and withdrew to his room.

The drink had only just started to take effect, however. By midnight, its hold was firm. She made her way into his darkened room, where he lay sleepless and consumed with lust for the raven-haired lovely. When her naked body insinuated itself next to his, a wave of fire swept through him. With a quick pantherlike twist of his elegant body, he held her pinned beneath him, his knee forcing her thighs apart. Delighted, she fought a little, straining her arms which he held fixed by the wrists, struggling to keep her thighs together. She would have the chaste knight force himself on her – and her groin melted at the thought.

They wrestled, skin rubbing, as she tested his strength. He was lost to everything in the darkness, his hunger to take her like a roaring in his ears. All he could think of was the sweetness of spearing her, whatever her resistance. Her hard nipples crushed against his chest as they fought – she was using her whole strength in earnest now, full of glee that he was so much more powerful – and it spurred him into a frenzy. His knee forced her open, his hips wriggled into the gap, and with one hard shove he sank to the hilt. Then he roared with pleasure, bucking and heaving in her slippery clasp.

He fucked hot and hard, thinking only of his gratification, the girl a mere sheath and a succulent shape to titillate him. He rode her to the crest of his pleasure, and shot his hot seed into her, then found it was not enough. After two minutes of gasping to catch his breath on top of her, his cock was painfully hard again without so much as withdrawing. Feral with lust, he began to slam into her again, squelching in his own juices. She was screaming, in pain or orgasm or both, he hardly cared, except that the sound made him even harder. He howled murderously as he came.

Through all that night, he kept taking her with his full brutal strength. Though he hardly cared to notice, her own orgasms kept pace with him five to one. Truly, the Black Knight was everything the sorceress had hoped and imagined.

The news quickly spread that the Black Knight had abandoned his true love for the sorceress and the kingdom he had defended for the enemy land. He lived with her in her castle, and her little cups of mead, always seasoned with a snippet of the precious golden hair, enslaved him. Every waking hour, he was consumed with lust for her, obeying her spell to the letter. He hauled up her skirts as she stood looking over the ramparts, and took her from behind. He seized her in the corridors; he dropped to his knees before her throne, and pushed his head between her thighs in front of everyone; he lay on her bed, splayed and lovely, permanently erect, gazing at her with hunger. The time was ripe to attack the king's lands, she knew, but it could wait . . . The Black Knight's hefty staff, always throbbing and ready to split her, could not.

Lily wept bitterly. Her wedding day, so close at last, had been snatched away; her lover, so famous for his fidelity, was screwing the enemy queen with – by all reports – unquenchable passion, little caring who saw his clench-ing buttocks or pistoning cock. She was fortunate, how-ever, to have a mother as clear-headed as she was far-sighted. The mother reasoned that only a spell could have torn the Black Knight from his beloved's side, and made him behave so out of character. Through her work as a wisewoman, she knew just what sort of spell, too.

It was not an art she ever practised, however the local maidens pleaded – love-spells are blackest magic.

In the lulls between her daughter's stormy sobs, she spoke reason. She knew the terms and requirements of the spell. It relied on the beloved's hair – that, for a start, guaranteed his love was true. The very extent of his lust for the queen proved how much he adored and desired Lily. The two women shaved Lily's golden hair, burnt it and kept her bald, letting it be known as the girl's way of mourning. Furthermore, the spell governed only the Black Knight's waking hours; it could not extend to his sleep. This was where her lock of his hair came in – not for a love-spell, which her mother would never perform, but there are other ways to use hair.

In the hot dog-days of harvest-time, even the nights were sweltering. There was no work in the sorceress's fields, for nothing had been planted, but the Black Knight ploughed her thoroughly and harvested their screams of pleasure. They lay asleep, their heads at opposite sides of the bed, their genitalia still clasped. The Black Knight's back bore long scratches from the queen's scarlet talons. She, splayed on her back, had a mouth swollen with kisses and slaps, and suckering bruises all over her breasts. The sheets were damp with their violent sweat. The door to the balcony stood open, letting in the scant breeze, and the moon stood high and small in the sky. The Black Knight dreamt.

In his dream, he lay by a fire on the roadside, dreaming. Twice asleep, he was twice removed from wakefulness. He dreamt with longing of a girl he'd just left, reliving their moments together. They'd followed the river deep into the forest, to a pool where the canopy of trees parted and midday sun fell on the water. The girl was tall, with golden hair, and beautifully formed. Most importantly, she was as gorgeous and desirable as only true love can be.

Teasing him, because she knew his long absence had made him ache fiercely, she darted out of his grasp and danced a few steps away to the edge of the water. Then she unbuttoned her gown under his eager eyes. Her light shift was almost transparent in the sunshine, showing the shape of the curving hips that he longed to be held within. She turned her back on him – he could just make out the slope of her buttocks, and sighed with longing to hold them against him – and she dived into the pool. He tore off his own clothes, clumsy with haste, his cock parallel to the ground. She stood up to her waist in the water, the wet white shift clinging in translucent folds to her breasts and hardened nipples. Trembling, slender and graceful, his shaft disproportionately thick, he waded towards her. The ends of her long hair were turned darker gold by the water and curled. She let him reach her, and his hands rose to cup her breasts as his head bent down to her mouth. The little gasp as his palms brushed her nipples was all he needed to hear.

Their mouths clashed fiercely, while shrieking moans flew like swallows from her. Together they fought the wet clinging fabric up to her waist, and as her thighs parted the cold slid over her opening. She wailed, falling back as he caught her and drew her towards the waiting spear. He pulled her slowly on to him, wedging her open. The heat of each other's skin supplanted the chill of the water inch by inch, until all of him was inside her and she was speechless. His strong arms supported her watery weight, keeping her lying on the surface, tugging her backwards and forwards on his cock, the water sloshing over her breasts.

Each time he withdrew, his exposed shaft was cooled by the water, then buried again in her slippery heat. She sobbed with joy. Her eyes fluttered open to see his lovely face, falling hair, steamy eyes, parted lips – then rolled backwards and closed, as a new thrust brought her closer to the peak. For so many nights, he'd dreamt of her body yielding to him again that now he could barely control himself. All he wanted was to let go and spurt plentifully inside her, but more than that he wanted to make her come repeatedly. Withdrawing further, he used the cold water to keep himself in check, though the sight of her was nearly driving him over the edge. She was writhing and wriggling against him, contracting so hard as she wailed that suddenly he could hold back no more. He pushed harder, thrusting all his length inside as a long pure scream tore out of her mouth. High above them, from the trees, all the birds took flight in fright as the two lovers capsized in orgasm.

In his dream, he woke by the fire on the roadside, the piercing song of passion sharp in him, his cock splattering his chest with purest lust. What strength it took to journey away from his darling Lily. Only the prospect of making the land safe for her to live in could induce him to do so.

'My darling . . .' he groaned softly, his arms so empty without her.

'I'm here,' he heard her whisper. 'Soon . . .'

He woke in the queen's bed, disentangled from her in his restless sleep. Unsure where he was, but peaceful, he watched the dawn through the open door. The edges of a few drifting clouds were burnt pale gold by the still unseen sun. The colour stabbed strangely at his heart. He lifted himself on to one elbow, a poem of languid male beauty in the early light, and took stock of his surroundings. The queen's face was hard in sleep, her body brazenly exposed. He felt a flicker of disgust towards her, then woke a little more, and realised he had to have her immediately. She rose from sleep with him already plunging in and out of her.

The queen was growing uneasy about her lover. True, his lust was unabated. If anything, it seemed to be growing stronger and fiercer – she could barely tear him away from her. He ravished her at every opportunity and long into the night. In sleep, however, he cringed from her touch and muttered in his dreams. Her supply of hair was growing low, too. She'd flown, crow-formed, into the valley several times, but the wretched girl was still in that ridiculous practice of mourning, and her scalp was bare. Angry and anxious, the queen arranged to bring the wedding day closer. Once he'd vowed himself to her, the spell would be sealed, and she needn't depend on the little bitch's tresses.

The Black Knight, too, was troubled. The queen's brew addled his every waking moment until he couldn't think of past or future, and his only present desire was to use her fiercely. Still, there was a discordant note, always strongest in the early mornings before he fully woke. When he fucked her, he worshipped her beauty and desired nothing else, but part of him seemed to be punishing her too. Whenever he tried to think about it, his mind fogged over, and all he knew was that he adored her and couldn't wait to bury himself in her once more. His nights were disturbed. Several times, he woke up walking around the castle, on the ramparts and once even out in the grounds. Some dream had led him out – some vision of a pretty running girl. He'd stand bewildered in the darkness, thinking his surroundings were a terrible place and he must leave immediately. Then, fully awake, he'd remember the queen and hurry back to bed. But all the time another dreamy desire was just out of reach, and he thrust harder, his cock straining towards that intangible ideal.

In the quiet valley, Lily grew thin and dreamy. Each night, she and her mother mixed their own collection of herbs with the morning's scraping of light fuzz from Lily's scalp and a snippet of the Black Knight's locks. Being practical women, they arranged pillows, blankets and cushions to support her comfortably, and then the mother would retreat to her room and carefully seal the chinks in the door with twists of old rags. It would not do for them both to be carried through the spirit-world thus. Lily would light the brazier, and let the smoke surround her, carrying her into a trance. One night, the mother heard Lily scream out, and sat bolt upright in bed with all her mother-bear instincts ablaze. If her child were in danger ... But then the scream came again, from high and shrill all the way down the scale to a breathless shuddering gasp that drew out, quavering. The mother lay down again, pulling the blankets back into place. Lily had found her true love, and found her way through the mist of the sorceress's spell into his heart's desire. All night, Lily gasped and moaned in her trance. When the dawn came, her mother took away the rags and opened the door. Her daughter was sprawled in front of the fire, her nightgown torn and a smile on her face as true sleep at last replaced the spirit-travel. So it went on, night after night, the mother sleeping with pillows over her head, the daughter sending her spirit in search of her true love.

By the time the queen's wedding plans reached their valley, Lily was grown so weak from her efforts that she could scarcely stand. The mother was worried – Lily was reaching her knight, true, but only in their dreamtime. She was keeping their love alive, but that only made the sorceress's hairy concoction more powerful.

'The memory alone can't break the spell,' said her mother, 'just as memory alone can't keep love alive forever. It must taste the sweetness of reality from time to time. He travelled far and often, for that, and now it's your turn.'

And so they borrowed a neighbour's horse, plodding but reliable, and left the village with the mother leading the horse and Lily barely able to keep upright on its back.

At each village, her mother enquired after the news. With the Black Knight's fame spread so wide, the gossip about him was equally enthusiastic. He had turned into a crow, said some, or the sorceress gave birth daily to fully grown knights, all with his strength and skill! As they approached the border, the rumours were less wild and more convincing. The wedding day had been brought forward. His passion had redoubled. The queen was now in the habit of discharging her sovereign duties, meeting emissaries, dismissing petitioners, and so on, while copulating with the knight. Sometimes he curled at her feet, while she sat at her writing table in the state room, his head making a bulge under her skirt while he drank between her widespread thighs. Just as often, her skirts were rucked up, exposing her to all the court, while his fingers made fast work inside her. She had been known to sign documents while bent over the table, her bottom bared, and his shaft shoving fiercely into her. However true or exaggerated, most reports agreed that the wedding was now fixed for winter's eve, the night that heralded two long moons of darkness. It was an evil and powerful time.

* * *

The harvest was taken in; the days were shortening fast. The earth's bounty had almost ended for the year – it still offered fat orange squash and late-ripening apples, but little else. The berries that hadn't been picked were shrivelled and vile, festooned with cobwebs. Over the black stubbled earth of empty fields, autumn mists crept thick and eerie. The bare branches of trees loomed out of the white weirdness and the road was hard to follow. In the queen's lands, the dying year's untidiness mingled with the pervading neglect and bleak weather to create a vista of desolation. The Black Knight saw it, and it brought misery into his heart. Bitterly, he sought his solace in the arid lands of her body, and found only brief satisfaction. However much he wanted her, he always came wanting more, as if it were not her at all he wanted. When winter truly dawned, so would his marriage. Perhaps, he wondered, that would fulfil the longing in his heart. And on the eve of his marriage, he dreamt of midwinter.

Snow was whirling around a little cottage, humble and snug. The chinks of wood were well sealed with pitch, and a fire blazed – a mixture of bright embers which had burnt long and low, and fresh flaming logs. He felt at peace, sitting cross-legged by the fireplace on a pile of rugs – but not so calm, because opposite him was the most bewitching girl he had ever seen. Their eyes met in shy heated glances as his hesitant hands unlaced her gown and opened it wide. The shape of her breasts was clear through her shift, making him swell painfully in his trousers. He swallowed hard, as his clumsy, nervous fingers slid her shift down. She was bare to the waist now, like him. He wanted to grab her close, feel her nipples against his chest and all that soft flesh compressed against him. Still, he was determined to be patient.

He always planned his first time back with her so carefully. He had enough time to think about it – night after night, hearing others' grunts and gasps, alone in his tent and yearning. But, once he was with her, it was always different. The Lily he returned to was so much more vivid and full-blooded than the pale shadow of memory that accompanied him. Her flame-lit eyes invited; she invented games to delight him. No doubt she, too, plotted each meeting with ardour, and so what played out was half of each, to the excited surprise of both.

Now she leapt up, her dress still wantonly around her waist. 'Come with me . . .' She giggled, moving to the door.

'But it's snowing!' he objected, and then followed anyway, thinking he could lick the snowflakes from her hard nipples and that she could lead him anywhere, undressed like that, and he would follow, cock first. Or maybe heart first, because, though his cock protruded alarmingly, his heart shot after her like an arrow. Into the blizzard they ran, her laughter guiding him.

In the dark castle, the Black Knight rose from the queen's bed, his eyes open but unseeing. He strode naked and hard down the cold stone corridors, following his dream-girl into the first night of winter.

Through whirling snow and over icy paths she led him, to a heavy door inset into stone. His veins pounded, thinking she meant him to take her there against the hard wood, the furnace of their lust defying the winter rage – but she was wrestling with the iron latch, and heaved her full weight to open the door. He had no memory of any such building in the village, but he followed his golden girl inside.

The sorceress's hall was festooned with ivy and sharp-edged holly, ready for the dawn wedding that would seal the somnambulist's fate. On the far side, almost invisible in the shadows, a woman beyond middle age staggered under her burden, and laid her entranced daughter on the steps. A bow was slung over the woman's shoulder and a quiver of arrows lay on her back. She loosened the girl's bodice, readjusted her skirts and withdrew into the shadows. She faded into the night.

Lily had crossed the interior hall, and sat on the low steps at the front. He walked slower, nervous now, until he was close enough to see her eyes. They shone with the same pure love they'd always held, since first he and she had found each other. Then he was reassured, and his aching redoubled with the wave of love.

'Let me take you,' he begged.

'It's not time yet,' she whispered back. 'But I want you, I want you . . . Touch me with your tongue . . .'

He knelt eagerly. Her thighs spread as his cheeks brushed them, and his tongue flicked on to her open petals. She shuddered and sank back, knowing his hands would always catch her. In thin wet lines, he traced her familiar shape – first the outer petals, and then the valley into which they led, then the slippery thinner inner petals, and at last the hard little stamen that made her scream out and beg for him. He was lost between her legs, drinking the salty sticky juice and pressing his tongue in for more, then nibbling again at that precious pebble. She cried with bliss, her legs pinning him to her, and when she finished shaking he kissed her more until the tremors started all over again. Eventually she stammered, 'Now – now – it's almost dawn – you need to be inside me, *now*!'

Outside, the sky grew pale, and the queen's subjects gathered around the hall. Still sleepy in their wedding finery, they yawned and rubbed their faces, waiting for the sorceress. Inside the castle, guards were scurrying back and forth at her shrieked commands, hunting for the errant groom while the maidservants arranged the bride's black gown.

Ecstatic, he pressed his tip against her and nudged it forwards. Always, after a long absence, she was tightly sealed and he had to strain to enter her. His fingers had done nothing to ease his passage, and as he wiggled deeper she screamed low and loud – but she screamed 'yes', and he knew to take her at her word. With each inch of penetration, she moaned blissfully, spurring him on. Her slippery well hugged him tightly, and he succumbed. A final heave, and their thighs met, his cock plunged deep inside; she held him entirely, both sobbing each other's name.

The queen was proceeding to the hall, angry and anxious, but sure her lustful knight would follow where her body led. And if he savaged her at dawn as was his way, even before the ceremony and in public, so much the better – her fury made her hot. Then all the unquenchable lust of that perfect body would be hers forever.

As they bucked, he seemed to be waking from a dream, seeing dawn light instead of darkness – but, if it were a dream, it was a good one and was continuing, because Lily's nipple still filled his mouth and his cock still filled her pussy, and the rising bliss still rose. He thought he knew where he was now: in a castle, not in the village at all – not even, he realised, as sleep fell away, in his own kingdom. But he was too consumed with lust-rage for his true love to care about any of that.

He heard the massive doors creaking and a babble of people, but it was too late for anything: she was already frozen in a parabola against him, completely still but for the secret muscles that drank and grabbed him greedily. His sap was rising inexorably, spilling over into her, and then jetting in burst after burst as if he had waited months for this. As they came, their eyes met, and he knew again she was his one true love, and he could never love or want another. So the dream met the reality, and no spell could withstand the cataclysm of that moment.

He was kissing her deeply when he heard a familiar scream of rage behind him. Leaping naked to his feet, he spun to see the sorceress in her bridal clothes, her face contorted with ugly wrath. The girl's mother stepped forwards, and passed the Black Knight his bow and arrows. The queen had a few final moments to observe his perfection: his long hair stuck to his brow with sweat and sweeping below his shoulders, his strong slender legs akimbo, his tool still thick and glistening with love, his biceps swollen as he pulled the string taut, his eyes shining with truth. Then his arrow found its home with keener aim than the first, and she was dead.

The Black Knight and his Lady Lily were married shortly after, in the king's castle, free at last to spend their every night together. In recognition of their brave deeds, they were given the sorceress's lands as a duchy. They ruled wisely and well, and in time the forests, the farms and the people recovered from her cruel reign. And, judging by the clouds of frightened birds in summer, and the plumes of steam in winter, they lived happily ever after.

An Earthquake in Leamington Spa Kristina Lloyd

I am having an affair.

There, I've said it.

Even the words make me feel giddy and alive.

I am having an affair!

Oh, God, how he touches me: his big hand in the small of my back, his big arms carrying me to bed, his big cock moving inside me. Everything about Harry is big, even his heart. *Especially* his heart.

'Well, well,' he said when I arrived in his attic room. 'Mrs Townsend.' He was sitting by his little cast-iron bed, knee raised as he polished a shoe, braces dangling, shirtsleeves to his elbows. A small coal fire glimmered in the grate, throwing an orange pool on the varnished floorboards, and shadows blurred the angles of that misshapen room.

He pronounced my name as if it were two words: 'Mrs Towns End.' And he had a randy mischievous grin that turned me to jelly. I stood pressed against the door, drinking in the sight of him. Oh, he's a handsome devil, no doubt about it. His dark hair feathers across his forehead and he always needs a shave. From the moment I saw him, I was a lost cause.

Considering what had happened, I wasn't as alarmed as you might think. I heard about it later: 3.2 on the Richter scale and apparently not uncommon in these parts. Something to do with faultlines in the Midlands Microcraton, whatever that is. The floor vibrated, the velux windows chattered and there was a rumbling like thunder that went on and on. I imagined tanks rolling up the Parade of Royal Leamington Spa, stucco columns trembling in their wake, baltis quivering in their woks. And then I thought: no, no, the world is ending. And then I changed my mind, thinking, dear God, the chimney's collapsing and I need to get out of here at once, because what use is a mother buried under rubble and plaster?

I turned, tugging the door open, and everything went calm.

Well, the attic stopped shaking, and all the junk we keep up there – the boxes, suitcases, extra duvets, toys they've grown out of and that sodding albatross of an exercise bike – vanished in a trice. For years I've been wishing that would happen, I thought.

So the room was calm, yes, but I certainly wasn't.

I was wearing a summer dress and a terrible tatty cardigan (I'd just been putting the washing out), and my heart was going wild. I might have been sixteen years old again, pale and petite, half mad with sensation, and smelling of Impulse, Juicy Fruit and menthol cigarettes.

'I'll get you a drink, shall I?' he said, standing.

The floor creaked, and I couldn't help but stare at his backside as he poured from a decanter. Really, it's not like me at all but there he was, broad-shouldered under his shirt, his smart trousers concealing buttocks I fancied would be taut and high, the flesh indenting perfectly as he walked. Excuse my French, but I hadn't seen an arse that good for a long time. What else could I do but stare?

It seems odd I wasn't more confused but my concerns were practically demolished by his strapping and kindly presence.

Smiling, he came towards me, the glasses diminutive in his hands, and, as I took my drink, he leant in for a kiss. Shocked, I turned aside, and instead he printed his lips to my neck, his broad hand on my hipbone, bunching up the cotton of my dress by an inch or so. His silky hair slid against my jaw and, carefully, I filled my lungs with the scent of his head, inhaling the faint smell of his scalp's natural oils. I may have even brushed my nose over his hair, its softness gliding past my nostrils. And, all the while, his lips were on my neck, his hand was on my hip, and everything I thought I knew about myself was as gone as my sanity.

Then he withdrew and returned to his chair, straddling it backwards, his wrists on its back, drink in hand. I stood there, too stunned to speak, fearing my knees were about to desert me. I hadn't felt so aroused since ... since I couldn't remember when.

He raised his glass. 'To your good health, Mrs Townsend.'

I drank. Believe me, I needed it. It was port, and the liquid seemed to seep into my lips, making them plump and sweet, full of ruby-red warmth and the first stirrings of surrender.

I struggled to speak, and, when I did, it all came out wrong. 'What on earth's going on?' I said briskly.

And I was no longer teenaged and hormonal. I was Ruth Townsend, 42 years old, part-time legal secretary, part-time picker-up of damp towels and other people's shoes.

'You've slipped back,' he said. 'It's 1909. I'm Harry Wilkins, butler, valet, footman and all round dogsbody.' He tugged an imaginary forelock, adding, with an ironic twinkle, 'Ma'am'.

I looked at him for too long before saying, 'And I'm married.' My tone, I'm ashamed to say, was no longer brisk. Rather, it sounded quite seductive.

Harry stood, swinging the chair aside. 'No, you're not,' he said. 'It's 1909. You haven't even met him. You're not even born.'

He took my drained glass and set it down on the washstand with his. He seemed so immense, and the attic so small. He isn't bulky or lumbering. He's tall and broad-shouldered, and has big sure hands that make me feel safe. How cruel to keep him up here, I thought. He was like an animal in a zoo, placid and accepting because he knew no alternative.

Clearly, we had a lot in common. I can't say I was happily married but 'unhappily married' wasn't true either. I was simply married. It was fact much as the sky is blue is fact. After a while, you simply accept. You stop noticing whether you're happy or not. You just keep turning up each day, cereals for breakfast, Radio 4 when they let you, a fortnight of foreign sun, and family birthdays ticking by. And, suddenly, that's your life. If I was unhappy, then surely everyone else was.

'It's 1909,' I echoed. His smile made me unusually bold and I plucked at my flimsy dress, murmuring, 'I imagine I'm somewhat underdressed for the era.'

Grinning, he strolled towards me, hands in his pockets. His eyebrows tipped up. 'I'd say you were *overdressed*, Mrs Townsend.'

I could see his intentions and I made to move but he grabbed me around the waist, making me stumble as he pulled me back to the door. His solid bulk sandwiched me to the wood, and his mouth fell on mine, wet and urgent, while his big hand pushed my dress up my leg, higher and higher. His rough palm grazed my skin and he kneaded my thigh with a touch that might have felt tender to him but to me it was dirty and crude, forceful and threatening. I swear, I nearly came on the spot.

'Oh, Mrs Townsend,' he whispered, dabbing kisses over my face.

His thumb found the elastic of my briefs, his other hand under my dress, squeezing my bottom.

'No,' I moaned. 'I can't do this. Please.'

He nudged my briefs down one hip, and then his hand swooped straight in there, parting my lips with one enormous finger. He held still, that finger lying along the crease of my vulva, its tip dipping into my milky entrance.

I rocked my head against the door, dodging his kisses. 'No,' I pleaded. 'No.'

He smeared kisses over my neck, his fingertip rousing my juices.

'I mustn't,' I breathed.

'No one'll ever know,' he said, and pushed his finger in a little deeper.

I moaned, bending my knees and bearing down because I was in agony, so desperate to feel a thickness inside me.

'*I'll* know,' I said, but I was starting not to care.

I cared even less when Harry dropped to his knees, pulling my underwear down my legs and scrunching my dress up by my hips. I was half-bared for him, conscious of how lewd the exposure was, my hair a wild brown flare beneath the decorum of my summer dress, my lust making me engorged and pink and shockingly sexual. I tilted my hips to him, and his hands spanned my thighs, thumbs running higher to rub my wanton sex-lips. My briefs were stretched tight between my knees and I couldn't open myself as wide as I wished. But, believe me, it wasn't a problem. Being dishevelled and half-dressed was sublime. I hadn't been seduced for years. Robert and I start from naked and horizontal, or we don't start at all. Mainly, we don't start at all.

Harry's big fingers took my lips in a gentle pinch and he peeled me apart, feasting his eyes on me, all spread and scarlet, and gleaming with greed.

'What a beautiful little quim,' he said. And then his tongue was right there, spread on my sex, and his two broad fingers twisted inside me.

Oh, what noises I made. I hardly recognised myself. I didn't give a thought to what lay beyond the door. Quim! I felt like a medieval fruit: quince or medlar, something unusual and precious, and not for the masses. I held my dress high as he plunged and lapped. He nipped my clitoris in his lips, sucking me softly, and then he built me up in a way that makes me eternally grateful, two fingers inside me, two more on my point, circling and circling as if we had all the time in the world. He was so patient, steady and focused, a gentleman of the highest order. My knees were bent open, briefs at full stretch, and I was sliding against the door, gasping and whimpering, my climax rising till I reached a sumptuous convulsive peak that left me fizzing from my toes to my ears.

Gosh. 3.2 on the Richter scale? I beat that hands down.

He held me gently, cupping my head to his chest and mussing my straggly hair. He must have known how much he'd affected me. Years of emptiness and despair were turning into something else. His shirt absorbed a tear or two, and it's hard to say whether they were tears of joy or sorrow. Each salty droplet held too much emotion to be named as one thing or another.

After a while, I whispered, 'Now what?'

Harry released me, planted his hands either side of my head and grinned down. 'Now you have to strip, Mrs T.'

I shook my head. 'I can't, I mustn't. I have to leave. How did I get here? Can I ... can I get back to my family?'

'You can get back,' he said firmly. 'Come to bed, why don't you, and I'll tell you how.'

Again, I shook my head, pressing my lips shut so as not to say a word but I was thinking of one, a big one: Robert.

Robert would know. He'd find out. He'd see the guilt

on my face and smell the man on my clothes. And yet, even as I was thinking this, I was correcting myself. As if Robert would notice! He stopped seeing me a long time ago. I bet he wouldn't even blink if I sat down to dinner with Harry's come in my hair.

'If I leave, can I return or is this it?' I asked. 'What happened? How did I get here?'

Harry covered my breast with a hard massaging hand. 'There's a temporal faultline around here. It shifts sometimes. A new gap opens up like it did today. You fell into it. And you can fall in again and again and again.' His hand caressed my flesh in time with his words. Again and again.

'I really have to go,' I said. 'Please, stop. I want to leave.'

He angled his big thigh across mine and began hoiking up my dress again. 'No, you don't,' he said. 'You want to stay. You want to throw yourself on that bed, naked as a bairn with your legs spread wide so I can fuck you like you've always dreamt.'

He was right. My God, he was right! But I fought against him. I'm a married woman. I am Ruth Townsend, mother of two, wife of one. I live in steady respectable Leamington Spa. I am not someone whose dreams come true.

I pushed against him, my hand having no impact on his chest. I pushed at softer bits, at his waist, his belly, his neck. My thigh wriggled under his. I tore at his groping hand. 'Get off me! Let go! You . . . you bastard!' I thumped my fist on his chest, my head rolling like a beast's. 'Don't you dare –'

And then I was back in our attic, slumped against the door, a shirt button in my fist, gasping for breath. Harry was gone. His bedroom had vanished. And instead I was surrounded by great piles of rags and rubbish, and that sodding exercise bike I used to pedal for hours every week. Round and round, staring at the wall, and it never got me anywhere. The kilometres kept mounting and I never fucking moved.

I sank to the floor, head in my hands, and, before long, I was weeping like I hadn't done for years. All those kilometres and I never fucking moved.

In the lingerie department, I held up a pair of lemon-yellow cami-knickers. In my mind I heard him speak, ending on those two distinct syllables: 'Mrs Towns End'. The camis went in my basket along with all the others, a watercolour swirl of ivory lace, pale-blue tactel, shrimp-pink silk and three new bras to give me an extra lift.

Lift? I didn't need an extra lift! I was as high as a kite and I wasn't coming down.

The beats of my heart kept saying, yes, yes. I didn't fret about my shoddy morals, or what my sister-in-law might say. I was falling in love and that trumped every-thing. I was the epitome of devil-may-care. I didn't even need an alibi because time stood still when I was with Harry. When I'd found myself back in the real attic, the hands of my watch hadn't even moved. Or, if they had, it could only have been by a couple of minutes.

At lunchtimes, I walked around the shops in a daze, trying on clothes I wouldn't normally dare touch. I preened in front of changing-room mirrors. Is this too low? Will they tut and mutter about mutton dressed as lamb? Do I give a monkey's if they do?

And no, I jolly well didn't because for once I believed that I *was* lamb. I was tender, pink, young and free. I was the lamb to Harry's huge, masculine, heedless slaughter. And I wanted him to do to me exactly what he said. I wanted him to fuck me like I'd always dreamt, right there on his little cast-iron bed.

But I didn't go back for a while. It was almost enough

that it had happened, a moment out of time I could treasure forever. *Almost* enough. I wasn't even sure I'd be able to get back, either. Something peculiar happened around the attic door but details were lacking. Should I simply stand there, wishing for an earthquake? But no. Again and again, he'd said. I could fall again and again. And oh, in so many ways, I believed that.

Before long, I made a decision: I *had* to return. At the very least, it would be rude not to. He'd brought me to a devastating climax and I hadn't so much as tickled his button fly or whatever went on down there in 1909. I ought to slip back a century to express my gratitude.

I was alone in the living room, rummaging through the bureau for a notepad to write a letter to Cora's teacher for the next day. 'Dear Miss Stevens, I'm afraid Cora doesn't have her PE kit today because I forgot to wash it, and anyway she hates Games.' I was wondering what I should wear for my return (another pretty dress and better underwear), and a song was running through my head: 'I'm just wild about Ha-ree! And Harry's wild about me!'

We don't have pets in our family so, when movement caught my eye, I was surprised. I turned to see a woman about the size of a cat on her hands and knees, crawling across the living-room floor. She was wearing a black housemaid's outfit complete with white apron and mobcap.

I screamed several short blasts because that was the only way I could breathe. The woman kept crawling, oblivious to me, but, by the time Robert arrived, she'd disappeared.

'A mouse! A mouse!' I cried.

'Where?' asked Robert, slamming the door behind him. 'Where did it go?'

'Behind the sofa,' I said, and it was true, although the mouse part was obviously a lie.

On the other side of the door, Cora and Lucas clamoured to know what the fuss was about. 'What is it?' asked Cora, worried. 'Is Mum OK?'

'Mum's fine,' called Robert. 'We've got a mouse, that's all.'

'Cool!' said Lucas. 'Can we come in?'

'Wait!' ordered Robert as the door handle tipped. 'We don't want it to get into the rest of the house.'

Of course, we didn't find a thing, not even a miniature maidservant.

'Are you sure you saw a mouse?' Robert asked later. 'I can't see where it would've got to. We've looked everywhere. How's your vision? Maybe you ought to get that bump checked out.'

'The bump's gone and my vision's fine,' I said.

I knocked my head during the earthquake, you see. The house didn't shake that much but I obviously turned too quickly and caught the edge of the door. Oh, I know what you're thinking: that I must have conked out and that 1909 is nothing but a dream. I do understand. I might have thought that too if I hadn't come back with the button from Harry's shirt. It was a tiny fragile-looking button, at a guess made of bone, white thread dangling through its holes. I would clutch it in my fist, thinking, this button is real and so is Harry. As real as the hunger that's coursing through my veins.

But I didn't dare visit him again, not after the housemaid. I thought it was my fault. Either guilt was making me hallucinate or I'd brought some of Harry's world into ours, managing to shrink it along the way. It was a warning. I had to stop before it was too late. Whenever I thought about returning, I'd imagine lots of little servants crawling around our house. How on earth would I explain that to Robert and the kids?

Oh, but it was impossible. I ached for him so badly I began to feel quite demented. I didn't know which was worse: the madness of going back to him or the madness of staying away. I was still undecided about this when the walls in Robert's study started to sweat. I was in there with the intention of closing the curtains one evening, and I'd been standing there a while, not wanting to close them because the sky above the white townhouses was such a beautiful sheet of peach. What sky does Harry look out on tonight, I wondered, and then I noticed a sudden rise in temperature. Moments later, tiny beads of liquid prickled on the surface of a patch of wallpaper. It looked not unlike condensation and, as the droplets began to trickle, another patch appeared behind the computer, and then another below the dado rail, and another and another.

I wiped my hand across the surface and my fingers were wet. I dashed out on to the landing to grab a towel that was hung over the banister (I wish they wouldn't do that), then began dabbing the walls dry, swabbing at patches as quickly as they formed.

It was hard to keep up and I don't know how long I was doing it for. I only stopped when I heard Robert's voice in the doorway. 'Ruth,' he said calmly. 'What's wrong with you these days?'

The walls had stopped sweating. There wasn't a drop to be seen. I felt such a fool, puffing and panting, clutching my crumpled towel. I righted the desk lamp and set the computer mouse back on its mat.

'I really think you ought to go and see Dr Chadwick,' said Robert. 'Perhaps you're overtired.'

Dr Chadwick left the surgery years ago. We have Dr Patel now, but Robert's not going to know that, is he?

'Yes, yes,' I said. 'I'll make an appointment.'

I didn't make an appointment. Instead, I went to hurl myself against the attic door when everyone was out, praying I'd go tumbling into that rabbit hole. It took several attempts and fortunately there was no one to see me because I must have looked a fool, trying to recreate my own earthquake by spinning and falling, the door banging shut as I pretended to stumble. My shoulder was quite sore the following day.

I might have been sobbing slightly when I broke through because I was starting to grow frustrated, fearing I'd never see him again. But suddenly I was in 1909, pressed against his door, and I dashed away a tear, calm settling around me. Harry wasn't remotely startled.

Standing by the washstand, he was naked from the waist up, splashing water on to his chest and soaping his armpits. I could have stood there all day, watching droplets spill over his pale healthy contours and explode at his feet in a pitter-patter of splashes. I felt such a happy sense of peace, and the urge to tell him about the strange goings-on at home slipped clean away.

Harry crossed the room, rubbing himself briskly with a small towel. His forearms were polished brawn, and his nipples were dusky-pink buttons within a haze of dark hair. His abdomen seemed deliciously old-fashioned, its muscled strength overlaid with a sub-cutaneous softness I wanted to clamp my fingers and lips to.

'Mrs Townsend,' he said, smiling. He flung the towel on to the bed before he reached me, brown twinkly eyes never once leaving mine.

For one tiny instinctive second, that towel irked me, then I remembered it wasn't my responsibility. To hell with damp towels! To hell with responsibility!

Resting his big hands on my hips, Harry bent to nuzzle under my hair, kissing my neck and making little noises like 'mmm'. I leant my head back, offering him the stretch of my throat before I tiptoed to suck on the damp skin of his shoulder. He tasted of fresh cool water and I was melting faster than butter in a desert, my hands scooting over the slippery skin of his hard wet back.

'Oh, Harry,' I said, adoring his name.

Our kisses were big and wild, his lips so moist and mobile. His body made damp patches on my dress, cooling the skin beneath, and before long I was practically faint with lust.

'I've been dreaming about you,' he said, and he undid the first button of my dress.

I'd chosen to wear a slightly shabby dress which for some reason I feel very sexy in. It was apple green with a pattern like creamy sprigs of elderflower, and those colours suit me because I have a pale skin and ash-blonde hair that, admittedly, gets ashier each year. The dress looks better than it sounds. It clings to my figure without being slinky, and I enjoy the way it swings when I walk.

I, however, look worse than I sound. 'Waxy,' Robert once said of my wintertime complexion, presumably thinking our marriage was strong enough he could insult me with impunity. He was probably right. Sometimes I do feel waxy, as if I ought to be in Tussauds, smiling blankly and giving the impression of life. But that's beside the point, isn't it? You don't go telling your wife she's waxy.

'Were they good dreams?' I whispered, as Harry undid the second button, big fingers fumbling on little fastenings. It was difficult for me to talk because he was gazing down at my newly boosted cleavage, and a hint of lemon-yellow bra. Let me tell you, there was nothing waxy there!

He raised a glance to my eyes. 'Bad ones, Mrs Townsend,' he cooed. 'Very bad indeed.'

I should perhaps mention that my dress buttons all the way down, so, when Harry undid the third and fourth button, I realised where this was leading. He gazed at my exposed flesh, untied the belt around my waist and continued with five and six. His fingers were ticklish on my belly and I held my stomach in and arched my back because you do, don't you?

'In what way were they bad?' I breathed.

Harry shook his head, feigning reproach. The edge of my pastel-yellow camis were revealed. Button seven, and I knew he could see the gold-brown of my hair crushed beneath the lace.

'Oh, the things you make me do to you,' he said, and he dropped to his knees to undo eight and nine. My thighs were on show, right in front of his face, and then, with ten, eleven, twelve, I was split all the way open, my dress parting like a pair of curtains. Harry looked up at me, his hands moving on the back of my knees, his gaze dancing over my near-naked stripe of body. Then he stood, and my heart was galloping as he eased the dress over my shoulders. I let it slide down my arms and fall, the buttons clattering lightly as they hit the wooden floor. The rough wool of his trousers brushed against one thigh as he reached behind me to unfasten my bra. His fingers were devilishly adept, and it was obvious he'd removed bras before.

My breasts are smallish but in his giant's hands and in his hungry mouth they more or less disappeared. Not that I was complaining. I was loving every moment of his attention. If I did have doubts, they were fleeting thoughts about perspiring walls and infestations of little housemaids.

You can't imagine how thrilled I felt when Harry swept me clean off my sandals. In one sweet easy scoop, I was in his arms, laughing and lustful, then seconds later, I was sprawled on his bed, the hard lumpy mattress bouncing inadequately beneath me.

He knelt over me, him still in trousers, me still in

camis, and he cupped his hand to my crotch, watching my face with mild fascination as he rubbed me there. He smiled kindly when I moaned, rubbing harder and deeper till he was pushing the pretty fabric into my wet swollen folds. I felt deliciously corrupted.

'You're not going to say no to me again, are you?' he murmured, wiggling my camis down my thighs.

I shook my head. 'No,' I breathed.

'No?' he echoed with a playful frown. He unbuttoned his braces at the front of his trousers, reached around and unbuttoned them at the back. He held them in his fists, tugging them taut, and the lengths of leather made a small snapping noise. 'What do you mean, no?'

'No,' I whispered. 'I mean, no, I won't. I promise I'm not going to say – '

'You keep saying no, Mrs Townsend,' replied Harry, and he took one of my ankles in his hand, making me squeal. 'I don't want you to disappoint me again.' He looped the braces twice around my ankle, then, quick as a flash, tied the remaining lengths to the bottom of the bedstead.

I confess, I was a little bemused by this turn of events. It wasn't at all what I'd expected, and I'd been expecting quite a lot. But I went along with it and, when Harry took another pair of braces from a drawer and began doing likewise with my other ankle, all I said was, 'Gosh.'

'Don't want you to go disappearing into thin air again, do we?' he said with a charmingly roguish smile. 'Not when I'm ready to fuck you.'

He tied my leg to the top of the bedstead then stepped back a couple of paces to observe me. There I lay, trussed up sideways along his bed, Ruth Townsend, with my skinny legs akimbo, wide open and ready to be fucked! Fucked by a gigantic beautiful Edwardian butler. Oh, and how ready I was! My knees were frogged apart and my upper body was bent against the wall, meaning it wasn't the most comfortable or elegant of positions. But I'd been comfortable for too long, and this unfamiliar discomfort was exquisite.

Then, to my great delight, Harry shoved down his trousers and underclothes, kicked them free and stood there, magnificent and immense, grinning slyly like the dirty rascal he is. And, oh, his thighs! His big handsome cock! And, oh, his torso, his hard slender hips, his muscular buttocks and, oh, Harry, Harry, Harry!

I'm not good at asking for what I want. I see myself as one whose role is to make others happy. But, spread-eagled on the bed, I discovered a new skill of begging for it. 'Please!' I urged. 'Oh, please, please! I can't wait any more. Please, Harry ... fuck me!'

The bed bounced dully as his knee pressed on the edge of the mattress. He slipped his hands under my bottom, cupping my cheeks and lifting me to his angle. When the big plum-tip of his erection nudged at my entrance, my senses reeled: this wasn't Robert! This wasn't Robert's penis! This man sliding inside me and filling me up with his enormous veined impudent virility was ... was far and away the most exciting thing that had happened to me for years.

'Oh, God, yes,' I said to no one in particular. 'Yes, yes!'

Harry slammed into me, sometimes pummelling fast, sometimes locking eyes as he glided with slow teasing strokes. The leather bonds chafed my ankles, and my neck and head bumped against the wall. When Harry spotted this, he withdrew.

'Forgive me,' he said, huffing and panting. He shifted the little table, tugged the bed from the wall and, as I wriggled for greater comfort, he drove into me again. I let my head and shoulders hang over the bed edge, blood slowly filling my brain as my body jerked, thrilling to the impact of Harry's big cock booming at my centre.

A man from another century who moves the furniture while making love! They'd never believe me. They'd call me mad. And, at that point, I was mad – mad with lust and sex, mad for Harry, mad with the delight of groaning and grinding like a shameless tuppeny slut.

'There! There!' I cried as my orgasm fluttered close. And, 'There, yes, yes!' as he tipped me over the edge, and all the pleasure that for years had been hiding in my thighs poured out of me, pleasure upon pleasure clenching around his shaft.

He grunted to feel me – Robert is so silent – then he pounded on and on, his dark feathery fringe stuck to his forehead, his neck taut and sinewy, until he climaxed inside me with a terrible yet heavenly noise of release.

Afterwards, we lay there stroking and glowing, and I was so blissfully relaxed I didn't even gasp when I spotted Robert in the room. Pint-sized and pacing, hands in his pockets, he strode from door to washstand, back and forth, quite evidently troubled. He looked as substantial as the little housemaid had done, and I could well imagine him clambering on to the bed to join Harry and I in our post-coital canoodling.

When Harry followed my gaze, he turned my head to face him.

'You need to bring the button back,' he said. 'The one from my shirt. It's causing problems.'

I frowned.

Harry nodded in Robert's direction. 'You mustn't take anything from my world to yours. Or leave anything here. The seal starts to degrade. Time gets leaky. It's imperative you bring that button back.'

I glanced at my dwarfed husband. 'I had a little housemaid,' I said. 'Crawling around on her hands and knees.'

Harry nodded, looking grave. 'Then it's started,' he

said. 'Sarah Smith, no doubt, searching for her engagement ring.'

'She was tiny, like a cat. Like . . . like he is. Why?'

'I don't know,' said Harry. 'Something to do with distance and time. I don't know why people appear smaller.'

'And the walls started sweating,' I said. 'Like condensation.'

Harry shrugged. 'I don't know about that either, I'm afraid. The leaks, the situations that slip, they tend to be connected to something . . . emotional. Traumatic times. Happy, sad, scared. Anything extreme. I don't precisely know, Ruth. You can only see it if you're sensitised to it. Maybe someone once had an outstandingly good bath. I can't explain it all. I wish I could.'

I looked at Robert, still pacing and clearly in another world, oblivious to ours and steeped in his own pain. Had *I* done that to him? Was that our future?

'Do you know what happens to me?' I asked. 'To this house? You knew my name. You must have other women. Ones living here before me, ones after. Have you –'

'None like you,' he said before pressing a kiss to my lips.

I kissed him back. 'I bet you say that to all the girls.'

'Only the naked ones,' he murmured.

After a while, I asked again, 'What happens to me?'

'You mustn't ask,' he said. 'You mustn't think like that. Someone once mentioned you to me. They shouldn't have done. It's dangerous to know. You end up wanting to change things. In your world, I'm long dead. You could probably find out when, how, where. But I mustn't know. And –'

'Oh, Christ,' I breathed, because I saw his death at once. He would die in the Great War. Of course he would.

They all did. And his strong youthful manly body would be as cold and heavy as the earth it fell on, just one in all the wasted thousands. 'Oh, Harry . . .'

He pressed a finger to my lips. 'Shhh, tell me nothing. And I'll tell you nothing. All we've got, you and I, all we can share is this little world of here and now. Nothing beyond the window, nothing beyond the door.' He glanced around the attic, thankfully now clear of shrunken husbands. 'Here and now. Me and you.' He kissed the tip of my nose. 'And, by my reckoning, that's a very beautiful world indeed, Mrs Townsend. I wouldn't ask for another inch.'

I gave him my word I would return the button at the first opportunity.

I was reluctant to do so, knowing it left me with nothing tangible in my world to hold as evidence of his.

Sometimes, I've found this difficult, particularly in the face of Robert's insistence I make an appointment with Dr Chadwick. (He means Dr Patel.) He still maintains I haven't seemed right since that bump on the head. But I feel right, deliriously right. It's all the years before that feel wrong.

Anyway, who do I need to prove it to? I know how I feel, and that's truth enough for me. I'm alive once again, giddy and alive. I want to squeeze the joy out of every moment I have with Harry. And with the button back on his shirt everything is sealed, everything except my heart which is leaking into Harry's just as his is into mine.

Stranger to My Shores
Sophie Mouette

He was behind me, hands on my breasts. I was braced against one of the benches as the hot tub bubbled around us and steam rose up to meet cold stars. It was spring on Cape Cod, and the parts of me that ended up out of the water must have been cold, but I wasn't paying attention to anything except him, his thick cock in me, our bodies rippling together. We'd been making love long enough for the moon to rise, all the time cradled by warm water. Floating as if in free fall while he licked me, drawing orgasm after orgasm from me with his clever tongue. Then floating joined, our bodies one.

It started slow and gentle, depending more on the contractions of my pussy and our co-ordinated movements than on his thrusting. I'd thought I could never come that way, pleasurable as it was. But his hands helped me over the edge the first time, and after that the dam burst.

But now we weren't slow. He was pounding into me towards his own finish and, as we rode the wave together, I felt his ecstasy build along with my own and, as his sinuous tail moved against my bare legs, I cried out.

Then I wept, and he did too, I think (though a creature of the water does not show tears as we do), both of us thinking, How can I let you go? But how can I keep you?

* * *

My cottage was on the water's edge. My grandfather built it as a summer rental, but I lived there full time – a perfect place for a marine biologist who cares more about being close to the water than about luxury accommodations. Two rooms, an efficiency kitchen that isn't, a huge deck and, on it, a hot tub. The unique thing about that was that it was filled with salt water.

'You're crazy, you know that, Maris?' Ben, my one and only lover, had said before he left. 'You're going to turn into one of your fish someday!'

I'd thought he understood how much I loved the ocean. He'd thought he could wean me away from working so much. We were both wrong. But, when things still looked promising between us, he helped me jury-rig a system to filter sea water into the hot tub, then return it to the ocean when I was done. The filter had worked better than our relationship, and for a long time I'd been enjoying the hot tub alone.

Which wasn't altogether a bad thing. Or so I thought.

My life changed on a brisk March morning. The sky was a bright flat blue, scoured by a storm the night before. I half-expected to be called into work. I work with stranded marine animals, and the storm combined with the suddenly cool weather after a few weeks of warmth made perfect conditions for a stranding. But it was my day off, so, although I took my cell phone with me, I set out to enjoy my solitary day.

Although my house has an ocean view, there's a lot of salt marsh between me and the water. I decided to go to the Cape Cod National Seashore, a ten-minute bike ride away. Teeming with tourists in summer, it was all but deserted now. The light was still young, the water still turbulent from the night's storm, a clear pale green.

Then I saw something ahead in the distance, sprawled out on the sand. I hoped it was trash, but my professional instincts kicked in and I took off at a brisk lope towards it. When I got closer, I broke into a run. The shape huddled on the sand looked human.

I hit my knees on the sand next to the prostrate form from a dead run. I reached out, then froze.

What I saw was neither human nor dolphin, not quite. But not quite not, either.

Part of me wanted to scream, but the biologist in me was fascinated. The upper body, to the hips, looked like a man, and a handsome and well-built one, too. That had to be a fifty-inch chest, and it looked muscular, though there was a sleekness to him that suggested he had a thin layer of blubber. Well-formed sensual mouth, Roman nose, thick hair that looked black at first glance, but at second look seemed to be a deep forest green. From the hips down, he was ... other. A casual observer might have compared him to a fish, but the closest proper comparison would be to a dolphin. No scales, but mammalian skin, adapted for water. He was dolphin-like in another way too: his genitals were retractable. In his distressed condition, though, they were not completely retracted and what I saw looked more human than cetacean – and, some utterly unscientific part of me noted, quite impressive. For a moment, all I could do was stare.

I knelt down and looked closely at his face. His eyes flickered under his lids, but didn't open. He drew a shallow raspy breath. It finally struck me that I was not only looking at a living legend, but one that might not be living much longer if something wasn't done. Both the humanoid and porpoise-like parts of his body were showing signs of deep shock. I could see no injuries but, with whales and dolphins, the stress of being trapped on land was enough to cause shock. This ... this *merman* might be suffering from the same distress.

I reached for my cell phone, then thought of the potential circus, of how the crew at the aquarium would react to this. The scientists would be fascinated. The PR department would go insane. This would be the biggest thing to hit the institution ever. And that's what stopped me.

I was scared of the press, the glare of attention – I could only imagine how terrifying it would be for him.

Instead, I started conducting a field exam, as best I could without equipment. I needed a vet, I thought, but realised a vet would be just as lost as I was. I made an educated guess that I could check a pulse at the throat, as I could on a human, and tried.

A jolt passed from his skin straight to my brain – or was it my clit? – filling me with his presence, and with a raw animal panic that tasted like desire. My first thought was heat, but it wasn't heat, but pure energy jarring me.

I've swum with porpoises before, and I know how their skin feels: rubbery, but soft, too, not unpleasant. Like wet velvet. Unbidden, I imagined how his wet velvet body would feel pressed against my naked one. His sensual mouth would move against my own, gentle at first, then more insistent, nibbling against my sensitive lower lip until my lips parted to let his tongue inside to flick against mine. His genitals would fully extend, and his penis would grow to press against my bare thigh, until he shifted his weight and nudged my legs apart . . . with his tail.

I'd never had fantasies like that, and I didn't know what made me start now. All I knew was that the reminder this was not a man woke me out of my sexual reverie.

Help me, I heard, or rather felt. His eyes opened. The pupils were dilated with shock, with no whites. What little I could see of the colour was a pure pale sea green. The meaning was unmistakable, even without words. *Help me, healer. Sick. Please help me.* And again that rush of energy. He was terrified, but so trusting, or so desperate, that he gave himself over to me, who must have been as alien to him as he was to me.

He put his hand on mine and tried to clasp it. His grip was weak, but the jolt he gave me shuddered through my entire body. I understood, not in words, that he picked up from my mind the media sensation he would cause, and feared it. Maybe he didn't have much choice but to trust me, or maybe he could sense my fascination and attraction. I was a sucker for stray critters and men with green eyes.

I raced back to my house and returned with my pickup. After some ridiculous manoeuvres involving a makeshift stretcher and the come-along on the truck – like a seal or dolphin, he was pure muscle, heavier than he looked – I bundled him in damp blankets in the back of the truck and headed home. He was cold to the touch, suffering from hypothermia. Perhaps, like the sea turtles that sometimes came ashore in winter, he was a tropical resident who got caught in the Gulf Stream and swept north. At the aquarium, we had tanks for recovering animals. I only had my hot tub, but it would have to do.

Getting him out of the truck was another adventure. I didn't want to drag him up the stairs with the come-along, but could think of no other way to move him.

At that thought, he put his arms around my neck and somehow made himself lighter. He was still an armful, but I could move him – it was as if he carried some of his own weight. I tried not to dwell on how nice his arms felt around me. That, I told myself firmly, was just twisted.

Why? he thought. *It's good to hold and be held.* Warm sensations of touching, teasing, mating, buoyant in clear water – yes, he was definitely tropical. *What's wrong with that?*

Then his momentary burst of energy gave out. *Must*

get well first, I sensed. *I'm not fit for mating*. Tail or no tail, he was all male.

I eased him into the hot tub. He smiled; then, as I had feared, started to sink. It wasn't deep, and he caught himself on the nearest bench, but I wasn't sure how long he could hold himself up.

When a porpoise is stranded, we'd take shifts staying in the pool with it, literally holding it above water until it gained the strength to swim. I didn't have anyone to take shifts with me. On the other hand, my patient was sentient. Once his body temperature started to adjust, I could probably put a life jacket on him. But, meanwhile, I had no choice. I didn't even dare leave him long enough to get a bathing suit.

I shucked my clothes and crawled into the hot tub. I tried to project maternal or medical images, but I'm not sure I succeeded. Weak as he was, he gave me a look that reminded me in no uncertain terms that he was male, gorgeous and untouched by human inhibitions. *Pretty*, he thought, or something like it. *Different but pretty*.

That startled me more than everything else that had already happened. Pretty? Me? Ben had never said I wasn't, but he'd never said I was, either. In fact, he'd often had small polite suggestions for me: 'You know, if you let your hair grow out ... if you wore a little blush and eyeliner ... if you tried some different clothes ...' But I keep my hair short and wear no makeup and choose simple clothes because I never know when my job will immerse me in water. In the end, Ben couldn't accept that. Couldn't accept that I'd rather walk on the beach than go to a nice restaurant, or read the latest scientific journal than see the latest movie. And so, in the end, he'd removed himself, leaving behind a few memories and a hot tub that ran on salt water.

Sad, the merman thought.

'Not really,' I said aloud, without thinking. 'It's just
... sometimes I miss what might have been.'

*Why spend so much time on what-might-have-been?
Why not think about what-could-be?*

Was I really doing that?

'I miss him sometimes,' I admitted. 'But, to be honest,
I wasn't right for him.' It didn't even hurt to say it any
more. 'I'm not right for most people,' I continued. 'I'm
very set in my ways, and I like being alone.'

The merman shook his head slightly, as if the movement tired him. *It is not natural to be alone*, he thought
back to me. *It is natural to find a mate and be joyous
with her.*

I got a mental picture of two merfolk playing in the
water. The sun above sent beams slashing through the
water, and the two played among them, darting and
slipping around the light shafts. They could see all the
way down to the ocean floor through clear turquoise
water, and that was their next destination. They shot
down, brushing through the swaying kelp in hot pursuit
of a school of neon fish, laughing silently as the fish
dashed between their webbed hands.

I didn't get a sense of great romance, or even of sex;
instead, it felt like exulting in being together with
someone you cared for. More than friends, yes, but more
than lovers as well.

The vision faded, and the emotions faded as well. I
looked at the merman. His eyes were closed and his
breathing even. Asleep. And I, lulled by the hum of the
hot tub and the feel of his arms, inadvertently joined
him.

When I woke, I was amazed to see how low the sun was
in the western sky. The morning's exertions had worn
me out. I looked at the merman. He seemed to be asleep
but, although his arms were around me, he wasn't

leaning on me for support any more. Instead, he bobbed gently in the hot tub's mild currents. His colour looked better.

I extricated myself from next to him. He didn't sink when I removed my remaining support. Good. I really needed to get out of the water.

I grabbed my flannel shirt and threw it over me as I scuttled, shivering, into the house for a much-needed bathroom visit. I checked back outside. The merman seemed fine, so I attended to the next demand from my body: food and drink.

I gulped a big glass of water, put tomato soup into the microwave and slathered butter on a piece of bread. I paused, the slice halfway to my mouth. If I was ravenous, how did the merman feel? And what was I going to feed him?

I continued to eat hastily once the soup was ready, standing in the doorway of the kitchen because it gave me a half-view of the hot tub on the porch. As I sopped up the last bit of soup with the last bit of bread, I saw movement. I was kneeling by the tub in seconds, reaching out a hand to comfort him when he glanced wildly around, not recognising his surroundings. I tried to project safety and healing. He stilled, and smiled up at me.

Thank you. He placed his hand over mine where it rested on his shoulder.

Nothing I could say to that. 'Are you hungry?' I asked.

The answer I got was clear. Well, he would eat raw fish, wouldn't he?

All I had available were some frozen salmon burgers. He grimaced, but was hungry enough to try them. I visualised the local fish market and promised him something better in future.

While he ate, I made a cup of tea, and dressed warmly in jeans and a sweatshirt against the chill spring night.

'How are you feeling?' I asked. It felt awkward to be sitting, clothed, apart from him, and for a moment I feared we wouldn't be able to communicate if we weren't touching.

He allayed my fears with a smile that reached his sea-green eyes. *Much better. I owe my life to you ... what shall I call you?*

'Maris.' Somehow, my parents had predicted my vocation – it means 'of the sea'. 'What do I call you?'

For the first time, he made an actual noise, and it startled me so much that I jumped, and would have overbalanced into the tub if not for his hands flying up to support me.

He'd made a sound not unlike the song of a whale or the squeal of a porpoise. I don't know why I'd expected anything else. Our 'conversations' hadn't been in English. He conveyed images, ideas, concepts.

His touch had set me trembling, and I didn't know why. To avoid thinking about that, I sat back up and continued on the language train of thought.

'Well, I'm not sure I can reproduce that,' I said with an embarrassed laugh. 'Do you mind if I come up with something easier for me?' At his mental assent, I thought for a moment and then suggested, 'How about Dylan? He was an ancient sea god.'

He smiled again, and I felt a warm rush of acceptance. I was surprised at how happy I was that he liked the name I'd chosen for him.

I cocked my head. 'You can't produce the sound of my name. What do you want to call me?'

His generous lips silently formed the shape of my name. What I received was a bombardment of images. I saw myself as I must have looked to him when I found him on the beach, looking down at him. Helping him into the truck, easing him into the hot tub. A disconcerting sensation of how he felt when I held him in the tub. And, with it all, a rush of something I tried to put into words: safetysaviourbravestrongkindprettypeltless-one.

I was stunned by all the compliments I had never heard before. So stunned, in fact, that I could only react to the last one.

'Peltless?!' I blurted.

Sensation of laughter, and the reminder of what I had remembered about Ben hating my short hair.

Sensible, the merman commented. *Short pelt on the head means easier swimming. Don't understand how you keep warm, though – no pelt anywhere else.* To emphasise, he placed his hand on me. On my breast.

The tingles I'd felt earlier exploded through me, much stronger this time.

I suppose that's why you cover yourself in this chilly climate, he went on. *Pity, though, because you have such a sleek shape and soft skin.* He didn't move his hand away; instead, he brushed it across me. My nipple sprang to life and I choked back a moan of pure desire.

'Yes,' I managed. 'We wear clothing to keep us warm.'

It is warm in here. He stirred the water with his other hand, the web between his fingers causing ripples as if from a near-surface fish. He cocked his head, green eyes watching me intently. *Will you . . . join me again?*

As he asked the question, he flexed the hand against my breast.

The scientific part of my brain questioned the ethics of the situation, but the emotional part refused to listen. I undressed again. The goosebumps barely had time to rise on my skin before I slid into the hot tub and into his arms.

My nipples stayed hard and puckered despite the heated water, and he wasted little time covering one with his hand again. The feel of his webbed fingers against my breast inflamed me further.

I've always felt somewhat clumsy during lovemaking, something about too many flailing limbs (and one arm always trapped somehow) and jerky motions. That all changed, here in the water. Here it was like a slow graceful dance. Instead of colliding against each other, we slid. Instead of random waving about, our movements were deliberate.

He claimed my mouth, one hand still trapped between us and teasing my nipple. I found myself trying to rub against him, and I felt his tail curl between my legs.

I tensed, intensely aware of how alien he was. Sexy as hell, but alien. It felt good – it felt amazingly good – but he was a different species.

Your body is new to me, too, Dylan thought at me. *But tell me we are not cousins, your kind and mine.*

I did. His eyes weren't human, but the emotion and intelligence behind them felt like home. *If you don't want this, we can stop,* he told me, *but I hope you do.* He showed me what he hoped, rather graphically. The combination of gentleness and desire overcame the last of my scruples.

I pressed myself against him, opening my legs so I could feel his tail there, and said, 'Teach me how to touch you.'

We'll learn together. His penis bloomed out of its sheath.

The area where his humanoid body and tail joined turned out to be remarkably sensitive. His tail flukes were remarkably adept at caressing my breasts and between my legs. Oral sex, I think, was new to him. I felt all kinds of questions when I took him into my mouth, but he shuddered with pleasure and his hands cupped the back of my head, encouraging me to continue.

Stroke around ... I got the image: as I sucked, he

wanted me to caress the slit into which his cock would retract. It was a little bit like touching myself, but not really, because he was so very male. The organ convulsed at my touch, and his cock jumped. I rubbed up against him fiercely, knowing I couldn't hold my breath much longer.

As I thought that, I tasted him and actually felt his ecstasy flooding me, triggering my own answering orgasm.

His first thought, when he could think anything coherent, was: *Does it work if I use my mouth on you?*

Fortunately, I didn't need to answer him in words.

For someone who had never tried oral sex before, Dylan had good instincts and more enthusiasm than Ben ever had. Of course, it helped that he didn't need to come up for air. *Delicious*, I felt him think. His tongue explored me fearlessly, even licking my ass before heading back to my clit and settling there. My right leg was draped over his shoulder, and I was clinging to the edge of the tub. It should have been terribly awkward, but all I could care about was the velvet of his tongue and lips caressing me, pushing me ... One hand braced me. He used two fingers from the other to enter me as he licked. I felt his anticipation at the tight heat of my pussy, his excitement, and I screamed as I came.

There was an awkward moment when we realised that, while we were both frantic to fuck, we weren't sure how to go about it. It was more like an awkward twenty minutes, during which we thrashed around, and laughed a lot, and got each other more and more excited and more and more frustrated. Finally, even though I'd never felt comfortable on top, I couldn't stand it another second. I straddled him, wrapping my legs around his hips as he floated, and eased his cock into me. Then I stretched forwards, my breasts brushing his chest. He pulled me down and kissed me deeply and began to move, thoroughly taking control.

I'd always thought of great sex – the kind I'd day-dreamed about – as crashing breakers, rough and a little frightening. With Dylan, it was more like a strong warm current, steady and powerful. We couldn't move together violently, but his rocking inside me was relent-less and wonderful, and I found an answering motion in my own hips. It was a slow build-up, molten and tender, and it seemed to me that we spent more time than usual looking into each other's eyes.

We were doing that when I came, and in his eyes I saw my pleasure echoing and triggering the same in him. Connected as we were, I felt that in the same way I felt his thoughts, felt the concentrated heat of a male orgasm, and that set me off again. This in turn gave him fresh inspiration, and he choreographed me into a float-ing 69.

I lost count, eventually, of how many times we came, and all the different ways. What remained clear, besides the great pleasure, was the tenderness in his eyes and his touch, and the feeling that I had somehow come home.

I didn't want to go to work the next day. I woke to the sunrise, still curled in a sleeping bag on the deck. My right arm was covered with dew because I'd slept with it stretched out so we could hold hands. He woke at the same time, and I crawled into the warm water and his magical hands. Eventually, though, I had to leave him, with a bowl of raw fish on ice.

Work was interminable. I was overseeing delivery of some sea turtles that had been stranded in the same con-ditions that had left Dylan collapsed on the sand. Some-how I managed to muddle through without harming any of the poor creatures. I left as early as I could and raced home to the hot tub and Dylan.

Dylan was floating on his back, which panicked me into a run. When he heard me, though, he thrashed around and raised his upper body out of the water. I ran to him (dropping the package of haddock on the deck) and we kissed over the side of the hot tub, our thoughts meeting and twining. Desire and pleasure – he had missed me at least as much as I missed him. More, because he didn't have the distraction of work.

But I liked watching the birds. You have different gulls here, and little songbirds. He visualised sparrows, chickadees, red-winged blackbirds. *And some not so little –* the Canadian geese in the salt flats. *Your land is different from what I know of the islands near me, but the sea is so different I shouldn't be surprised. Things are quieter colours here, but it matches the grey climate.*

'You're from the tropics, aren't you?'

I was rewarded by an answering nod.

'Did you get lost? You're a long way from home.'

I was curious to see other parts of the ocean. And where we live, the last few seasons, it has been almost too warm. The coral is suffering, and it's harder to find food. Where the water is colder, there is more plankton, and so more fish. We have never been migratory, but I wished to see if it were possible. But I went farther than I meant. I was learning so much!

I must have registered surprise at the scientific curiosity, not to mention his understanding of El Niño, because he laughed at me.

We already know we are cousins, your species and mine. You love to learn more about the world. Why should I not be the same?

Why indeed? Because we spoke to each other 'in translation', communicating more with feelings and impressions than with words, I had thought him naive.

But, like myself, he was a student of the ocean – only he could know it in a much more intimate way than I ever could.

Once we figured that out, we spent the time we weren't making love 'talking' about the sea. Among his own people, it turned out, he was the equivalent of a biologist. They had no written language, but their telepathic abilities helped them share knowledge.

From all our 'conversations', I got a very distinct impression of Dylan's underwater home. Based on the wildlife, it was somewhere in the southwestern Caribbean. But where? I was dying to know. He didn't know our names for the islands. One day, though, something he'd said about turtles sparked my memory. Excusing myself, I ran back into the house. Dripping water everywhere, I leafed through a stack of magazines until I found some articles on the turtle sanctuaries on Turks and Caicos that showed underwater views. When I showed him, he nodded sadly. *We used to live there, but too many of your kind dive there now. We moved.*

Of course. The Turks and Caicos chain was quiet compared to flashier tourist meccas in the region, but it was popular with divers. It would be far too crowded for his people's safety.

Where had they gone? I found myself reviewing scenery from the area, but I hadn't spent much time in the Caribbean. I tried to remember underwater scenes from the internship I did during my senior year of college at a remote, almost uninhabited island, and my follow-up visits there when it became the field station for the region's first Marine Protected Area.

Yes, he told me, *there! You have been there?*

I love it there. I didn't need to explain to him that I could say that about few other places besides that tiny island and Cape Cod. He knew.

An image of us swimming together in those clear

warm waters. *Then you can come with me when I go home. You must live on land, but we would be close.*

Then he physically pulled back from me. *You don't want to?*

How could I explain it to him when I couldn't even explain it to myself? I'd felt lost during my time at the field station. I'd only gone as far as U-Mass Dartmouth for my undergraduate degree. I'd done my master's at University of Rhode Island so I could commute. This spit of sandy land and the ocean around were in my blood, almost literally. My ancestors were among the first white settlers in the area, and I knew just which overgrown cemeteries held their graves – or the marker commemorating a death at sea. I couldn't possibly leave . . .

I was *afraid* to leave, I realised suddenly. I hadn't thought of it in those terms before – but that panicky feeling in my gut had more to do with the prospect of leaving the area than with the realisation I was in love with someone who wasn't even my species.

He swam back to me now and put his arms around me. *Your home is beautiful, but there is so much more to see, friendloveplaymate. The ocean is vast. And change is scary, I know, but I'll be there with you.* And then he kissed me with such tenderness and yearning that I resolved I would try to get over my fears of leaving.

I meant to think it through rationally, I really did, but instead, that night, I ended up in the hot tub with him, unable to think about anything except his hands, his cock, his tail. For the rest of that week, we tried not to think of the future.

By the next Monday, I realised I couldn't let him go forever. I didn't know if we could really have a future together, but I had to try. And I had to see his part of the ocean with him as my guide.

I started small. The idea of actually selling my house and moving to the Caribbean was still too scary. But I talked to co-workers about planning a dive vacation in a very off-the-beaten-path location. Not surprisingly, given where I worked, I got some good advice.

We enjoyed our idyll until leaves covered the trees, and the water off the Cape, while still frigid, was warm enough for Dylan to tolerate. We dreaded the idea, but he couldn't stay in the hot tub forever.

We made love one last time, frenzied by the prospect of our coming separation. Then, under the cover of darkness, I helped him out of the tub and spotted him down the steps. Now that he was healthy, he could move for a short distance on land, hunching along like a seal. Like a seal, he looked rather foolish that way, but could move surprisingly fast. Too fast. We reached the water's edge before I was ready.

Don't worry. We will meet again. I saw what he was dreaming: us, together, in the clear waters of the Caribbean, among coral and brilliantly coloured fish.

I tried to echo his hope back to him, but I found it hard to picture. I was still frightened.

We will meet again, he repeated. *I will be waiting for you, near the island you know. You'll love it. I can show you so much, so much your people don't know. Besides*, he added, after a brief blankness, *I love you*. Only he didn't say it. Because he was Dylan, he showed me what he felt, opened up to me completely, and I could not doubt that he meant it now and forever.

I couldn't say anything because I was crying too hard to talk or even think clearly. But I kissed him, and I think he knew.

I watched out to sea for a long time after he was out of sight. The biting spring air, which I'd always loved, seemed too cold.

Now I wait on the beach, feeling the rich tropical night cloaking me. This is my third visit to the island. The first two were vacations. By the time I dragged myself back from that and asked my boss if she had any connections to people doing research in that area, she grinned and accused me of being in love with some island boy. I didn't deny it. She was close enough.

Luck was with me. She knew someone who needed help with fieldwork. I was back for six months this time, possibly longer if we got the grants worked out. Dylan didn't know that part yet, but he knew I was here. As soon as I went into the water off the island, I felt him, unseen, but present. So I waited in our favourite cove.

I didn't have to wait long. I heard splashing, saw a form rise out of the water to greet me. I ran into the warm water and dove into his arms.

Simply seeing him, his eyes, made my chest constrict, the joy so intense it threatened to burst forth. I hadn't realised how much emotion had pent up inside me: fear that he wouldn't come, nervousness about seeing him again, the ache of missing him. Now all the feelings crashed together inside of me. I felt exultant.

When he touched my hand with his, so cool and sleek – I'd almost forgotten how he felt! – I whimpered. I felt the answering overwhelming emotion in him. I saw him smile, and suddenly I couldn't wipe the grin off my own face. I held out my arms and he pulled me to him, crushing his lips against mine. We kissed to make up for all the time we'd been apart. When we finally pulled apart, we were both gasping for breath. With a sound that was his own unique laugh, he took me by the hand and pulled me into the deeper water.

The full moon gave a surprising amount of light in the clear depths. The water felt like silk being drawn across my skin, enveloping yet not hindering me. Startled fish darted out of our way, into the safety of coral shadows, as we swam by. I pulled my hand away, tapped him sharply on the head, and began swimming in the opposite direction, daring him to chase me. Which, of course, he did. He caught me easily, webbed fingers wrapping around my ankle. I surfaced, desperate to breathe. Dylan rose up in front of me, his entire body sliding against mine as he did so. The sensation of his wet-velvet flesh almost made me cry out – and then I did, as he ran his hands over my breasts, found my puckered nipples and caressed them.

Then, with a cheeky grin, he tapped me on the head and dove beneath the water.

Oh, that was the game, was it? I followed, less successful at catching him, both because he was far better suited to underwater chase and I was trying not to laugh or moan. I suspect he let me catch him, which was fine. I gulped a mouthful of air, slithered back down, and took his cock in my mouth.

Oh, yes, I felt him say. *So special . . .*

I don't know how long we teased each other, arousing one another before indicating 'Tag, you're It!' and diving away, only to be caught and teased again. I only knew that suddenly we were on the surface, and the teasing had turned serious.

Dylan lay on his back, and I straddled him, facing away. The need to have his thick cock inside me was overpowering. I slid down on his hard length, sobbing, 'Yes, yes!' He grasped my forearms and pulled me down on to him, so I lay with my back on his strong chest. His lips nipped at my earlobe, his hands kneaded and tweaked my breasts, my sensitive nipples. He began undulating beneath me, driving his cock in and out of me; all I could do was hold on, feeling my climax build and build. Then his tail arced up between my legs and flicked at my exposed clit, and I screamed as my body exploded into a million bright floating pieces.

When I came back to myself, we were still lying, floating gently in the warm soft water. Dylan's arms were wrapped around me and I could feel his heartbeat against my back.

And there, in a sea reflecting tropical stars, I knew that I was home.

Lust for Blood Madelynne Ellis

That night ... The night my world screwed up, started with the same ghastly routine as every Friday night: work, pub, restaurant, club, trying to blot out the numbing emptiness of my life. The invasive greyness of Messers Cox, Cooks & Evans, accountants and soul-suckers, is what pushes me to these shallow pools of warmth and comfort. I knock back alcohol, gyrate with strangers on the dance floor, anything to rub away the feel of old paper and tweed.

Blondie by the bar has been flashing his eyes at me all evening. He's cute in a seedy pimpy sort of way, dressed in a Lycra T-shirt that's torn at the neck and offers just a tantalising glimpse of what's below. My palms itch at the prospect of sliding them up his snake-skin-covered thighs to his tight behind.

Snow-blond hair shrouds most of his face and falls in a ragged line along his jaw, but through that veil his eyes are piercing and intense. Sex with him I anticipate as an edgy place, full of surprises and riddles. It will absolutely not be straight and vanilla, which I guess makes us a match, because, while I'm not exactly far out, I am here for escapism, and I like to take risks.

So, when I catch him staring again, I return his gaze and lick my lips.

Instead of sauntering straight over, he just breaks eye contact and looks away, leaving me in a predicament over whether to be just a bit more pushy.

I can do it, but it's not something I like doing, because I want them to make the first move. Mostly they do, so tanked up that a brush-off will barely dent their soporific shells. Maybe that's how I know he really is different. He's not drinking.

I mull him over, stealing glances while he lounges against the bar, his tight arse barely on the stool, one booted foot hooked around the metal rungs. Just the way he poses makes me want him, but it's obvious that he's worlds away from me. I'm a dull little secretary with Tippex on my fingertips, and he looks as if he's fallen from a stage, or maybe a constellation.

Then, just when I'm finally drunk enough to go over and introduce myself, somebody smashes a glass on someone else, spilling first one liquid, then another. There is screaming and shoving, and I lose him in the ensuing panic.

To avoid getting dragged into the fight, I run for the loos. Which is where bad goes from bad to fucking diabolical.

In I dive, and I'm thinking pee, phone, powder nose, by which time the drama outside will be all over and security will have done their thing. I did mention I'm stupid when I'm drunk, didn't I? OK, so I'm not exactly a genius sober, hence my dead-end job at Boredom Inc. This is my idea of a safe place while people outside are scheduled for plastic surgery.

Anyway, I pee . . . I hear moans . . . seems that, despite the commotion, some lucky girl has managed to pull and is not far off her very own crisis just a few doors down. My head automatically turns that way as I exit from my own cubicle.

The door to the end stall is open, enough for the reflection in the mirror to tell me that I have things seriously wrong. For starters, she's alone.

I watch her writhe, both appalled and aroused by her lascivious display. Her 'Hello Kitty' T-shirt is pulled up above her bare breasts and her sparkly hipsters are undone, showing flashes of pussy hair. What's she playing at? I wonder. Putting on a show? Trying to attract an offer? Or, worst of all, is she having a bleeding fit?

One of my classmates once had one during a really heavy physics practical. She flopped on the floor like a drowning fish, her eyes rolled up in terror, the same terror that freezes Hello Kitty and holds her fast against the chipboard, gasping for air. Her mouth goes slack. She starts to gurgle, like there's something sticky in her throat.

Abandoning my lipstick, I scoot along the line of basins, my phone already in hand, ready to dial whatever number presents itself. If I'm lucky, she'll have one of those medical bracelets that say diabetic, epileptic or celiac. If I'm even luckier, I'll just end up watching her puke the remains of some euphoric or a recent blow job, while I reassuringly pat her on the back.

Except . . .

I'm wrong on all scores, because, contrary to what the mirror is telling me, she's not alone.

'Shit!'

I back away with my hands raised.

His eyes are feral, wild green and slit like a cat's – my Mr Blond. He's *done something* to the girl.

I realise that this could've been me. If it hadn't been for the fight outside and my weak bladder, it would have been. Might still be.

Blood soaks him. It splashes his face, giving the illusion of tears while it bubbles from her throat. He releases her and she stands for maybe a second before her legs crumple and she falls like a rag doll.

Shocked, I just stand there.

What are you? What have you done? The questions echo inside my skull. I know what I am seeing, but my mind doesn't want to comprehend it. It refuses to accept it. I have to break the image into pieces. His arctic fringe. Cat's eyes. Hello Kitty disappearing into a red stain.

And he advances.

Perversely, he's prettier now than he was on the edge of the dance floor. It's an ethereal otherworldly sort of beauty, frighteningly cold and horribly arousing. A montage of images enters my mind from somewhere outside: licking the blood from his face, smearing it across his chest, him going down on me while I bleed. I can see his tongue delving between my pussy lips, and somehow that seems horribly wrong.

There's a girl dying, right now, because of him.

My sensible self fights its way through the fog in my brain, yelling, 'Run! Run! You stupid bitch.' But I don't run. I'm numbed. I just shuffle backwards until I hit the sinks, which dig into my back, cold and impossibly real.

'What are you doing to me? Don't come any closer!'

My fist tightens around my phone and I wish for the nineties and something a bit heavier. This slender silver shell won't cause more than a slight bruise before it snaps.

'What am I doing to you?' His voice is in my head. His eyebrow asks the question. '*I'm* not the one with these fantasies.'

He slips into my personal space and entwines himself around my body like some exotic snake. He sways as if he's scenting me, and closes his hypnotic eyes. His breath is wet and cloyingly iron scented. He rubs his nose and his cheek against my neck. Then licks the sweat from my skin.

That touch sends a shiver right through me. I burn, anticipating darkness, but the sharp-sweet pain doesn't come.

'Oh, no,' he whispers into my ear. 'I'm saving you. Are you frightened? I can smell it on you. You reek of it.'

His hand slithers up my arm and takes the phone from my fingers. It falls, skittering off under the sink.

'I'm already sated. Lucky for you.' He cups my cheek with his other hand, and paints my lips with his thumb. 'But I've a mind to take you home ...'

A midnight snack, the ever irreverent part of me thinks, though this is no joke. I'm in serious danger. 'I can't. You just ... to that girl,' I say.

'To satisfy a different kind of hunger.'

He pushes my hand down between our bodies to where his cock lies hard, trapped beneath his snakeskin. It's my dance-floor fantasy come true, with a horrid twist. I guess it's true that you should be careful what you wish for.

'You want me,' he says. 'I can feel it in the rhythm of your pulse.'

'No!' I shake my head and try to pull my hand away but he holds me firm.

'You can't resist. It didn't save her, it won't save you.' His gaze flicks towards the girl.

Kick him and run. Put as much distance between you as you can.

'Try. You won't get further than four paces.'

And I know he's right, so I don't even try. Instead, I let his erection bruise my palm, and I try to ignore the fantasy that plays out in my head, of me taking this velvet-dressed rod and slipping it inside me, of riding it hard and making it weep. My fingers curl around him. Oblivion looms, as I see us coupled at the point of orgasm with his lips pressed to my throat.

My lips part, ready for a kiss, but, though he's close, he doesn't press into me, and he doesn't share the blood smeared across his lips.

'Let's go,' he says instead. 'I hate fucking in toilets, it's so crude.'

* * *

We walk out across the dance floor, shoes crunching on broken glass and the disco lights still flashing. Everyone's still in shock and one more bloodstain goes unnoticed. We continue out through the foyer and into a waiting taxi. Nobody questions us, and he has stolen my voice.

'Help me,' I mouth to a tramp on a bench, before the car door closes.

I stare at the rain-streaked windows and the shimmering lights reflected endlessly in the windscreen. The multi-tones of traffic lights blur into a kaleidoscopic haze, but all I see are blue, blue eyes so full of terror. Was it really too late to save her? Is it too late to save myself?

Up front the driver's radio crackles and cuts between static and late-night radio. It's easy to drift between the music and white noise, to remain entranced and still, and not to think too deeply, but slowly the fog rolls back from my mind.

The taxi driver is slumped over the wheel, although the car is still moving. I wonder if he was alive when we got in. The rear-view mirror is cracked and there's a crimson smear across the dashboard. I wonder how long it will be before I'm broken too.

I stare at my captor's hand where it lies beside me on the scuffed upholstery. His fingernails are black, not with nail polish or grime, but because he is something born out of a nightmare. Still, it's significant, for it means he's no longer touching me.

I realise this little freedom is probably my one chance to escape. I need only open the door, jump out and it'll all be over, or would be if I had the courage. But I've seen the films. If I run, I'll die. It's a given.

I feel his gaze on me, then, but when I look his head is turned away. Another image floats between us: I'm laid out across the road. Sirens scream. All around us blue lights brighten the sky. He's cradling me like a child. The onlookers think he is mourning a lover and give him space though they stare, while really he's supping from my injuries.

I find I am staring at him, and without movement, he is staring back.

The angles of his face are sharp, and his eyes glow an unearthly green. He has wiped away most of the blood splatter, but a smear still stains his lips. Hesitantly, I touch a finger to it.

He clasps my hand and sucks my finger into the heat of his mouth.

'Where are you taking me?'

'Home,' he says cryptically.

I feel a stab like a needle, then his tongue massages the pad of my finger, and he starts to suckle.

His eyes glaze, and he seems lost in the moment. Gradually, his sucking deepens and slows. I feel the caress of his tongue not on my finger but between my thighs.

'Mmm ... It's so good. You taste sweet.' His voice is a low mellifluous burr inside my head. 'I want you, Kristy.' He sighs, looks me deep in the eyes, and the effect is magnetic. 'I want all of you.'

And I want nothing more than to clamp myself around him and merge our bodies into one. It already feels like he's supping down my soul.

'Kristy ... Kristy,' he murmurs.

How does he know my name?

Panic paints a chill sheen down my back. I pull away, though he still holds my hand tight.

'How do you know me?'

'It's written in your blood,' he says. 'Every tiny detail of you runs through your veins, all your memories and all your thoughts.'

'No.'

There are too many things I don't want anyone to know about me to take this admission calmly. There are things I've been thinking while he's sucked my finger that I don't want him to know.

'Too late,' he says, and he keeps on licking. 'I know all your dirty secrets now.'

'No.'

Light from a streetlamp streams in the window and lights up his eyes like reflectors.

'Like how you want your handsome but dull boss to lean you over his desk and chastise your pert little arse.'

'Stop it! I don't.'

'No use denying it, the longing is written across every bead.'

I shake my head. 'You're wrong.'

It's just his hands. Mr Cox has the most beautiful hands, with long tapering fingers and baby-soft palms. I want to see them flushed with the pain of punishing me.

'No more,' I beg. 'Don't tell me anything else.'

He scratches his nail down my cheek where the skin is now burning. 'But, Kristy, that spoils all the fun.' He licks at the stinging red line he's made. 'Besides, I think you'll stomach a little indulgence. It's what we all do for ... our lovers.'

He tilts his head to one side and brushes his fingertips down the pale white expanse of his own throat, then peels back the torn collar of his T-shirt. I don't understand what he is showing me at first. Then I see it, a red impression just over his jugular – a bite mark. He tears away the T-shirt, and there are many more marks spread across his torso.

'I don't understand.'

'Once is rarely, if ever, enough,' he says.

He leans over me and opens the car door. It's only

then that I realise we've been stationary for several minutes.

'Run, Kristy, run. Run until your heart's fit to burst.'

I bolt on to the verge, but I don't run. I don't run because he wants me to, and there is no hope in being chased. Better I accept my fate now.

'Fool,' he hisses, and strides past me to a wrought-iron gate, beyond which steps lead up through a tangle of briars to a redbrick house.

He disappears along the path of thorns, and I find myself drawn along behind as if the thread of destiny is tugging me. I can't escape him any more than I can escape the images in my head. I see him naked, his chest smooth, his two nipples pointed. Blood trickles in tiny rivulets down his thighs, and his cock juts proudly towards my mouth.

I lick at the offering, suck him deep. I know what I'm doing is crazy, that I'm not in control, but I want what he's offering. I want it, the whole fantastic dreamscape.

Inside, the walls are fiery red. The hall is tiled in black and white, and each step echoes. There's a soapy floral smell in the air, too, that reminds me of a funeral parlour. I pursue him straight upstairs to what I assume is the bedroom, and not just his coffin repository.

I'm not disappointed. The room is airy and dark, lit by a single bubbling lava lamp that paints inky-blue colour on to the thick swathes of velvet on the bed.

He's waiting for me just inside the door, where he stops me with the icy press of his hand against my chest.

'What?'

He presses a finger to my lips, but too late, apparently . . .

An ear-splitting shriek breaks the silence. From out of

nowhere, a man lurches towards us. There's a sharp clink and he jerks to an unsteady halt in the middle of the room, and only then do I realise he is shackled.

'Show her to me, Lucius. Free me.'

I cling to my date as if he's going to protect me. Crazy really, all things considered, but, of the two men in the room, he seems the tamer option. The prisoner is naked, with skin as pale as porcelain and hair so black it betrays obvious Eastern ancestry. Even chained, he exudes power.

I tremble under his gaze, but still allow myself to feast upon his form. He's cut like an athlete, all pecs and abs and triceps. His legs are long and broad across the thighs. It's just a peek from there to where his cock slumbers in a nest of dark curls. He's beautiful, but in a different way to Lucius, who is all hipbones and wiry perkiness. And my capricious body responds to him, warming my cheeks yet again.

'Lucius,' he demands.

Lucius takes my hand and twirls me before him, showing off all my most obvious assets – bottom, thighs and bust, all of which fail to soften his gaze.

'Raffe,' Lucius drawls. 'Go easy on her. You can't say she's not what you want.' He pulls back my hair and reveals the unblemished buttermilk expanse of my throat.

Raffe's eyes immediately blaze with hunger. 'You haven't tasted her!' His voice sounds as choked as I feel.

'Just a drop.' Lucius offers up my hand for inspection. He squeezes the incision until blood beads in the wound again. This he then smears across Raffe's tongue.

The effect is startling; he swallows and groans, writhes as if tormented. 'More,' he demands. 'Release me. Give her to me.'

'No!' I struggle but Lucius's fingers bite hard into my wrist.

'Soon,' he promises Raffe. 'I just need to decorate her a little first.

He strokes my neck, runs his hands all over my body and finally settles his attention on my breasts. My nipples grow tight and tingly. I lean into his body, and a hand delves lower, under my skirt to exactly the spot I need to feel him.

'The chains,' Raffe demands.

'A little precaution first.' Lucius fastens a spiked collar around my throat then throws him the key.

Far from pouncing, Raffe stalks me like a panther, slowly circling and showing his teeth.

There are no boltholes in the room for me to run for, no place to hide except the bed or in Lucius's arms. Except his attention is now all on Raffe.

He drapes a silk kimono around Raffe's shoulders, which falls away moments later when he closes in for the kill.

In desperation, I scuttle backwards until I hit the bedpost.

Raffe's hands land upon my shoulders, pinning me. 'Do you have a name, girl?'

'Kristy.' I look up into his face like a frightened rabbit. His eyes are fathomless pools of deep magenta, not feline like Lucius's but infinitely more knowing and, if not wiser, definitely older. 'Please,' I beg. I'm not ready to die.

His lips curl. He strokes away the tears that are forming in my eyes. 'Do you enjoy pain, little Kristy?' he asks.

'No!'

'Liar!' says Lucius.

He entwines his arms around Raffe's neck, and presses an idle kiss to his jaw. Suddenly, I understand where all the bite marks have come from and at least part of their significance. They are lovers, of sorts, and the marks denote just how much they have shared.

Lucius watches my reaction to the kiss, then slides his hand down Raffe's front to his crotch. He teases Raffe's slumbering cock, massaging it in a fashion that is both dirty and deliciously crude, but fails to rouse its full attention.

'Not enough blood,' says Raffe.

He turns so that their bodies press together from shoulder to knees and kiss aggressively. The lamplight plays across their skin, shading the contours of their bodies in tones of ink and frost. I try to slip around them, but I am also mesmerised by them.

When they part, I'm no more than five paces away, and Lucius's lip is torn and bloody.

'Come,' he says to me and holds out his hand.

My heart flutters. I look to the door, to the bed, the window. In the end, Raffe simply grabs me and hoists me on to the bed. He covers me, and his lips skim over mine. His kiss is smoking hot. It invades and penetrates. It is so much more than a melding of mouths and tongues. And I love it, and I loathe it. I struggle beneath him, trying to push him away, while my pussy grows wet and my body aches for more of him.

The first bite is more painful and more exquisitely sensual than I could ever have anticipated. I drown in its intimacy; my treacherous body alight with hurt as Raffe's teeth dig deep into my breast.

The second bite lances into the tender flesh of my inner thigh, and is a thousand times more painful. It is bitter and sharp, and makes me feel dizzy.

Like decadent twins, they cover me. I kick and whimper, but cannot push them off. Raffe alone is easily twice my weight and far more muscled, and, so pinned, I stare up into the canopy only to find its darkness chased with silver. My reflection stares back at me; spread alone and naked on a bed apart from a bunched-up skirt that hugs my hips like a girdle.

Lucius finds my clit, and I writhe like a whore, but his touch is flighty and teasing, not insistent, as I want it. He toys with me, pushing a thumb inside me while Raffe takes possession of my mouth again.

This time, he tastes of fresh blood, *my* blood. His lips are flushed crimson, and his cock has risen. It brands my hip, pushes eagerly against me seeking admittance.

'Yes . . .' he murmurs, 'yes . . .'

Then he straddles my head, and pushes into my mouth.

His hands weave themselves into my hair. The taste of blood in my mouth grows stronger, and I realise he's weeping tears of it from his cock.

'Take it. Take it all. Drink me down,' he urges.

Above me, his eyes glow red. His hips buck faster. He begins to pant. His rhythm almost chokes me.

'Stop it!' Lucius drags him from me. 'Not yet.' They roll on to the sheets beside me, spitting and hissing like cats, and tearing at each other with sharp black claws.

'I need to possess her!'

'Stop it!'

'A few love bites won't hurt.'

'Control it, Raffe.'

'Ow!'

'Fuck! Get off.'

They fall still with Lucius on top, one hand wrapped around Raffe's balls and his other pressing into his eye socket.

'Be calm. Don't spoil it. Concentrate and you can salve both thirsts at once.'

'The burn's too strong,' Raffe's voice is husky and choked. 'We've left it too long this time. You should have let me out days ago. I warned you it would be like this.'

'It's not too long.' Lucius strokes his hair and brow.

He bites into his wrist and offers it to Raffe, who latches on like a babe and sucks greedily.

Watching them together like that makes my cheeks burn. I feel I am spying on something desperately intimate. I pull myself up on to the mound of pillows and draw my knees up to my chest. They are beautiful, frightening and strong. I want to watch them forever. The bond between them is so strong. Lucius's eyes glaze with pain, but still he lets Raffe greedily quench his thirst.

'Are you still here, Kristy?' he asks.

I nod and shuffle forwards a fraction so that I can touch him.

'You're not very good at escaping.'

'No,' I admit.

'She likes what she sees too much,' says Raffe.

He offers Lucius's wrist to me, but I shake my head. Then he offers his own, and I'm forced to shake my head again. I don't want to be like them. I just want to watch them.

'Next best thing, then,' he growls. 'Let's fuck.'

He pushes Lucius on to his back and peels off his snakeskin trousers. Bite marks cover the whole of his body. He focuses on me next, and pulls me astride Lucius, whose hands warm my thighs, then mould my breasts.

Raffe straddles him too and presses up close against my back. His erection slides between my cheeks and brands me with promises. They are both too near and too far. Everything grows slippery and warm as we writhe together, tongues and fingers exploring each other's flesh. My muscles flutter as Lucius massages my clit with his cock. I want them inside me now – together.

'Together?' Raffe whispers into my ear as he teases the lobe with his tongue. 'Do you think you'll fit us both in your cunt?'

I know he knows that wasn't what I meant.

How can they know my every thought?

Lucius's eyes are black with hunger and his breathing is heavy. Raffe licks incessantly around the edge of the spiked collar.

Is it even possible, outside of extreme pornography? I'm in unknown territory being explored by ghostly fingers. Raffe's tongue creeps up beneath the collar, as he releases the buckles. Lucius urges me forwards for a kiss. He slips inside me. He urges my hips down on to his, over and over. Raffe massages my back. He rubs circles into my arse, then scissors his finger down around Lucius's cock as he slides in and out of me. It's pure magic. I feel like I'm glowing, but I know that the best and worst is still to come.

As I rise and writhe, Raffe holds me still. He clasps their cocks together and when I fall it is on to both of them.

They are like iron twinned inside me. Stretching me so the pleasure is intense. But it's still not enough for them. They sink sharp teeth into either side of my neck. And I'm lost in a world of cocks and claws, of teeth and hair and light-headedness. My heart is beating three rhythms at once. They know everything about me now, what every little touch will do, how to make me sing and weep. I can't fight the inevitable. They've drunk down more than just my blood – part of my psyche too.

When my orgasm breaks, I'm weeping ruby tears of my own.

I don't wake the following day, or the next. I sleep through a week and into a fortnight. When I finally come round, I'm in a hospital bed with no memory of how I got here. Pain streaks through my body like electric fire. Any light is too bright. Not even morphine dulls the pain.

They won't let me eat. They just feed me constant bags of saline via a drip.

Everything is very white.

Why is the room full of lilies?

I wish I could remember. Then I do and wish I couldn't.

Messers Cox, Cooks & Evans let me go. I'm not sure they can do that, but I don't care enough to fight, because I've a burning thirst that the ice cubes they bring me to suck won't quench.

It's a lust for the pale skin of the two dark angels who led me along this path.

A lust for blood . . .

Sun Seeking Janine Ashbless

He had the most beautiful arse.

I'd seen a lot of naked backsides that morning, male and female, big and small, but one glimpse down the length of that hall took my breath away. It was ... just awesome. Not a bum; bums are soft and round and a bit silly. There's no muscle in a bum. Kids have bums. Women have bums, particularly when they're worrying about whether their pants are too tight. Even builders have bums. This was emphatically *not* a bum. It wasn't a nearly non-existent student slacker rear either, or a slightly hairy squared-off male backside.

No, this was an *arse*. A truly magnificent arse. He stood tilted on one hip as if about to take a step forwards, the right buttock clenched. Both cheeks were distinct, the crack between them a deep cleft. I felt an urge to grab those proud glutes and run my tongue up that crack. It was something to do with the dimples at the top of his cleft, something about the easy line of his spine, and the way the long folds of his cloak hung off one shoulder as if he'd just let his clothes slip and casually revealed himself to me. As I walked up the Archaic Sculpture hall, my flip-flops snapping on the flagstones, I realised my pussy had suddenly grown warm and puffy, and I blushed.

Nobody was supposed to get hot looking at sculpture, I told myself. I'd been round the Archaeology Museum in Athens on the first day of my holiday and I'd been in this little museum on Delos for nearly an hour already, admiring the marble torsos of athletes and deities and heroes, and they'd never had this effect on me before. They were certainly beautiful. But this statue – far bigger than life – he was *sexy*.

I looked at the typed label on the plinth as I drew close. *Kouros: 5th Century* BC: *Parian marble*. They weren't into long explanations in here. *Kouros* just meant 'young man'. I looked up again. Now I could see the cracks where they'd pieced him back together. They hadn't found everything; he was still missing most of his arms, both feet and, most obviously, his head. But they had his long thighs and his broad shoulders and lithe hips and that fantastic edible-looking arse.

God, I was really letting it get to me. The barren room with its stone exhibits suddenly felt warm and airless. I wanted so badly to run my hands up the old marble. I wanted to touch myself.

'D'you like him?' said a voice at my shoulder.

I jumped and spun around; I'd had no idea there was anyone else in the room. All the other tourists had gone to look around the ruins first, before the museum.

'Huh? Yes.' I went pink again.

The woman was taller than me and wore shades propped to the top of her head, where her mahogany hair was pulled back in a long plait.

'He's lovely, isn't he? Apollo. My favourite piece in the museum – I always make sure I look in on him.'

'Right. Do you come here often?' Then I realised what I'd said and dissolved into flapping embarrassed giggles. 'I mean – do you work here?'

She raised her eyebrows, smiling. She really had the whole Lara Croft thing going; khaki shorts over long legs, a webbing belt and a tight sleeveless top that displayed tanned and toned upper arms. Not the pneumatic breasts though – or the guns, of course.

'I do some consultancy work,' she said, 'for the archae-ologists.' Her accent was almost inaudible; it might have been Greek or French. The archaeologists on Delos were mostly French, I recalled.

'Wow. What a great place to work.'

She tucked a stray wisp of hair back behind her ear. 'Better than most. Plenty of sun. No mud. You're from England?'

'That's right.'

'I lived in London for a few years. Are you staying on Mykonos or on a cruise ship?' She kept her eyes fixed on mine, which was a bit disconcerting.

'Mykonos.' I'd come over to Delos on the first ferry that morning.

'On your own? Or is your girlfriend around?'

Boy, was she direct. I blinked. It was an easy mistake for her to have made; there are a lot of gay holiday-makers on the party island of Mykonos.

'Well, I was supposed to be here with my boyfriend,' I admitted, slightly emphasising his gender. 'Only, we split up just before the holiday. Actually, I dumped him.'

'So you came out on your own? Enjoying yourself?'

I shrugged. 'Yeah. It's great.'

Actually, I'd been shocked to find out how much of my confidence, after three years, had been dependent on having Lee around. It had taken a couple of nights for me to work up the courage to go to a club.

As if reading my thoughts, she asked, 'You like the nightlife?'

I winced inwardly. Everyone else on the island seemed to be with a pack of friends. It was impossible to break into a group of women, though it was easy enough to hook up with some lads – in the same sense that a side of beef can hook up with a tank of piranha.

'I'm not that much of a party animal,' I said, trying to sound casual.

My first attempt at a two-fingers-up-to-Lee holiday fling had been a huge disappointment. I'd gone with an

English lad back to my room in the small hours; sex had been over within minutes, and then he'd hogged the bed, snoring, for the rest of the night. In the morning, we'd had nothing to say to one another. My exciting stranger of the previous evening had turned out to be, well, just an ordinary bloke from Sheffield, not particularly good looking and no conversationalist for sure. 'Cheers,' he'd said as he'd slipped out. *Cheers!* – I ask you!

Don't get me wrong, I wasn't looking for romance or anything. I just didn't want it to be so ... ordinary.

'You're more interested in this sort of thing, then?' The flick of one wrist somehow indicated the museum, the island of Delos and more than three thousand years of history. She had lovely hands with long fingers.

'Oh, yeah.' Why not? I thought, then panicked that she might call my bluff. I was really here because there isn't much to do in Mykonos if you're on your own, other than lie on the beach or take the half-hour crossing to Delos. 'I mean, I don't know that much or anything ...'

She put her arm on my shoulder, riffling her fingers up the hair on the nape of my neck. My heart skipped and I froze.

'I'll show you around the island then,' she said. 'Would you like that?

'Great,' I said numbly. I have a very long fuse; I never react quickly to a surprise. Hey, it took me two years to get round to dumping Lee.

Her hand gripped the back of my neck. It should have freaked me out but it was weirdly reassuring. 'I'm Phoebe.'

'Ness.'

'Good.' She looked up at the statue. 'You finished in here?'

I nodded. My heart was doing uncomfortable things

under my breastbone. She released me and I followed like a lamb, with only one look back at my *kouros*. I consoled myself with the thought that it would only have been a disappointment to have gone round and taken a look at his front elevation; Greek statues always have teeny little dicks.

Phoebe knew her stuff. She walked me right round the ruins on the tiny island, starting with a climb up Mount Kythnos – more of a hillock really, but it was a steep incline and against the fat surface of the Aegean it looked taller than it really was. I was grateful for my straw sunhat. Below us, we could see the excavated ruins stretching from the hill to the harbour where the tourist boats waited: the theatre, the stadium, the residential districts, the many temples to gods Greek and foreign, and the sanctuary area dedicated to Apollo and Artemis, who'd been born on the island and had promised to hold it in their care. For thousands of years, Delos had flourished as a centre of pilgrimage and as a trading station.

Then she led me back through the ruins, which were a maze of mostly waist-high walls, restored in some places so that the pillars and pediments stood again. Diving into different houses, she showed me wall paintings and intricate mosaics: a god riding a leopard, gurning theatrical masks and grinning toothy dolphins. On returning to the harbour area, we visited a terrace on which stood a row of curiously slender lions. I took a photo of her leaning against one. She had her glasses back over her eyes now that we were outdoors and they made her face look masklike. I was growing dizzy from the sun, despite my hat. The light struck up off the marble roads as fiercely as from the cloudless sky overhead.

'Let's get a drink,' I suggested. 'There's a café by the museum.' I was enjoying the tour but all the names and dates didn't mean much to me. I knew I wouldn't remember most of them in 24 hours.

We cut back through the ruins. 'You've got to see this,' Phoebe said suddenly, taking my elbow and drawing me aside. 'This is the sanctuary of Dionysus.'

I looked obediently. There wasn't much to the temple itself; another low ruined enclosure. But out at the front were two pedestals, and on them balanced the biggest stone phalli I'd ever seen, angled like guns at the heavens. My mouth fell open, then I couldn't help laughing.

'Great, aren't they?' Phoebe waved her hand at the nearest. 'Give me your camera; I'll take a picture of you.'

For a moment I wondered if she'd put all this effort in just to run off with my new digital camera, then I decided I didn't care. I handed it over and went to stand by the plinth, looking up at the monstrous stone phallus above. Balanced on its oval tightly drawn-up testes, it was thick and ridged and ready to salute. What a pity it was broken off part way up the shaft, I thought.

'Stand against the pillar,' Phoebe ordered, shoving her shades up her forehead once more. 'That's right. Smile.' The camera clicked repeatedly as she ran off the snaps. 'Lean back. Lift your hands over your head.'

There was no one else around. I did as she'd said, grinning cheekily, jutting my hip. My fingers brushed the marble. Wasn't this what I'd come to Greece looking for – sun and big cocks?

'Very nice,' she said, squinting at the viewscreen. 'Stick those pretty boobs out, Ness.'

I essayed a jiggle, trying not to crack up. Phoebe closed in until she was right in front of me, still snapping away. Then she lowered the camera and looked me right in the eye. There was one long silent moment when I could have said something or broken her gaze. I didn't. She leant in and kissed me full on the lips, her mouth as ripe and juicy as the tomatoes in the taverna salads. I trembled. Something hot and wet writhed inside me. Her tongue broke the seal of my lips and slipped into my mouth. I made a little noise in my throat; not protest, just surprise.

Phoebe chuckled. I could smell the suncream fragrant on her skin. I'd never kissed a girl. She was softer to the touch than a man, her lips fuller, and her tongue stirred rather than thrust. Her breasts were now brushing up against mine and there was a heavy feeling in my sex, so heavy that my legs were weakening under the strain. And now she had hold of my skirt and was drawing it up, sliding her hand up my thigh. Her fingers were cool on my burning skin. She released my mouth and pulled back a little so she could look me in the eye as those fingers found the edge of my panties. I was quivering like a leaf. I'd waxed to hell and back in preparation for the holiday, and she was finding only the softest, smoothest skin, even when she slipped a finger under the edge of the cotton.

There, over the centre line of my mound: the last tufts of pubic fluff. She stroked them up and down. She broke the seal down there too, releasing a tiny trickle of moisture as she stirred my clit. I pressed my rump to the marble, needing the support. We were in full public view. What if someone saw? I couldn't tear my eyes from hers.

'Good girl,' she whispered. 'What a lovely thing you are.' Then she tilted her head. 'I know somewhere we could get a drink and some lunch. Much better than the museum café. It's on the beach, out of the way of all the tourists.'

I'd not heard there was a beach on Delos. 'Is is far?' I asked, my voice husky.

'Not far.'

'I've got to get back to the boat in an hour, remember,' I said weakly. 'You know how strict they are.' Under

Greek law people were forbidden from spending the night on Delos. I didn't know why, just that I had a timed ticket.

Phoebe laughed at me. I noticed that she wore a necklace, a silver crescent which rested at the top of her breastbone; I wanted to touch its smooth metal. 'We've got our own boat, Ness. We can get you back to Mykonos any time.' She withdrew her hand from my knickers, flicking the elastic. 'Come on. You might learn something new about . . . island life.'

Why not? I asked myself. I'd wanted something that wasn't ordinary.

She was right about the beach, and it wasn't far. She held my hand as we walked. My head was spinning and I didn't pay much attention to our route, but in a few minutes we passed beyond the excavated area and over a low headland, and there in front of us was a narrow strip of sand, the dark Aegean washing up against it. Right at the far end was a taverna.

'See? You can meet my brother. He's staying there.'

I ran my free hand under my chin. 'Oh . . . It's so hot.'

'It's Greece, Ness, what did you expect? Did you bring sunscreen?' She brushed a finger down my breastbone, awakening little tremors right through my limbs. 'What about a paddle in the sea?'

She didn't wait for my assent this time. Pulling me firmly in her wake, she tripped down the path to the shore. The sand was coarse underfoot, like demerara sugar, but the shallows were blue and inviting and I went with her willingly, right over my knees in the water. My pink skirt swirled around me.

'Too warm still?' she asked, scooping up water in her cupped hands.

'Oh no,' I protested, shrinking back, but she poured it over my head anyway, and it ran right through the straw hat. After the first shock, it was lovely, but I yelped.

'Quiet.'

I froze at her peremptory tone, pouting at her from under the rat's tails of my normally sleek hair.

'That's better.' She dumped another scoop over my right shoulder and breast, drenching my clothes. I shuddered, wondering what it was that gave her the right to do this without me putting up any sort of fight, but the ache in my body answered that. Phoebe held me out at arm's length for inspection. 'You're so pretty.'

I felt I should return the compliment but I was tongue-tied. The cotton of my skirt clung to my thighs so closely that I could see a dark mole on my skin through the wet fabric. My blouse had turned translucent too and the bikini top I was wearing instead of a bra was quite visible beneath. Phoebe bit her lower lip, smiling. I couldn't see her eyes through the tinted glasses but I was sure there was a wicked glint back there. She slipped her hands up my back, under the wet top.

'Hey, no,' I protested as she pulled loose the first bikini tie and my breasts swung free. 'This isn't a topless beach.'

'You're not topless.' She transferred a hand to the nape of my neck where the second bow was. I grabbed to stop her.

'No!'

Knotting her fingers in my hair she pulled my head back firmly. 'Don't,' she said calmly, 'be such a baby.'

I went quiescent in her arms. She pulled my bikini top out through the neck of my blouse, leaving my nipples to rub on the cotton, then tucked her trophy into the front pocket of her shorts, letting the bright-fuchsia straps hang out.

'Better,' she said, looking down at me.

I have boobs big enough that I really do need a bra – otherwise I jiggle wildly when I walk. Now, under the wet cotton, both orbs were quivering. My nipples were prominent and so sensitive they felt sore. Hot and cold waves of embarrassment washed up and down my body, all emanating from the cauldron that was my sex. That cauldron, neglected for too long, was simmering over and the contents were soaking my knickers.

'Come on.' Phoebe was amused at my obvious shame. She led me up the beach. I was raw with self-consciousness. My breasts jounced with every step and the skirt gripped my legs, displaying the contours of my bum-cheeks and the pale triangle of my panties. I was grateful that the sands were empty – or nearly so. As we passed a scattering of boulders, some lads sitting in their lee looked up and spotted us. It didn't need the St-George's-flag shorts to tell me that these youths were British; I could tell that from the jeering tone of their catcalls, even before I caught the words. Blood flamed in my cheeks. I stumbled, trying to hide my face. Phoebe glanced sharply at me and then at the boys with a look of chilling hauteur. Interposing herself between me and them, she put one arm around me, her hand on my buttock, and we walked on together. My embarrassment vanished at her firm touch, to be replaced by a feeling of dizzy calm. I no longer felt vulnerable. I felt owned.

By the time we reached the ramshackle taverna, my clothes were no longer dripping. I hesitated before the structure as Phoebe took the steps two at time. Old fishing nets had been draped over the wooden frame and vines were intertwined with the mesh, effectively screening the interior. Outside on the sand were a few plastic tables and chairs and an unlit charcoal grill. A dog with a curly tail took one look at us and fled. Inside, someone was playing an acoustic guitar.

'Come on, Ness,' Phoebe commanded.

I followed her. The space within was filled with tables and chairs. Thick sand covered the floor, but in here under the dappled shade of the netting it was cool to the feet. A dozen people were sitting around; all but one were obviously local. That one was the man playing the guitar, and the others watched him in absolute silence. Phoebe pulled out a chair at an empty table and waved me to sit next to her. I sank down and held my hat over my breasts, grateful for the shade and the anonymity. An old woman dressed all in black brought us two bottles of cola from a battered fridge and Phoebe accepted them without a glance, her attention on the guitarist at the next table.

He was worth paying attention to. Wearing only cargo pants slung very low about his hips, this was pure surfer dude; the kind of beach-bum who'd never realised that you're supposed to give it all up at some point and get a proper job. His unruly brown hair was bleached corn-blond on top and he carried a deep tan that offset the pale-gold strands on his long shins and the muscular arms that cradled his guitar. He flashed a smile at Phoebe and I saw that his eyes were a blue like the clear Aegean shallows.

'That's Xander,' she whispered to me.

God, could he sing. I don't remember the lyrics now but I remember his voice and the sweet pain of the emotion stirred by it; a terrible hopeless longing for something forever out of reach. He switched to Greek and it made no difference; everything was carried by his tone. In moments, I felt the tears prickling in my eyes. I looked around and saw the same tears streaked down the faces of everyone in the taverna – all except Phoebe.

She sat with a cool smile, tilting the cola bottle to her lips.

When he finished, it felt like the world had stopped. I wanted to applaud, but no one else moved.

'Xander, this is Ness.' She waved a hand at him. 'This is my brother.'

'Ness?' he mused, tightening his tuning pegs. 'Short for . . . ?'

'Vanessa,' I confessed. 'But no one calls me that.'

He smiled and I felt it strike me like a kiss, leaving me tingling. It's unfair that men like that should exist; women have no defence against them. Except, I supposed, women like Phoebe.

She rose from the table. '*Doste mo mezedes*,' she ordered the old woman, and went to the back of the room to look in the cabinet and the fridge.

I took the opportunity to ask, 'Are you really her brother?' They looked nothing like one another.

'We're twins, actually.' There was a twinkling almost-smile in his eyes. 'Guess who's the elder.'

'Her,' I said without hesitation.

He lifted one eyebrow teasingly, then broke into another song – something about the last apple left on the tree.

Phoebe returned with a platter of pickles, olives, cucumber slices and dips, which she dropped on my table. 'There's not much of a selection.'

'That's OK.'

'*Feyete*!' she ordered, waving at the Greeks – and without a word every one of them rose and filed out of the taverna. She followed up behind them like a sheep-dog herding ewes.

I was stunned. Not just by her rudeness, but by their obedient attitude. Xander caught my expression and muted a complex instrumental improvisation long enough to explain softly, 'Our family owns this island;

the Government just rents it from us. Some of us keep some bad old habits, I suppose.'

'Your family's Greek?'

'Originally. We live all over the place now.'

Shipping millionaires or something, I guessed. Men might be from Mars, but the rich are from another galaxy altogether. Over by the taverna entrance, Phoebe tugged down a swathe of netting to block the gap and the speckled gloom deepened very slightly. I shivered. My damp dress was less comfortable now.

'Come on,' Phoebe said, switching off a tablecloth and laying it clean side up on the sand at Xander's feet. Taking the platter, she sat herself down picnic-style and patted the cloth next to her. I slid out from behind the table, feeling a little weird now that there were only three of us left. I felt worse when I'd sat down and she scooted behind me so that I was reclining back against her. With a snort, she snatched away the sunhat held casually at my breast. The damp cloth of my blouse still clung in places it was supposed to conceal. I squirmed inwardly. I hadn't bargained on getting cornered by a strange man; it seemed far more risky than just going off with a girl. But, I thought naively, a woman would be on my side if it turned nasty – wouldn't she?

'Pretty, isn't she?' said Phoebe, and Xander nodded, his enigmatic near-smile teasing.

His fingers rippled up and down the strings of the guitar, weaving cascading tapestries of sound. Phoebe fed me the appetisers from the plate with her fingers, piece by piece. I tasted reluctantly the salty feta, juicy black olives, creamy tzatziki. I wasn't feeling hungry. There was something creepy about the intimacy here; the way she was flirting with me in front of her brother's steady gaze.

The trouble was, the more uneasy I felt, the hotter and wetter I grew. She traced my lips in yoghurt and I lapped at her finger. She dripped olive oil on my tongue and I tilted my head back to receive it. Each new transgression forced me to find the courage to accept it, and each act of submission made my pussy burn. I wanted to squirm my bottom on the sand. When she slid one hand up under my blouse to cup my breast, I excused it to myself by saying that Xander couldn't actually see my naked flesh. When she pulled back my head against her shoulder and kissed me, long and wet, her tongue sliding in and out of my mouth, I told myself I shouldn't be prudish. When she rolled up my top to expose my nipples and took those points in her fingers, pulling and pinching them until they stood up fat as pink olives, then I mumbled in my head that every tourist in Greece went topless and it didn't mean a thing. And all the time my pussy grew plumper and more slippery until I felt like I was all writhing cunt and pleading tits.

She kissed all the strength out of me. She kissed me down to heavy, to passive, to open and empty, needing her forcefulness to fill me. When she withdrew from my mouth, my lips were slack and swollen. I made little helpless noises in my throat.

'Let's get this off,' she murmured, easing my blouse over my head.

I whimpered, my eyes pleading, but I didn't resist. What difference did it make, after all, if my breasts jutted out from beneath the bunched fabric or whether my shoulders were bared too and the blouse discarded in the sand?

'Shush,' she ordered, pulling my head back by the hair so that she could lick my tongue.

I was grateful; she understood me. My whimpers didn't mean that I needed her to stop; they meant that I needed her to make me go on.

Once I was resting back in her arms, she cupped my breasts from below, squeezing them as if fascinated by their weight and softness. 'Beautiful,' she whispered. 'You have beautiful breasts.'

She looked up at Xander for confirmation and he nodded, one eyebrow raised, cool and distant. But his hands had slowed upon the guitar and the rapid intertwining notes were grown simpler now, as if the music were vying for his attention with something more elemental.

'I could eat them up,' Phoebe whispered in my ear. She took up a piece of cut cucumber and rubbed its wet cold flesh across the stiff tips of mine, glazing them shiny as the cucumber turned to pulp. 'Do you like this?'

I nodded faintly. I couldn't speak any more.

'Let's see.' She pulled my skirt up slowly, finger over finger. Xander's eyes, a merciless blue like the cloudless skies above the islands, were fixed upon us, barely blinking. 'Yes. Let's have a look.' She cupped her hand over the mound of my sex and my hips twitched, my bum grinding into the cloth and the sand. 'Yes. See this? She's wet already, Xander.'

There was no denying that. The gusset of my tiny panties was soaked, the cotton already translucent from the sea water but more slippery with my juices. My thighs spread wider under her coaxing; he could look straight down between them. She pressed the cloth up against me. Then she slipped her fingers beneath the cotton and ploughed my furrow for real.

'Beautiful pussy too,' she breathed. 'Oh Ness, is that nice?'

I mewed like a kitten. Her fingertip was stirring my clitoris to flames.

'Pussy's so wet. Pussy's being naughty.'

There was no denying, either, what was happening here: if they really were siblings then this had gone way beyond kinky. It struck me with a kind of terror, which rendered me helpless as a rabbit in headlights. I was sagging against her arm, her right hand hooked up under my breast and tugging at my teat while her left hand delved deeper and deeper into my sex. Her fingers made little wet noises as they spread me wide.

'Can you hear how wet she is?'

Xander dipped his chin in acknowledgement. His lips were parted. The notes fell slow and distinct from his fingers like drops of rain.

'Dirty little pussy,' Phoebe breathed. 'Showing yourself for my brother.'

I began to come. She wasn't even trying to bring me off, she was just touching me up, but I couldn't bear her gloating judgement or the lancing blue of his eyes or the knowledge that she was exposing me and I was doing nothing to cling to my dignity. Electric sparks flashed through my clit.

'Oh, what a slut. What a filthy little slut.'

And she was right, wasn't she? I thought as I convulsed, hips and belly jerking, thrusting my tits up, longing for Xander to see them shaking, longing for Phoebe to enslave me further. The blood thundered in my ears.

Even as I came down, the pulse jumping all round my body as it does with that first easy orgasm, distress started to return in the backwash. But I had no time to think what to do next. Phoebe slipped from beneath my limp body and laid me back on the sand, pulling my arms over my head. I could feel the cool firm ripples of sand through the tablecloth. I could see the fishing nets and the vine leaves overhead. I felt her shift her position, pinning my arms to the sand under her shins. I heard the last note of the guitar fall silent. I looked down the length of my body and Phoebe slipped her hands under my head for a moment to support it. I saw the skirt rucked up around my hips and the pathetic wisp of cloth over my pubic mound and my sprawled open thighs.

Beyond them, Xander laid his guitar gently aside and stood, and I knew that Phoebe was offering me to him as a gift.

I should have been angry; I should have been afraid – but I was in a trance of submission and drunk with desire. And Xander was beautiful, so crazy fucking beautiful that I lost myself just looking at him. Dappled patches of sun gilded his smooth torso; he had surfer abs to go with the legs and the arms, and his pants hung so low on his hips that the hair mounting from the base of his flat belly peeked out. He slipped the top button of those shorts, taking his time. Two more and he could drop them over his thighs and step out. As I'd anticipated, there was no hint of a tan-line; he was bronzed all over. He put his hand on his cock and tugged it once, just guiding it to full erection. The lazy strokes he gave it after that were purely gratuitous, but helped emphasise its length and grace and the utter solidity of its stance. I whimpered low in my throat, knowing a dark hot pleasure in submitting to their incestuous game.

Without any hurry, he knelt between my thighs and tugged down my knickers. He tossed them to Phoebe, not looking at them, not lifting his gaze from mine. I think he wanted to see my helpless horrified need. Phoebe took the sodden scrap of fabric and pushed it between my lips. I opened for it willingly, tasting myself, accepting the gag as I'd accepted every one of her humiliations. She stroked my face and whispered, 'Good girl.'

Then Xander slid his hand under my hips and lifted me and guided his prick into me and fucked me – steady, implacable, slow at first so that I could feel every thrust, then faster and harder and higher. I've never been fucked like it. He held my bum off the floor, my cheeks on his locked thighs, my back arched across his hands.

He must have been strong – he must've had an arse like steel. Phoebe let my head fall back and instead ran her hands over my breasts. Only the fact that she was pinning me down at the shoulders kept me braced against the sand. While he towered above me, his cock slid in and out, mashing my sex until the heat built to a blaze. Not once did he stop to touch me or bestow a caress. His expression was taut with strain now, his eyes fixed on an ineffable distance, his beauty magnificent. Then Phoebe leant forwards into the light; a moon eclipsing the sun. I looked up and saw them meet, her lips against his, their tongues dancing together.

Xander groaned into his sister's mouth.

My orgasm came like a burst of light. It was white, it was golden – and it was not gentle. I only came back to myself when he withdrew, lowering me to the floor. I opened my eyes just soon enough to see his cock withdrawn into the shadows, still erect and nodding sagely and glistening with my butter. My muscles clenched yearningly around emptiness. I was awash with his come, I realised.

'Oh my pretty pussy,' whispered Phoebe, crawling headfirst down the length of my body and lying against me, one thigh draped around my neck. My arms were suddenly free and I took the chance to pull the knickers from my mouth so that I could draw more air with each gasp. I needed to; the next thing she did was wrap her head and shoulders over my pelvis and lower her face to my sex. I bucked in shock. She pushed into me, her tongue writhing, and I squirmed under her as she lapped up her brother's semen. Aftershocks chased my previous seismic orgasm and I clasped her waist and tilted my pelvis towards her, welcoming her mouth. Eyes shut, I blindly sought the cinch of her belt and loosed it, undid her button and fly and slid my hand into her shorts. I found no hair, only smooth skin and then slippery wetness. She heaved under my hand; it was the first reaction I'd ever got from her.

Then she was wrenched from me. From behind and above, Xander seized her hips and pulled her arse high, and in a few brief movements he yanked down her shorts, before flinging them aside. Phoebe cried out and clung to my thighs. Xander planted her knees firmly either side of my head and knelt up tight behind her; I was looking straight up at the sweet shaven folds of her sex when he pressed into her with the head of his cock. I got a ringside view. Inches from my nose he pushed home, and I could hardly believe that he was still hard after all he'd done to me, or that he could fit into that tight slit. He took her all the way – and she took him. His balls, fuzzed with their golden corona of hair, slapped up against her. 'Yes!' Phoebe cried into my muff.

He pulled back for the next thrust and I could see the sheen of her juices lacquering his shaft. I could smell her excitement and I could smell his heat. Her clit was quite visible; if I could've reached it with my tongue I would have licked it like a sweet. Sweat ran down the inside of his perfect thighs, his rhythmic thrusts building wave upon wave as she arched and writhed against him. She forgot to mouth at my sex and her hot face banged against the inside of my leg. I longed to feel her pleasure. I ran my hand up her belly and then, after laving my fingers in my own spit to lubricate them, laid them upon the pink pearl of her clit. I heard her sharp mew. In stroking her, my fingertips brushed Xander's hard shaft and were pummelled by his balls, and I added the friction of my splayed fingers to the grip of her cunt on his girth, my palm massaging the slick softness of her pussy.

Phoebe shrieked as she came. Xander's rhythm stuttered and for a moment he seemed to lock inside her, but I only really knew he was climaxing when he pulled out and, pressing his hand down on his cock to angle it better, ejaculated in great wet splashes on my face. Warm jism fell on my lips and lashes. I was shocked by how much those big clenched balls were able to produce; he was still jetting as he stuffed his prick back into his sister's hole to finish the job properly.

When it was all over, he bent forwards and kissed her bare shoulders before withdrawing. The expression on his face was exactly what you'd expect: smug. Phoebe slumped into a sitting posture at my side and pulled off her top to wipe her hot face; there was a wicked complicit grateful glitter in her eyes as she looked first at Xander, then at me.

She had a small crescent moon tattooed on one beautiful breast and silver studs through her nipples.

There was one last benison. She knelt to neatly lick his spunk from my face, kissing the last drops from my lips.

That was when the jeering and whistling started. At first I'd no idea where it came from, then as we looked around I spotted them, silhouetted on the netting wall. The obscenities in English identified the spies as the youths from the beach. Phoebe scrambled to her feet and I could read the fury in every taut line of her frame. She strode without hesitation across the taverna and ripped aside the nets at the entrance. Out into the sunlight she stalked, the boys whooping and gesturing before her; they fell back a little but they weren't really afraid. They were nearly killing themselves laughing.

Phoebe pointed her hand at them. She spoke in Greek. They fell to the floor. Then they turned into dogs.

I didn't have the best view, knelt up between the tables, but I know what I saw. They hit the sand and writhed wildly, kicking it into the air, and when they came up they were ragged-looking dogs with curly tails who fled howling with fear, tripping over their feet and falling again and tearing at their own limbs with their teeth in panic. Phoebe stalked after them, still shouting words I couldn't understand.

I turned in shock to Xander.

He shrugged. 'Old habits die hard.' Then with an exasperated sigh he heaved himself to his feet and followed his sister out on to the beach. 'Phoebe!'

His arse was *exactly* like his statue's.

Power Play Katie Doyce

Late-morning light poured through the patio doors of Jessica's high-rise flat. The sun-warmed carpet felt delicious against the soles of her feet as she padded across the living room and into the kitchen, sparing only the barest glance outside, checking the skies out of unconscious habit. Twenty-three floors above the streets of Mercury Bay, Jess never worried about peeping Toms or privacy blinds, even when (like today) she was still wearing nothing but a pair of white panties and a threadbare but much-loved Sonic the Hedgehog T-shirt at eleven in the morning, pushing sleep-tousled auburn hair out of her face to peer at the boxes of breakfast cereal in the pantry. In the two years she'd had the flat, she had never caught anyone watching her patio from an adjoining building; no telltale glint of a telephoto lens or binoculars, and no wall-crawling voyeur lurking behind her deck furniture with a video camera.

Certainly, no one had ever come crashing through the safety glass, collapsing in a heap in the middle of her living-room floor.

Jessica had just turned away from the counter, already munching on a hefty spoonful of muesli, whole milk and sugar, when all that changed. A split second before the stranger came sailing through the window, there was a deep resounding *clang*, like a large but cheaply made church bell; looking over the wreckage later, she would be able to deduce that her visitor had actually struck the patio railing first – and hard – before arriving in her flat. Glass flew into the room, scattering across the living-room furniture and ticking off the back wall. The man, dressed mostly in black leather with a few red accents, first somersaulted, then rolled length-wise along the floor before colliding with the heavy coffee table.

Another young woman in this situation – perhaps *any* other young woman – might have let out a yelp; even jumped back, prancing comically, flailing her arms and inadvertently throwing the bowl of cereal against the ceiling and stepping on several of the small cubes of glass that lay scattered across the kitchen tiles.

Jessica did not. She was not a normal young woman, and Mercury Bay was not a normal town.

Still chewing, she craned her neck to peer around the couch at the man on the floor. She swallowed noisily, set the bowl on the counter next to the sink and picked her way to the hall closet, where she retrieved an old pair of slippers and pulled them on.

Arms folded across her faded shirt, she made her way back to the living room, grabbed the shoulder of the man's leather jacket and rolled him on to his back. She turned her head left and right, trying to view his face right-side-round without actually moving.

She wasn't surprised to recognise him.

'Nathan . . .' she drew out the end of his name, shaking her head like a disapproving aunt. 'Have you been a bad boy again?'

She looked back at the ruins of her patio door. Another chunk of webbed glass fell from the top of the frame. Without the double-paned glass door blocking it, the sounds of the street could be heard fairly clearly. Rather than the low murmur of auto traffic, Jess picked out an electric crackle and several low vibrating thumps she could feel through the floor. She moved around her prone visitor and managed to reach the (bent) patio railing and look down. Brightly clad figures circled one another on the street and in the air above, strobe-lit by too-white flashes.

Again, she wasn't surprised to recognise them, or the blue-and-white figure – large, even from twenty-plus stories above – staring up at her.

'Bugger,' she muttered. She turned back to her flat at the groan from within as her visitor rolled on to his side and pushed himself to a sitting position. 'Bugger, bugger, bugger.'

'Sorry?' He was leaning on one arm and had the heel of his other hand against his temple, his eyes closed.

'You –' Jessica glanced from him back to the street, where the large figure was backing across the street, still looking up in her direction and completely ignoring the chaos all around. 'Shit.' She turned back to him, gripping the rail behind her. 'You have to move.'

'What d'ya mean?' He blinked his eyes several times, shaking his head in a way that indicated he thought it might come loose.

'I have no idea,' she muttered, wondering what the hell she thought she was doing.

'What?'

'Nothing. You have to move,' she repeated. 'They're coming.'

He looked in her direction, wincing at the sunlight. 'No. It's all right.' He sounded resigned.

She clenched her jaw. 'Fuck that,' she said, stepping in over the doorframe. 'Run.'

'Oh.' He smiled, not showing any teeth, his lips a curl of self-mockery. 'I don't think that's on the cards, love.'

She looked around the room, searching for inspiration. She marched over to him (as well as one can in cotton knickers and old slippers, through broken glass) and grabbed the collar of his jacket. 'Then crawl.'

Amid general and pained protests, she pulled him into the kitchen, behind the central island and out of sight, half-dragging him and half-leading him like a dog on a leash.

Not a moment too soon. A heavy impact on the patio shook the crystal baubles in the light fixture over the coffee table. Jess heard the crunch-squeal of someone heavy stepping on the bits of glass on the cement pad.

'Don't be alarmed.' The voice was radio announcer smooth and pitched to project. Jessica also happened to know that it was essentially an act. 'I'm only here to help.' A pause. 'May I come in?'

Strange phrase to hear from someone who'd just broadjumped onto your 23rd-storey balcony, but understandable: a pile of breaking-and-entering litigation had been accumulating in the Mercury Bay courts concerning these kinds of situations.

'Umm, sure,' Jess replied. Her hands were restless. She couldn't decide between resting them on the countertop, tucking them behind her (a bad bet, with the way her T-shirt stretched), resting them on her hips (which reminded her she was still half-naked), or folding her arms. They moved from one position to the next like nervous pets.

The doorway darkened almost entirely, eclipsed by the mass of her new visitor, who stepped through as gingerly as possible and still managed to knock more glass loose and dislodge the bent frame of the sliding door itself. The huge man, clad head to foot in a blue and white bodysuit, surveyed the rest of the room before focusing a leading-man smile in her direction.

'Hello, miss. I'm the Blue Brahma, a member of the Vindicators and a fully sanctioned representative of both the Mercury Bay and national law enforcement. I apologise for the damage done to your flat. On a related note, I'm looking for the, ah, individual known to the public as Cinder.' He motioned to the scattered glass. 'The fellow who made this mess.'

Jessica stared at him. 'You've got to be fucking kidding me.'

Her other guest, sitting on the kitchen floor with his back to the island, shifted and opened his mouth to speak. Catching the slight movement, Jess dropped her left hand down and pressed her fingertips to his lips, hard enough to make the message clear.

Blue Brahma paused, but his smile remained. 'I'm sorry? I assure you that my goal here is entirely –'

'Dwight,' Jess interjected. 'Open your eyes, for Chrissake.'

The man blinked, clearly taken aback by the use of his name. His gaze shifted ever so slightly, actually *looking* at her; the effect was not entirely unlike a television anchorman focusing past the cameras and looking straight at the viewer for the first time after ten years on the air. 'I'm sorry, I don't –' He paused. 'Jessica?'

Jess nodded, her eyes wide and the movement slow, as though she were communicating across language barriers. 'Yes, Dwight. Jessica.'

Again, her first visitor shifted, this time turning his head as though trying to clear the obstruction to speech. Jessica slid her fingers around to grip his jaw, and, when his movement subsided, relaxed.

The big man in her living room frowned. 'What are you doing here?'

Jess tilted her head. 'I live here, Dwight.' She made a show of looking around. 'This is my flat.'

This didn't seem to clear anything up for the Brahma. 'You're supposed to be on holiday.'

'I am.'

'But . . . you're here.'

'Yes.' She nodded again, slowly. 'This is my flat.'

'But you're supposed to be on holiday,' he said, his expression shifting from charming to dogged. 'You're supposed to go away when you go on holiday.'

'I did go away, Dwight.' Jess tried to keep her tone patient, but Blue wasn't her favourite conversational partner at the best of times, and her silent guest was moving again. Though he didn't seem to be trying to ruin the whole thing by talking; he just kept turning his head from side to side. His lips were brushing across the palm of her hand. It was distracting.

'But you're here,' Blue Brahma repeated.

Jess sighed, clearly exasperated (though her breath caught a bit at the end; Cinder – Nathan – had grazed his teeth over the pad of her index finger). 'I went away from *work*, Dwight. Just work. That's why I'm not down there with the rest of you, wreaking random property damage.' She closed her eyes for a moment, already tired of the conversation. (Not trying to concentrate on what Nathan was doing with her fingers. No.) 'Clearly, I should have gone further away.'

Brahma's smile came back at that, and he laughed his television interview laugh. 'I'd have to agree.' He switched to a concerned expression and started to walk over to her. 'Are you all ri–'

She started and took a half step further behind the island, away from him. 'What are you doing?'

Blue Brahma paused again, brought up short in mid-hero performance for the second time in two minutes. 'I was making sure you were all right.'

'I'm not exactly dressed for company, Dwight.' She looked at him, looked down at the midriff-high counter-top meaningfully, then back.

She had to look up again – *had* to – her silent guest was teasing the end of each fingertip and watching her face. Looking down, she'd met his eyes and simultaneously become aware of how much closer she'd moved her panty-clad hips towards him. The realisation made her face hot and her knees a bit weak; robbed of blood supply that was rushing elsewhere.

'Oh.' Brahma's eyes dropped to the counter again, then widened. 'Oh! I . . . Oh!'

'Yes.' Jess agreed, biting hard on the end of the word for several different reasons; one visitor was annoying, and the other was sliding his fingertips up the inside of her left leg, over ankle, then calf, and higher. 'So if you could please . . . ?'

'Absolutely.' The Blue Brahma nodded, stood for several seconds, seemed to remember himself and stepped back on to the balcony. 'Very sorry, Timbre.' He called from out of sight. 'Jessica, I mean. Sorry.'

'It's all right.' Jess bit her lower lip, dropped her head forwards until her hair obscured her face.

Nathan's fingers traced the curve on the inside of her knee. She looked down at him, moved her fingers along his lips, bracing herself with her other hand on the counter. What the hell, she thought, I'm on holiday. With that, she took another step and placed her feet on either side of him, bringing her sex within inches of his face. She met his gaze, then closed her eyes. 'It's all right.'

His hand reached higher, while his lips opened under her touch and he sucked gently on her fingertips. Jess pressed her lips together to keep a moan from escaping. His touch skimmed her leg from inner thigh to the sole of her foot, and back again, each time travelling higher, lighter, closer. He'd just brushed against the damp cotton between her legs with his knuckle when another piece of glass crashed to the floor, and Jess jumped, looking over at the door.

'Sorry, very sorry.'

'*Yes*, Dwight?' Jess braced herself against the counter's edge and flipped her hair back, putting a hardly feigned look of annoyance on her face. 'What is it?'

'Sorry, I didn't mean to bother . . . it's just . . . well . . .'

He slipped back into official superhero mode. 'I was looking for Cinder. He was part of that fight, below, and obviously he was here.' He indicated the scattered glass. 'May I search for him?'

'Hell, no, Dwight. Do you ask Batman if you can poke around the Batcave?'

Dwight looked confused. 'Batman's not real.'

Jess sighed, her breath catching for a moment, as the object of the Brahma's quest slid his finger under the elastic of her panties. 'I know! I'm saying, um ... Look, he's not here, OK? He took off right after crashing through my door. Didn't stop to say anything.'

'Very well, then.' Brahma ducked his head back outside, then back in again. 'Keep an eye out for him though, would you? You know his reputation as well as any of us. He's not exactly a respectable citizen.'

Big Blue bounded off the balcony again, but Nathan's attentions didn't resume. Jess let her gaze drop to his.

'I should go,' he murmured, brushing her fingers with his lips.

'You can't. They'll find you.' She pulled her hand away from his mouth to run her fingers through his black hair, tugging on it as she forced his gaze to meet hers.

'It doesn't matter.' He rubbed his forehead against the soft curve of her belly above her knickers, his nose pressing into her. His teeth caught at the cotton and pulled, gently. 'You heard him, I'm not respectable.'

'I don't –' Her fingers clenched in his hair as his fingertips played along her slick wet slit. 'Please, stay.'

Cinder complied, and slipped a hot finger into Jess's core. She moaned as he flicked her clit, warmth building like an inferno. The heat radiated out from where he touched her, where his fingers slipped inside her and teased, flicking, playing, toying. Jess pressed her palm against the granite countertop, and a delicate glass flower vase shattered as she came in a molten explosion. She sagged against his hands, but managed to remain standing.

When the shuddering aftershocks of her orgasm faded, Cinder slipped his hands back to (slightly) less enticing locations. 'I really should go.'

'Maybe I won't let you.' She nudged at him with a roll of her hips. 'Maybe I'm going to have to make a citizen's arrest.'

She pulled at his hair again, and he looked up, smiling. 'You think you can keep me here?'

It was Jess's turn to smile. Hadn't he heard anything? Then again, he had been somewhat distracted while she and Dwight spoke. Maybe he didn't catch that Brahma had called her Timbre, or that she'd just shattered a perfectly good vase. Then again, maybe it didn't matter if he had.

She pulled at the front of his jacket, drawing him away from the cabinet and pushing him down to the floor. She dropped to her knees on either side of him and leant forwards, one hand pressing against the tile floor while the other gripped the leather. 'I *know* I can,' she whispered.

He heard a low-level hum. The sound built, peaked and the glass on the floor rattled away across the kitchen, clearing a space around them.

He glanced to either side, a small smile on his lips. 'That's pretty impressive'

She arched an eyebrow. 'Wanna see what else I can do?'

Ask anyone within the news agencies that specialised in 'paranormal personalities', and they would tell you that the sanctioned Mercury Bay hero known as Timbre was a 'sonic', that is to say, someone who did something with sound. What that 'something' was varied, depending on the paranormal in question, but, in almost every case that Jess had encountered, it involved screaming at the top of one's lungs like a distraught jilted banshee with PMS.

Jessica didn't do that. The fact of the matter was that Jessica's powers weren't actually sound based at all. Yes, they *produced* sound, but so did Dwight the Blue Brahma, and Jess could attest that his ability to do so didn't in any way make him special.

What Jessica did was produce vibrations in anything she could physically touch, as well as control the direction and intensity of those vibrations, anything from a mild hum to foundation-shaking tremors. She'd lost count of the number of times that some 'criminal mastermind' had tried to 'take her out of the equation' by clamping some wondrous gizmo (or sometimes just their hand) over her mouth, only to start jerking around like a taser victim as soon as they touched her.

She didn't mind that almost no one knew how her powers worked – it's why she'd called herself Timbre in the first place instead of something like 'Tremor' or 'Seismiss' or, God forbid, 'Vibro Lass'.

She didn't bother unfastening Cinder's jacket or pants yet; she let her eyes unfocus and simply feel where he was beneath the layer of leather. The first pulse spread across his chest like gooseflesh, intensifying as it reached each nipple. He didn't gasp, but she could feel the muscles in his thighs clench and allowed herself a small distant smile.

'I could make this last a while,' she said. Her voice sounded dreamy in her own ears. 'But you were so good and so fast for me, I'll be nice.'

She slid further down his legs, letting her hands glide over his chest and abdomen, spreading the slow low vibration as she went. At his waist, she tugged the button of his pants loose with one hand, pressing the palm of the other against the rigid length of him, wrapped in the cool black leather. Here, though, she didn't enhance the contact with her power. Not yet. He didn't seem to mind. His legs flexed again, lifting his pelvis against her hand. Jess used the motion to help pull the zipper down, then gripped both sides of his pants and pulled them down as far as she easily could, bunching them around his knees. It wasn't pretty or elegant or romantic, but that wasn't what this was about. The rest could wait for later.

The stretchy-tight cotton fabric of his briefs strained to contain his sex. Jess caught the top edge of the elastic band with her fingers and pulled it down to reveal the crown, dragging the fabric along the shaft as she stripped him to the knees. Before she'd even got the cloth entirely out of the way, she was bending forwards, tracing the thick bulge along the underside of his cock with the tip of her tongue.

Here, she used her power. Any kind of contact worked, after all – it didn't have to be her hands. The inaudible hum she sent into the shaft elicited a very audible groan from him. She was inclined to drag that out as long as possible, but she stopped herself and intensified the vibration instead. His back arched and he pressed the shaft of his cock blindly against her mouth. She slid her lips and tongue along the shaft again, first down to the thick fuzzy base, nuzzling, inhaling the musky scent, then up to the head, already slick and glistening with his own fluids. The tip of her tongue circled once, twice, and on the third rotation, she slid him into her mouth and amplified the vibrations again.

There was something to be said for immediate gratification.

Her hands free, she slid them up his thighs, sending shivers into him from three different directions. He writhed, tried to talk, but only managed half-words; at a guess, Jess thought he was trying to get out 'Don't', 'God', 'Fuck', and 'More', in roughly that order. She focused on 'more'. Moving slightly to the side, she cupped his balls in her left hand and gripped the base of his shaft in her right, sliding the taut skin over the shaft in time with the smaller motions of her mouth – more than enough to please any partner, even without the waves of additional sensation that radiated out from those points of contact and into the rest of his body. She could tell from his ragged breathing that he was already close to coming – all it would take from her was a small push to put him over the edge.

She decided to throw him over instead. Hard.

She splayed the fingers of her left hand, pressing the palm against the very base of his cock and starting a low thrumming pattern that pushed into the core of him. He let out a strained moan that seemed to come straight from his chest. With one finger, she teased down even further, circling his anus in softly vibrating torment. His body arched to the point where it seemed only his shoulders and heels were actually touching the floor.

Something smelt like it was burning, but she ignored it. Her left hand sent tremulous probes into his core, her right continued the steady hard rhythm along his shaft, and her lips formed a tight ring of sensations just below the head as she swirled the sensitive tip over and over with her tongue. Then she intensified every point of contact until he was straining upwards beyond the capacity for breath.

There was no way she could take more of him into her mouth than she already was, but Jess knew that

that really wasn't important – it was making him feel everything she was doing, right through his climax.

He left scorched handprints on the kitchen floor.

'What the–?' Nathan's bellow would have shaken knick-nacks from her bookshelves if she hadn't long since given up on fragile tchotchkes.

Jess popped her head around her bedroom doorframe. 'You're awake.'

He was a bit more than awake; 'outraged' seemed a good word for it. Surprised, maybe, at the very least.

'I'm tied up.' His voice wasn't much past a growl. 'And I'm naked. I'm fairly certain these are both new developments.'

'Not entirely.' Jess moved into the room and leant on the corner post at the bottom of the bed, making sure her eyes stayed on his. 'Anyway, I thought we should have a chat.'

He gestured – tried to gesture, at any rate, with one hand. The movement was hampered by the heavy leather straps securing each of his arms to a bedpost, and the hand (like its mate) was covered in what looked like an oven mitt made out of a shiny sort of neoprene. 'This how you chat with everyone you have round?'

Jess found she was actually blushing, struck by the simple fact of what she'd done – taken a man (one who'd arrived in her flat, fleeing authorities, then serv-iced her and been serviced in turn), who was little more than a stranger in the best light and a criminal adver-sary at the other end of the spectrum, and finally strapped him, stark naked (except for the hand cover-ings), to her bed. It wasn't as though she could claim innocent intent. She tilted her head, suppressing a smile and trying to let her hair conceal her face. 'No. This is a first.'

He was watching her, his expression balanced

between suspicion and something she couldn't identify. 'I honestly can't tell if that's a good thing or a bad thing.' He glanced at his left hand. 'Flame-suppressing synthetics?'

She nodded. 'We were issued them when you broke out last April.' She didn't see the point of denying her connection to the Vindicators – he'd obviously heard Brahma use her 'public' name. It didn't matter much in any case; most professional heroes only used them to avoid paparazzi.

His gaze moved to the heavy leather straps holding his arms. 'These look a little more multipurpose.'

Again, her face flushed. 'They're from when Captain Conundrum escaped from Utumno Prison last year.'

'Ahh.' His brow arched. 'Now that you explain, I can see they're *completely* innocent.' He let his gaze travel down the length of his body, dragging hers along with it. 'Though I suppose I should take heart in the fact that this is not otherwise anything like the usual method of detainment for the Mercury Bay Vindicators, or the police.'

She returned his look. 'You should know.'

'I do indeed.' He watched her face for several seconds. 'So –' he crossed his legs, but just at the ankles, and leant his head back, looking for all the world like someone sunning themselves on a beach without a care in the world '– you wanted a chat?'

The conversation hadn't started out the way that Jess had hoped, but this was the opening she thought she could use to turn things round again. 'Actually, I thought I'd do you the favour of explaining what was going to happen to you, rather than...' She paused, letting the corner of her mouth curl up. 'Rather than letting you find out the hard way.'

He tipped his head a bit to the side. 'That sounds a bit sinister; have you suddenly decided to switch sides?

Am I hearing your first monologue? If so, I'd have to say –'

'Shut up,' she snapped, 'unless you want me to black you out again, pull your clothes back on and give the police an anonymous tip.'

He started to reply, then changed his mind and waited.

Jess nodded. 'That's better. You see, I *could* turn you in, but the thing is, I'm on holiday.' She moved around the post of the bed and sat down on the edge of the mattress. 'I didn't really have any plans, but I knew without a doubt that I wanted to get away from work. Turning you in would *be* work, and that rather misses the point.'

'You'll forgive me for saying so,' he replied, 'but in this particular case you've taken procrastination to an entirely new level.'

'Well –' she laid a hand on his leg, toying with the fine hairs '– we get on a bit, also.'

He shifted on the bed, just enough to move the leather straps around the bedposts. 'Aside from the obvious contradictions, I'd have to agree.'

'And . . .' She watched her hand as it moved – almost entirely on its own – up to his thigh. 'It's like I own you.'

'Excuse me?' Though his words could have been spoken in outrage, his voice was soft.

She shrugged. 'Well, I can turn you in.' Her fingernails grazed his hip. 'Or you and I can play a little game for the rest of my holiday. I own you.'

He was looking at her, but she didn't meet his gaze. Cinder wasn't a 'serious' criminal – no assault charges or any kind of violent crimes, actually, despite the nature of his powers – but he was a very prolific thief, a notorious safe-cracker in dozens of bank heists and sole escapee of three hitherto 'impenetrable' prisons and many lesser institutions, in most cases without any apparent use of his powers. She had no doubt whatsoever that, if he had actually wanted to, he could have been dressed and out of her apartment before she'd even realised he was awake, and even less doubt that he could escape whatever holding cell the police might put him in. He didn't have to be here, and she wasn't really blackmailing him.

In short, they were already playing a game.

The thought made her breathing tight. She shifted on the edge of the bed and felt a telltale slickness between her legs. Her hand grazed over his cock, fingers running up and down the shaft in an unconscious rhythm.

'All right.' She was so wrapped up in the sensation that his voice almost made her jump. She looked up at him, finally. His eyes were half-closed, but she could see he knew what was going on as well. 'What do you want me to do?'

A dozen ideas popped into her head – plans and half-formed fantasies that she'd entertained while cleaning up the mess in her kitchen and living room, waiting for him to wake up – but the way she felt right now, she wasn't in the mood to prolong the anticipation. 'This time,' she said, her voice low, 'nothing fancy.'

She stood and pulled off her T-shirt, tossed it to the floor and shook her hair back behind her head as she hooked her thumbs into her knickers and smiled, then slipped them down over her smooth hips.

She crawled up the bed, lowering her face and running her tongue up the underside of his cock, circling it around the head. She heard him groan, as he tried to reach for her, the move blocked by the leather straps, and smiled to herself. She took the head in her mouth, sucking hard, working on just the end with her lips and tongue until his breathing started to get ragged, then she sat up and straddled his abdomen, letting his cock lie against the crack of her ass and lowering her breasts to his mouth. He sucked roughly, like a starving prisoner finally given his daily water ration, and she heard her own moans and gasps. She moved back and forth, alternating breasts, then edged even further up his body, dragging her sex along his bare chest. She could feel her wetness against his smooth skin as she moved her pussy up to his mouth, grabbed the headboard and began riding his tongue. Unable to use his fingers as he had before, he thrashed her clit and lips, sucking at her, building a heat she didn't think possible. Her hips rocked back and forth over his face, and he stabbed his tongue into her, fucking her with it, then sucked on her clit, building pressure as she hunched against him, hips jerking, barely breathing until she came, hard, gasping air like a drowning swimmer that finds the surface, before finally dropping back on to the bed.

'Enough?' His breathing, Jess was gratified to note, wasn't much more even than hers.

'Just –' she flailed her hand around, trying to get her arm under her '– just fine.'

When her limbs were able to obey her again, she crawled up the length of him, bracing one hand against his shoulder and gripping his cock with the other. She slipped it into her and slid down on to it in a continuous motion that made him gasp. She moved over him with a slow steady rhythm for several minutes, watching his face, leaning down to nip at his lips and neck and whisper perversions in his ear. He arched his body upwards, groaning, pushing his hips up to meet her, trying to push into her as far as he could as she rocked, dragging her clit across the base of him with each downward thrust, as the pressure and heat built in both of them. She reached up to brace herself against the headboard, pushing down against him with each thrust, riding him, sweat gleaming, then dripping on to his chest as she came again, the tight shuddering grip of her slick pussy around his cock pushing him over the edge only a few seconds later. She rode him through it, rocking her hips, squeezing him with her core. Sweating. Smiling.

She hadn't even used her powers. Not yet.

Jess returned to the bedroom, towelling her hair and smiling at Nathan, still sprawled underneath the duvet. It had been easily the best holiday break in history, in her opinion. The week had been a blur punctuated with food delivery and interrupted only once when the repairmen had come to fix the patio door. Otherwise, she'd turned down the volume on the answerphone and left the television off.

Now, she disappeared into the depths of her closet and pulled a pair of red slingbacks away from her shoe rack. The back wall swung open to reveal the rest of her closet, containing her uniform, accessories and the various 'special situation' tools of the trade that she'd been re-employing in various ways over the course of the last week. She sighed and pulled 'the suit' off its hanger.

'Back to work?' Nathan peered at her, muzzy and adorable, from the bed.

'Duty calls.' She didn't look at him.

'I suppose this means our little game is over, then.' He watched her dress. She didn't reply. 'Jess?'

'I was thinking,' she said, still not looking at him. 'I could say something on your behalf, maybe get them to give you a second chance.'

'You *really* don't have to do that,' he said, after a pause. 'It's sweet, and I adore you for it, but it's really not necessary.'

'I want to,' she interjected. 'I'll get the Major and Jasmine and Blue Brahma into a proper sit-down meeting and –'

'Why's he call himself that, anyway?' Nathan interrupted. 'Blue Brahma. He's not even Indian.'

He was changing the subject. Letting her win, really, when he didn't have to. She was just starting to understand him, and she didn't want that to stop because of her stupid job. She walked towards the bed and sat down on the edge, her hands in her lap, his leg just touching her back. 'You know, I asked him that once. Y'know what he told me?'

'What?'

'He said that, if he actually were Indian, he could never have called himself the Blue Brahma, because then it would have been disrespectful.'

Nathan searched her face, clearly hoping she was joking. 'I find myself embarrassed *for* him, and I don't even like him.'

'Well, he did knock you through my patio door, so that's understandable.' She traced his jaw with a finger. 'I'll have to remember to thank him for that, someday.'

His eyes searched hers. 'Don't talk to them. Don't bother.'

'I want to.'

'Jess –'

She covered his lips with her fingers, just as she had in the kitchen only a week earlier. 'Don't make me tie you up again.'

That made them both grin, and a few minutes later she had to flee the room before things went so far that she missed her first day back on the job.

Jess slid, literally, through the front doors of the Vindicator headquarters. It wasn't the most glamorous way to get around – she intensely envied the metas who were able to fly – but, by using her powers, she could keep herself in perpetual motion along almost any surface using vibrations to control direction and speed. It

POWER PLAY **133**

wasn't flashy or very fast, but there were upsides, not
the least of which was popularity with the citizens of
Mercury Bay, who saw her as a more approachable hero.
There was even a group of 'grrrls', somewhere between
a fan club and a well-meaning gang, who tried emulat-
ing her moves as much as possible using skateboards.

'Timbre!' Anna Davida waved as she crossed the
lobby. 'You're back! You look great!'

Jess made a face. 'Do I? That's funny. I didn't really go
anywhere.'

Anna's eyebrows rose. 'You didn't?'

'Timbre used her holiday to stay home.' Blue Brahma
stood just inside the doors to the main meeting hall. He
sounded bemused and, somehow, disapproving.

'Hi, Blue,' Jess said, careful to use call signs inside the
headquarters. It wasn't a habit that had come easily.
'Did I miss anything exciting, after you broke my patio
door?'

Brahma frowned. 'I didn't have anything to do with
that, Timbre, other than my brief stop to look for Cinder.'
Brahma's tone went sour at the mention of Nathan's
public identity.

'Sure.' Jess smirked. 'Did you ever find him?'

Brahma sighed. 'Finally, yes. Just this morning.'

She stopped dead, only a few dozen feet into the
meeting hall. Most of the Vindicators were present and
milling about in clusters of various sizes, chatting before
the actual meeting started up, but Jess could barely hear
them over the roaring in her ears. 'You caught him?'

'Caught?' Brahma shook his head. 'Those days are
over, I'm afraid.' He nodded to Night Sparrow as the
hero walked by. 'No, he just showed up this morning,
like a badly trained dog that finally remembered where
the food was.'

'Blue, that's hardly fair.' Jasmine appeared next to
Brahma. 'Hello, Timbre.'

'Hi, Jas.' Jess followed, stunned, as Jasmine turned and started walking towards one of the larger groups near the Major's podium. 'What do you mean, he just showed up? He surrendered?'

Jasmine smiled. 'Of course n– Oh!' She shook her head. 'Of course, you were on vacation during his court hearing.'

'*Whose* court hearing?'

'That would be mine.'

She knew the voice – knew it better than anyone else in the room, she was quite sure – and still she couldn't believe it. Cinder (in his full outfit, which Jess distinctly remembered stowing in her secret closet) slipped out of the knot of people near the podium and pulled himself to mock attention. 'Hi. Don't attack me. I'm one of the good guys.'

Jess gaped. 'How? Who?'

'Court order,' Brahma explained. 'The judge said, if I remember correctly, that any prison term would be shortened inexcusably by either probation or Cinder's well-documented abilities, so he assigned community service instead.' He looked down at Cinder with undisguised distaste. 'Ten thousand hours of it, to be served as a provisional member of the Vindicators.'

'That's five years, give or take, if I don't pull any overtime.' Nathan grinned and swung a light punch at Brahma's shoulder. 'Big Blue here is my parole officer.'

'Don't call me that.'

'Right.'

'But . . .' Jess's voice trailed off in silence.

'All right, everyone, let's get this started, moving and finished.' The Major had stepped to the podium, calling the Vindicators to order as he always did. 'We've got work to do.'

Conversations dwindled and died out as the heroes found their seats. Jess dropped into hers, stunned and numb. She jumped when Nathan leant forwards from the row behind her and whispered in her ear. 'You OK?'

'I . . .' She shifted in the chair. 'I'm just not sure what to do.'

'No?'

She shook her head, eyes staring at nothing at all. 'No.'

'Hmm . . .' Nathan murmured. 'That's interesting. You see –' he leant in another inch closer. She could smell his hair. It smelt like her shampoo '– I was thinking that tonight, we could play a *new* game.'

The Shadow of Matthew
Gwen Masters

Alison opened the bedroom door.

It was a simple thing, opening a door that she had opened a million times before. So why did the knob seem to burn in her hand, and why did the door open so slowly, like it was just as afraid of her as she was of it?

There were his jeans on the floor, his shoes right beside them. There was his book and that was on the floor, too. A bookmark held the place where he had stopped reading. A pair of glasses rested on the bedside table, in front of the little sound machine that mimicked ocean waves. The quilt was thrown back and the pillows were rumpled. There was an indentation where he had laid his head.

Alison flinched violently at the sight of that, as if an invisible hand had risen up to strike her.

She had expected the bed to be the worst. The bed where they had read books while lying in companionable silence, his hand occasionally brushing across her arm in a gesture of marital contentment. The bed where they had made love during long and lazy days and even longer nights. The bed where their whole marriage had been played out, in arguments or in lovemaking, in one way or another, for the last ten years.

Alison sat carefully on the edge of the bed, as if it might leap up and swallow her. She waited out the earthquake that didn't come. Wind rattled the branches of the big oak tree against the windows. A cold front was coming through and, by the time night rolled around, it would be snowing. There would be four inches, maybe more, or so the forecast said. Matthew always loved winter. She remembered when they would lie in bed and watch the first snowflakes together.

This was nothing but a bed. This was nothing but their house.

Hers. Not theirs, not any more.

A month ago, her husband had gone for a walk in the fallen leaves. It was his favourite time of year, right before the first of the snow fell. It was his favourite time of day, right before the sun went down and the moon went up.

It was a simple walk down a simple road that no one ever travelled – but that day, someone did. Someone was travelling that road at a speed fuelled by one too many drinks, a kid who shouldn't have been drinking and maybe shouldn't even have been driving in the first place. And that kid certainly shouldn't have been driving that big SUV, the one that was too big for her to keep under control.

The SUV wrapped itself around the tree, an old maple whose leaves were all but gone. Alison's husband had seen it all. She could imagine the horror on his face, the paralysis of watching it happen, then the sudden break into a run, the determination to help.

During the time between life and death, Matthew had done everything he could do to save that girl. That's why he was in the SUV with her when the engine caught fire, and that is why he stayed there too long.

It was just like him to do that, so many people had said to her at the visitation and at the funeral and in the days beyond, as if it was something that would bring her a measure of comfort. It was his nature, they said. It was just like him to give all of himself for someone else.

Alison's husband died a hero.

But that didn't change the fact that he had *died*.

Alison blinked at the sudden tears. Here it was, surely – here was the tsunami of pain. She held tight to the edge of the bed and focused all her energies on her heart, listened to it pound within her body, not going too fast, not yet . . .

If she didn't fall apart, did that mean she didn't care enough?

There across the hallway was the open door to the bathroom. Alison walked to the door and looked in. The light wasn't on – Matthew was always good at conserving energy, it was one of the things he harped on until Alison wanted to tell him to shove it – and the winter sunlight came through the skylight, as if showcasing everything for her to see.

Matthew's razor was right there on the edge of the sink. There were little black stubs of hair all over the white porcelain. She stared at them for a very long time.

His toothbrush was there. The bristles were dry. The toothpaste tube was squeezed out of shape in the middle, twisted into the shape of his hand. Another tube sat beside that one, neatly rolled from the bottom. Years of marriage had taught them that, while some things had possible compromise, other things were just best accepted.

But he had *died* on her. Where was the compromise in that?

'Liar,' she said out loud. Her voice echoed, the only answer she was going to get. The fury rose up within her, two steps ahead of the guilt. How could she be angry with him? This was the man who had given the last measure of himself in an effort to save the life of someone else. He made the front page of the national newspapers. Complete strangers mourned him. How could she not see him the way everyone else saw him?

But he hadn't left everyone else. He had left *her*.

Alison picked up the toothpaste tube. Her fingers almost fit in the places where his fingers had squeezed. She thought about his hands. He was obsessive about his nails. He kept them clean and clipped and tended with a nail buffer that was grey on one side and pink on the other. He made such a strange picture, his broad shoulders resting back in the chair, his strong hands wielding something so dainty and feminine.

She dropped the toothpaste tube into the trash can. There was nothing else in there, and it looked lonely at the bottom of the wicker basket. She picked up the straight razor, the one that frightened her when she watched him use it, but, sure enough, he never cut himself. Not once. Not a single drop of blood.

She dropped the razor into the trash can. It bounced once and landed neatly beside the toothpaste tube. The sunlight found it and dazzled in starbursts along the sharp edge.

She opened the medicine cabinet. There was the aspirin. She had never been able to take aspirin, but he took them three at a time, sometimes four. She often imagined his blood thinning out to nothing, growing lighter as it pumped through his veins, until there was nothing but the outline of cells in something as clear as water.

The aspirin rattled as she dropped the bottle into the trash.

The toothbrush, the one with the neon colours that looked so out of place. The soap he used, the sandalwood stuff that dried her skin, but made his feel smooth as silk. The shaving soap and the mug and the brush, the old-fashioned way he did things, it all went into the trash can, sometimes with a thud, sometimes with a crash.

She didn't realise she was crying until her tears fell

on the prescription bottle of Valium, the one that was out of date by five years, the one his doctor had given him after the death of his mother. Matthew had sworn he didn't need them and there they had stayed in the cabinet, but when she looked at the bottle now she realised most of the Valium were missing.

Matthew was with his mother now, and Alison was the one who needed the Valium.

She spun on the balls of her feet. She flung the bottle into the hallway as hard as she could. It bounced on the hardwood floor and skittered across it, then found the steps and clicked on exactly five of them until it hit the carpet at the bottom. The silence inside the house echoed even with the sound of the wind picking up outside.

Alison slammed the door of the medicine cabinet. Light flashed in the mirror and it shook in the frame, but did not shatter. She swept the cologne off the back of the sink, *his* cologne, the expensive bottle she had purchased at Macy's less than a year ago. It shattered in the porcelain sink and the scent filled her nose, reminding her of him, overwhelming her.

The tears came harder then, hard enough to run down her cheeks and scald her pale skin. If it was from the unbearable strength of his cologne or from the pain, there they were. She was glad, in some dull and joyless way, that she was finally crying. Not a tear here and there, but really *crying*, after all this time.

'And there you have it,' she intoned, and the sound of her own voice in the empty space was spooky as hell. She turned to look behind her, then chastised herself for being a sissy. This was *her* house now, not theirs any more, because there wasn't a couple to be reckoned with. Her name was the only one that mattered so far as the bank was concerned, and she had damn well better get used to the empty house and the echoes that weren't his, but hers.

Alison.

She froze in the hallway and looked down the staircase. The bottle of Valium lay at the bottom of it, looking up at her like some single accusing eye. She took two steps towards the stairs and then stopped again, listening for something. Anything. The only thing that finally came to her was the winter wind and then the steady click of the grandfather clock in the dining room, a sound so steady that it might as well have been her own heartbeat.

'I am going crazy,' she said. 'That's why I can't grieve. I'm going crazy instead.'

She turned back to look at the bedroom. Everything was just as it was before. She wiped the tears from her eyes and willed more to fall, but none did. Her tear ducts were again dry as a bone when they should have been working overtime. The guilt was almost as overwhelming as the scent of his cologne from the bathroom.

She walked through the unforgiving sunlight and looked down into the sink. The cologne bottle was in a half-dozen pieces. She picked up little shards of green glass with careful fingers and dropped them into the wastebasket. Then she turned on the water and washed the majority of the cologne down the drain. The scent was still in the air.

She turned the water off and looked at the sink. There were drops on the side, high on the edges where the water didn't normally reach. She dipped her finger into one and sniffed. Yes, it was cologne. She put it on her wrists, on her throat, behind her ears. The scent of Matthew surrounded her.

She started to cry again, but it was a quiet and gentle cry, not the sobbing hysterics she thought she needed. She turned on the water again, used the closest washcloth to sweep out the sink and tidied everything up again.

Alison.

This time she turned with a small scream, sure there was someone in the hallway looking at her, certain there was someone in the house. She stood stock-still and waited. There was nothing again, nothing at all. She stood there for what seemed like an eternity, afraid to move, lest she miss some little sound that would give away the fact that there was an intruder in the house. She was aware of the grandfather clock, the ticking of it from down the staircase and down the hallway and around the corner, and she wondered, if she could hear *that*, why couldn't she hear someone breathing?

The logic of it relaxed her, and she stepped towards the door again. She looked out into the hallway. The sun had reached that point Matthew always loved the most, when it found the half-moon windows in the top of the house and spilt light through them in shafts that were so strong they looked almost solid. The light danced across the floor and dust motes danced in the beams, reminding her of how long it had been since she had been in the house. Avoidance had seemed the right thing to do, but looking at those shafts now she wondered if she had waited too long, if Matthew's memory had somehow evaporated during those long weeks she slept in her old bedroom at her mother's home, afraid of the memories this house would hold.

I missed you.

Alison stared at the sunlight and waited. The fine little hairs on the back of her neck stood up and she broke out into goosebumps, the same way she always did when Matthew kissed that sweet spot right underneath her ear. She listened and heard nothing and decided she really *was* going crazy, bonkers, bound for the funny farm, one brick short of a load, not playing with a full deck . . .

Stop it, BeeBop.

Alison was suddenly dizzy. She groped for the wall and leant against it. The voice was shocking but the words were so astounding that she couldn't utter a single sound in response. No one called her BeeBop; no one even knew that name existed. Not her best friend or her mother or her sister or anyone else.

No one but her husband.

She took deep breaths and looked down the staircase. There was the bottle of Valium. She had thrown it. It had bounced down the stairs. She had thrown it and it was there and so all this had to be in her head, right? She was awake and not dreaming.

You're awake, BeeBop.

She shook her head against the wall. It was cool against her forehead. A breeze picked up and ran over her skin, pulled her hair away from her face, made those goosebumps happen again, only this time they happened everywhere, the way they used to when Matthew had her good and riled up and then blew his warm breath into the sweet cove of her ear.

But she was in her house, the home that was built to last, and there wasn't a draft. This house was built tight – tight as a virgin in church, Matthew had once said, and laughed out loud at the way she blushed.

There was no breeze. There *couldn't* be a breeze.

'I am imagining things into existence because I want them to be so,' she said out loud.

This isn't real?

The breeze was there again, this time moving across her midsection, just the way Matthew's hand used to do. He would ride his fingers across her belly, right where it started to curve out a bit. It was the sweetest spot, he would say, perfect for his hand.

Her knees went weak and her legs threatened to spill her on to the floor. Before they could, she braced both hands on the wall and breathed deep. She took in great lungfuls of air, and all of it was tinged with the scent of his cologne. She turned from the wall and staggered into the bedroom. She sat down on the bed just as black shadows began to cross her vision.

Stay with me, BeeBop.

The voice was sharp. It was enough to get through the lazy blackness that was creeping up like water over a lens. She spread her knees and dropped her head, trying to get it lower than her heart. She took deep breaths, counting as she went, holding each for a few seconds and then letting them go. The darkness began to recede.

Good girl.

The breeze came again, this time over the back of her neck and down her spine, like fingertips across her skin. She felt them even through the sweater she wore. She sat up slowly and looked over at the window. It was closed, locked down tight, and the wind was blowing around what had to be snow flurries, even though the sun was still shining.

The breeze was *warm.*

Alison closed her eyes and sat there on the bed where they had made love so many times, the bed that held so many memories, and waited. She didn't know what she was waiting for, but suddenly it didn't seem to matter so much as the fact that she *should* wait, that she should just give herself over to whatever it was that was in this house or maybe even just in her head. She knew what she felt even if her logical mind railed against it. If she was going crazy, well, so be it. And, after the hellish weeks since Matthew died, who would blame her?

You're not going crazy. You knew I would be here.

Alison flinched at the honesty of it and opened her mouth to protest, but the insanity of that struck her and she clapped her mouth shut. That voice knew everything about her whether she wanted it to or not. Why attempt to lie to a ghost?

A ghost?

Alison bit down her on her lip. She tasted blood. She dug her nails into her own palms. The pain was vivid and fresh, flowering up through her arms. She moaned and opened her eyes. There was nothing there but the *feeling* was there, it was definitely there . . .

You knew, BeeBop.

Yes, she supposed she did. She knew there would be memories and maybe even some sort of message waiting for her, some final goodbye. Perhaps it would have been in the form of a quick handwritten note that she had missed that fateful afternoon, or a page in a book he had turned down, or a rose he had bought for her and put in a vase, one that would have long since turned brown but a surprise nonetheless. There would be some kind of sign. She believed in such things.

But she never expected, even in her most comforting daydreams, to find *him* in the house.

'Why did you do it?' she asked aloud.

There was silence that stretched forever, and she began to doubt that he was there, after all.

You aren't asking why I did it. You're asking why it turned out the way it did. I can answer the first question, but no one can answer the second. It is what it is.

She closed her eyes again, this time to hold back the rising flood of tears. Here it was, the grief that she had known was coming, but now that it was here she wasn't prepared for it, not at all.

Then the breeze was back, touching the back of her hand, caressing her palm, kissing slowly on that sweet spot right in the centre of it. It travelled up her arm and found the inside of her elbow, teased lovingly there before moving up to her shoulder and trailing across her collarbone.

Cry later. Not right now.

The flash of anger was sudden and choking. Cry later? Why the fuck was he OK with letting her cry at all?

Then there was the breeze – no, more than that, because there was heaviness to it, a weight that hadn't been there before. The touch slid down the centre of her chest and suddenly a button on her sweater popped open. And then she knew what he wanted.

The anger spilt away like the cologne down the sink. She laughed out loud. The sound was melodic in the empty space of the bedroom. It felt foreign, and she realised it had been weeks since she had laughed.

The laughter filled up the space and suddenly it seemed as though he *was* there, not just a presence but a real physical being. It seemed as though he had drifted through whatever veil there was separating this world from the next. His touch slid down her chest and her hands joined his. She opened a few buttons but he got most of them himself. The breeze touched her lips and her laughter settled into a sigh.

'You're here,' she said.

Don't think. Just feel. Feel me, Alison.

She didn't open her eyes. She lay back on the bed and then he was above her. The breeze wasn't so much fluid any more as it was solid, and there was heat – so much heat! Matthew had always been warm as a furnace. During the summer, they slept in the bed without touching, because his body was always too hot, but during the winter she cuddled up to him. The heat was there now, as unmistakably real as the bed beneath her.

'I feel you,' she said.

He chuckled and the sound seemed to settle right between her thighs.

She lifted her hips. Her slacks slid off with a whisper, and her panties followed that, with a bit of a fumble at her ankles to get them free. She threw her arms up above her head. Hands settled on her thighs and gently pushed until she lay open for him.

The first touch was undeniable. There was no mistaking that for a breeze, or a whisper, or a breath of air. That was Matthew's tongue, and he was using it in all the ways only he knew. He licked around her lips with feather-light touches and then delved deeper, swirling his tongue but not going inside, making her want him deeper. Then he flicked at her clit, not quite touching it, but moving close enough that she arched her back and growled deep in her throat.

He chuckled again, and this time his tongue made a slow trip from the tip of her clit all the way down to her ass – firm, solid, not yielding in the least, even when she struggled against the intensity. It had been too long since she had felt him and, now that she was, she couldn't help but respond with every fibre of her being. She wanted more even as the feelings threatened to consume her.

It's just as good as always, BeeBop.

The breath from his words shimmered over her. She arched under them. Every nerve was alive and waiting. His tongue came back up and this time he delved deeper, almost reaching inside her. She spread her legs wider for him and he moaned in approval. His tongue moved in lazy circles, reaching farther and farther, until she was holding her breath in anticipation. She knew what he would do.

His tongue swept up then, riding hard on her clit. He pressed on the little sensitive nub and she burst into an orgasm that was so sweet she could almost taste it. She pushed against him and he pushed right back, keeping up the pressure, making it last. Finally, she collapsed and drew her knees up to her chest and rolled over to her side, almost as if she could hold it all in.

'Matthew,' she said.

Yes.

'You're here.'

The smile came through in his words. *Oh, yes.*

She smiled right back, and slowly rolled over on to her belly.

'Just how *here* are you?'

Matthew's chuckle ran over her skin. The heat of him was against her back and the heat of something else was against her thigh. She wiggled back against him and his touch found her hair, then he was pulling gently, pulling her head back while she whimpered a single word.

'Please...'

You always did like it this way. More than any other way.

'So did you.'

It struck her that she was speaking in the past tense, and the grief threatened to rise up inside her like a tidal wave. But before it could that heat of him was pressing into the wetness of her, and she cried out as he slid into the place that was still reserved only for him. The hiss of his breath told her how much he liked it. The grief gave way before the thrusting of his body into hers. His words were in her ear and his hands were all over her, blankets of warmth sliding up and down her arms and her back, and that hardness was so deep inside that it took her breath away.

I've waited all this time. Aren't you glad you came back?

Alison smiled against the quilt. Matthew was always cocky about sex. He was the best lover she had ever had, and she had once made the mistake of telling him so.

'Your ego is bigger than your dick,' she said, and his laughter was both a sound in her ears and a wind against her shoulder. She got up on her knees. Then she had to brace herself on the bed because he was fucking her from behind, pummelling her from behind, slamming into her. She moved lower, meeting his thrusts until he hit that one certain spot that always did it for her. She gasped when she felt it and he chuckled breathlessly.

There's the spot, honey. You get tighter around my dick when I hit it.

She stayed as still as she could and let him pound away at that little spot. Her hands dug into the quilt. Her teeth ground down so hard her jaw would hurt later. Then her mouth fell open and her hands went weak. Now he was caressing that spot with the head of his cock, and she knew that feeling – that was the way he moved when he was going to come. She waited, rode it with him, until he pushed deep and called out, a long and low sound of relief and release.

Alison...

The flood inside her was more than real. For a moment she was transported back to when things were perfect, when they were happily married and he was still there with her, waking up beside her every morning. She could believe for a moment that she would turn around when he withdrew from her and he would be right there, his hair damp against his forehead, his eyes glassy with pleasure, a goofy smile on his face.

Then the weight pushed her down on the bed. Her knees went out from under her. The wetness crept out and stained the bedclothes. She wrapped her arms around the pillow, the one that had the indentation of his head still in it.

The grief came then. It was unimaginable, a pain that ripped from the centre of her and made her feel as though her whole body would come apart, not just her heart. She screamed into the pillow and, even though the weight was there and the voice was in her ear, she couldn't stop.

The sun set an hour later. The house had gone dark. The wind had died down outside, and there was the sound of sleet pinging against the windows. Her throat was sore from the screaming and her eyes hurt from the tears. Her whole body felt like she had been dealt a dozen good whacks with an out-of-control baseball bat.

But the hand on her back was soothing and constant.

'Matthew?'

Yes.

She listened to the sound and thought again that she might be going crazy.

You wanted a sign. How did I do?

She nodded against the quilt. One more sob came out, and then she was silent, thinking over the question that had been burning in her mind since the moment she realised he was really there.

'How long can you stay?'

There was a very long silence. Something was missing. As she lay there and listened to the rhythm of their breathing, she realised that the grandfather clock was no longer ticking.

I'm here right now.

It was enough. She turned in the bed and, though she couldn't see him, she knew he was there. Under the cover of darkness, it was all the same, just like he had never left.

In the morning, the snow had covered the world, including the skylight. Even so, the vision in the bathroom mirror was clear enough. She saw the marks on her throat and her breasts, the marks left by the eagerness of his lips. There was no mistake as to what they were, and how they got there.

She touched them and, though her eyes were red and bright with tears, her lips were smiling.

Magic for Beginners
Sabine Whelan

'What are you reading fantasy for? Again?' asked Susan, plopping on to the chair next to me. 'Most people grow out of fairy-tales by the time they get to university.' She hoisted her feet on to the desk, hiked up her flouncy skirt and began to examine her stockings for snags.

On the cover of my book, an elderly wizard was consulting his orb amid a storm of lightning. All flying robes and fluffy hair, he didn't look like any magician I knew – particularly not our master – and his magic was extremely ropey. This was Susan's issue with my choice of reading matter.

'I like fantasy, Suze. I've liked it before you-know-what, and now you of all people should understand how real fairy-tales can be.'

'But they're not true! They just aren't real. Is that a dragon in the picture? Well, dragons don't exist.' Satisfied that her stockings were intact, she banged her feet back on to the floor. The thin carpeting of the Riverside auditorium hardly deadened the boom of her chunky heels.

'Whether dragons exist or not is not the point,' I said. 'Next you'll say magic doesn't exist.'

'Who says magic doesn't exist?' asked Alberic, walking into the room. As always, we hadn't noticed him enter until he spoke up.

Our master moved like a dancer. His jeans looked as though they had been spray-painted on to his legs, and his shirt was delectably crisp. My mouth watered. Not for the first time I wondered whether he was aware of the effect the closeness of his body had on his pair of apprentices.

As soon as Alberic was in the vicinity, it was as though somebody had switched on the lights in Susan: she sat up, straightened her shoulders, flicked back her ironed locks and said in the sweetest voice, 'Meg is reading childish books again, sir, with all the unrealistic wizardry.'

I snapped, 'When somebody writes a novel with real magic, send me a card, will you?'

Alberic shook his head. 'A little maturity, please, ladies. Meg, put your book away.'

Susan beamed. I sulked, stuffing the book into my purple and white tote with a golden Durham crest. Neither of us spoke while Alberic prepared the auditorium.

With little gestures we knew so well, but couldn't begin to imitate, he rearranged the room to his taste. He beckoned at the door, which smoothly clicked shut. A short nod, and the curtains fell, covering the room from any stray glances of passers-by. A breath, a gesture and the blue scribbles left on the whiteboard from the previous lecture obediently faded.

'Let's get to work,' he said, clapping his hands together. 'Uh, excuse me, Meg, may I ask where your thoughts are?'

I started. I had been thinking about the muscles of his round compact posterior encased in his customary pair of tight black jeans. The muscles had rolled as he had walked away from me towards the window and, when he twirled back to confront me, I had glimpsed how full and stretched his trousers were at the front.

'Nothing, sir,' I said, feeling my cheeks grow hot. 'Only magic.'

* * *

I had come to Durham to study French with Mediaeval History in St Cuthbert's, the college by the river, only to find myself swiftly transferred to the College of John Dee.

It is not in any university prospectus you will ever encounter. It isn't on the terrible out-of-scale map every fresher gets with the information pack. It consists for the most part of staff and researchers all assigned to the same tiny department.

Even so, Dee's thinks itself to be a part of Durham, stuck to it as a mollusc to the side of a cliff. Just like all other colleges, it has a bar. Alberic brought us here for an introduction on the first night. That day Susan and I had found out the real reason for the unassuming sequence of puzzles all freshers had been asked to complete during registration. She and I were all the new blood the college would get this year; two new apprentices a year was the average result, though the current third year had three people, and some years, they said, yielded nobody suitable.

Even the perfect Susan could hardly stand from shock and fatigue that day. Still, she and I had smiled, and shaken hands, and filed away names, and watched filled glasses whiz across the room straight into waiting hands, and the air was thick with something we couldn't yet explain, but would never again fail to recognise. We longed to learn to do the same.

To the toll of the cathedral bell, I braved the cobbles of the Bailey in my best evening heels, and thudded down a tunnel of wooden steps into a little room with unpainted beams and a whitewashed ceiling. It was still empty, though I supposed for a midweek night, that wasn't surprising.

As was the tradition of the college, there was nobody to serve our drinks. I went behind the bar to pour my own large lemonade and upend a shot of vodka in it; it would be a long time before glasses and bottles would do my bidding.

No sooner did I camp on a high padded stool, than a voice behind me said, 'So. Have you done it yet?'

I swivelled around, only accidentally succeeding in holding my glass upright. 'Hi, Tom.'

He was in the third year, spoke with a cut-glass accent and felt he knew everything. I forgave him his cosmic arrogance in return for a continuous stream of practical advice.

'Have I done what?'

'Have you screwed each other's brains out yet?'

'Ha,' I said glumly, and sucked on the straw. It was oddly comforting that I was not the only person in the college with nothing but sex on my mind.

'It's that time of the term, you know,' said Tom, planting his bottom on the neighbouring stool. 'Just about now, you and Suze should be banging each other's brains out.'

'Me and who?' I spilled my lemonade on to the lacquered bar surface.

With only a slight flush of effort, Tom glared the sticky puddle out of existence. 'You and Susan. This is where the two of you discover that, out of magic and sex, magic creates the deeper bond, and you're expected to have this bond with every object to which you apply it. For all intents and purposes, I've just fucked a puddle of lemonade.'

In my mind I saw Alberic's arm rise in a silent command; the sun glinted between his slender fingers, every piece of wood, plastic and living flesh in the auditorium his eager servant.

Tom stared at me with as much intensity as he devoted to performing his magic. 'For most apprentices this translates into a simple piece of logic: magic matters, sex – not so much. Let's have a lot of sex. Don't tell me you aren't as horny as hell right now.'

I swallowed.

'Don't tell me you wouldn't like to come and sit on my lap while we talk.' He patted his knee. He was sporting a wicked grin I didn't quite trust.

'Are you using some sort of magic on me, Tom?'

'No. The magic is in you. Come on.' He patted his knee again.

It was a large lap, sturdy and inviting. I slid off my stool, walked over to him and allowed him to hoist me up. He was warm and smelt of cinnamon. In this position even my impossible heels didn't quite brush the floor.

'So,' said Tom into my ear from behind, snaking his arms around me. 'The answer is: no, you and Susan haven't done it yet. Why not?'

'Go to hell,' I said, squirming on his lap. I was aware of the stirring in his jeans, and even more aware of beginning to respond to it with a stirring of my own.

Tom's hands slid up my back to my shoulders; his thumbs found a knot of sensitive muscles. I bit down a moan, and prayed that the bar remained empty for a little while.

'You need to get laid, girl. It's no joke; you're so tense there's a horny aura all around you. Everybody can tell, even Alberic.'

'Really?' The idea that my infatuation should be so obvious stopped the breath in my throat.

Tom's hands slipped around me again. Warm palms smoothly covered my breasts.

'No,' he admitted, giving me a little squeeze, which made me squirm and press my legs together. I was very aware of my nipples pushing against the lace of my bra as Tom's fingers made little circles around them. 'Not really, but everybody went through the same thing their fresher year. Every last researcher in Dee's could get a degree in quantum erotica.'

'I'm not everybody,' I said petulantly, barely stifling a gasp when one clever hand found its way into the stretchy waistband of my skirt, slid down past the flat of my tummy, and pushed between my clamped thighs. I liked to believe what I said, but Tom was playing my body as knowingly as at times I had played it myself. Still, I persisted, even as I pressed myself against his fingers. 'It's not just because I'm learning magic.'

'Uh-huh,' said Tom, playing deftly with the soaked gusset of my panties. I wriggled in his lap, stifling embarrassing little moans. 'And you're not up to getting frigged right now, wishing I was Alberic. Because you don't want to shag Alberic at all. Because you are unique, and an apprentice's crush hasn't touched you at all.'

The rush of blood to my face was so sudden and violent that I thought my skin would burst, like an over-ripe tomato. Tears sprang to my eyes. I pushed his hands away and hopped off his lap, by some miracle landing firmly on my feet despite the murderous heels.

'Hey, sorry,' he said. 'Sorry. Just illustrating the point. I know what it's like, because you're my recent past, apart from being a girl and all.'

I remembered that Tom was, in fact, apprenticed to an impossibly glamorous researcher by the name of Veronique, who always walked around with no fewer than three fellows in tow. I wondered if it would have made any difference if his master had been a man.

'Is this all there is to magic?' I asked miserably. 'Moving things, and being horny all the time?'

'It might be easier to find out what there *is* to magic, if you got over being horny. I offered you my services, but you're so busy overanalysing everything I may as well go and find Susan instead.'

My panties felt slippery as I perched on my own stool again. I could still feel the ghost touch of his fingers, though he was right: I wished they were Alberic's.

'Story of my life,' I said with a crooked smile. 'Everybody would rather go and find Susan instead. I bet she's in bed with Alberic right now.' I knew this wasn't true, but saying it gave a perversely pleasurable twist to my nerves.

'Damn,' he said. 'Bad luck, girl. I guess you'll just have to shag me after all.'

'Fuck you, Tom,' I said, now smiling in earnest. I slid off the stool once more, and headed around the bar to top up my lemonade.

'Yes,' he said. 'Exactly.'

I didn't fuck him that night, even though I would have liked to. Thus, I punished myself for being the same as every other apprentice in John Dee's, horny and confused. Instead, I went home and read more of my fantasy novel, losing the taste for it with every new page. Their lives were easy; none of them walked around with a huge crush on their master. Their magic sucked. In the end, the book had all the fascination of yesterday's weather forecast.

I hoped I'd feel better when Alberic moved us on to doing some proper magic, but he was in no hurry to make academic progress. As the days grew cold, and the term dragged on, our master set us exercises that wouldn't have been out of place in my school's drama club. We threw invisible balls, strode across the room and back to an irregular rhythm it was our task to guess, and for our homework we studied poetry – pages at a time. Alberic claimed it developed concentration, and became disproportionately cross when we failed at committing five-page ballads to memory without a hitch. When he grew cross, the fake daylight in the room dimmed. I suspected he was unaware of this.

We had spent the entire tutorial so far failing an infuriating exercise Alberic had called a *Mirror*. Susan and I had faced each other in the middle of the room, and taken turns trying to guess each other's next move. It was her job to make small simple motions – lift her arm, shake her hand, stick out her tongue – while I had to do the same thing at the very same time. Not an instant later: our motions needed to be simultaneous. My only consolation, when the exasperated Alberic called an end to this torture, was that Susan's efforts weren't any better. I got far more pleasure out of this than a mature person should.

His next words brought me even more guilty pleasure; he said, 'Meg, I'd like you to come to the front and have a go at the *Mirror* with me. Susan, you will have your try in a minute, but, in the meantime, I'd like you to turn your chair to the wall, and engage yourself in something else. Try not to peek.'

Like a blushing bride, I stepped into the aisle between desks. The whiteness of Alberic's crisp shirt blinded me.

'I think doing it with me might give you a little push in the right direction,' he said, putting a hand on my shoulder.

Oh, you bet I'd like to do it with you, I thought, trying not to purr with pleasure.

His hand pressed me down; I folded on to the floor, and he followed me; soon we both sat on our heels opposite each other. I could feel the coarseness of the denim on his knees through the gossamer of my stockings. In a false flash of modesty, I gave the hem of my skirt a feeble tug, but it wasn't long enough to cover my knees. My heart hummed with contentment.

'You'll know what to do,' said Alberic. 'I promise, it's easy once you've figured it out.'

After this, he fell silent, leaving me to find a quiet place in my head, where all my stores of intuition and concentration lay dormant.

Having leave to stare at him directly was a real wonder. His black eyes were so close that it seemed that his gaze was a secret velvet voice inside my head.

His lips moved. 'Engage,' he commanded.

I watched, daring for the first time to look directly at his face, *into* his face, study it close, knowing that at that moment he was also studying mine. Something moved in his eyes, but I knew – though I couldn't tell how or why – that this was a trick; his limbs rested still, and so I remained still, too. There was a connection, a charge, and it was hotly disquieting, like an uninvited confession.

Alberic's stillness unnerved me. Usually my concentration would have drifted here, and I would have tried to sneak a look at his hands just to see what he was doing, but now I had permission to look into those eyes – and I would never be able to look away. Even once it was over, I would think of Alberic's face, search it with my inner eye, appeal for the calm and connection, and ... I felt my hand rise to rest on his shoulder; the instant my palm touched the cotton of his shirt, my own shoulder felt the warmth of his hand.

We were connected. Now that I knew how to do it, I couldn't imagine not being able to repeat, without stopping to think, any move he made. He inclined his head to the side and righted it again; a compliant mirror, so did I.

His eyes lighted with mischief, and I tensed, not certain where we were going now. He smiled – very briefly, but not so briefly that I didn't reflect his mirth back into his face – and leant towards me. Unthinking, for magic is quicker than thought, I leant towards him.

Our lips touched with the same deliberate care that he had invested in the rest of the exercise. When his tongue pushed forwards, I met him with mine, half-caressing, half-fighting a battle of mouths and teeth. I wanted to throw my arms around his neck and lock our bodies together for this long kiss, to make it last and to make him come back for more, but even in this turmoil my mind followed his lead on instinct: just as his tongue invaded my mouth, his hands hung by his sides, and so must mine.

His lips were drawing away, his mouth was closing against me. In my obedience, I didn't pursue the kiss, leaning back instead like I knew I should. Oh, but I want you, I thought petulantly.

Out loud, he said, 'I know.' And at once: 'Disengage.'

As though a supporting hand was withdrawn from around me, my back and shoulders slackened, and I allowed myself to let out a long breath. My head hummed.

'And this is what you do,' said Alberic conversationally, addressing Susan as much as me, even though she had no idea what had just happened. 'That was very good, Meg; return to your desk. Susan, would you like to have a go?'

Even the grimace on Susan's face when she realised she would have to sit on the mucky carpeting didn't make up for my disappointment. Alberic hadn't told me to turn my chair to the wall, and so I petulantly glared as he guided my rival into the very same spot on the floor where I had sat a minute before, and drew her into his gaze.

I had seen couples kiss before – you couldn't live in a pretty town filled with students without encountering snogging youngsters in every romantic spot. That said, I had never had a front-row seat. Their lips met precisely in the middle of the empty space between them. Faces slightly tilted, they carefully pressed their mouths together in a deliberate measured caress. He didn't close his eyes, and neither did she, and hers were huge and astonished. I could tell the exact moment when their tongues met. I wondered if my cheeks had been as flushed as Susan's were getting now. It was unfair that she should be such a pretty girl.

I felt a little sorry for her when our master drew back from their kiss and commanded her to disengage. At least I hadn't been watched in my frustration and confusion, while Susan was too aware of her jealous audience.

Alberic didn't allow us even a minute's pause before he launched into a lecture.

'Magic is a bond,' he said, walking there and back in front of us. Like charmed snakes, we turned our heads after him. 'Once you have let yourself be drawn into a magical connection, no other form of intimacy will ever live up to it. You have felt it now. How was it?'

We were both silent. Susan didn't even attempt to rise from the carpet.

'Was it pleasant? Shocking? Claustrophobic?'

'It was invasive,' I said, surprising myself. 'I wanted to hide. It felt great, though.'

'I didn't want it to end,' Susan echoed from the floor, and I thought, I bet you didn't.

'Yes,' said Alberic, striding back and forth. 'It's invasive, which is why your instinct will always be to close yourselves off. But then it worked this time. Why?'

I looked at Susan, and she looked at me. For the first time since the day we were chained to each other by our destiny, we looked to each other for help. I realised that it disturbed me to see her so lost. I volunteered my ignorance. 'No idea, sir.'

Without a pause, Alberic leant down, grasped Susan under the arms and yanked her on to her feet. Before she could as much as squeak, he was kissing her with aggressive gusto, one hand fixed in her hair. One moment, two – and it was over; he allowed her to breathe again. Her eyes were glazed with dreamy pleasure, but for once I felt no jealousy.

'This was invasive,' he said calmly. 'Yet, you didn't resist at all. Why?'

'It felt really good,' whispered Susan, flushing a deep red.

I had never thought she was capable of blushing.

'Not only is it nice of you to say so, but it's the right answer,' said Alberic. He grinned a toothy grin, and walked over to me.

I couldn't yet be sure what he was going to do, but I knew what I craved, and I lifted my face to him. He leant down towards me, and pressed his mouth to mine. Our teeth clashed together as I hurried to welcome his tongue, which pushed and pushed deep into me. His fingers dug into my hair at the back of my head, holding me still for his insistent exploration. It took just instants but, when he withdrew, I felt exhausted from the intensity of this one moment.

Unlike with Susan, he didn't let me go. His hand still holding a firm grip on my hair, he drew me up from my chair and guided me around the desk. My head leant slightly back; I took little breaths, giving myself up to the lesson. Alberic gently pushed me forwards over the desk.

'Come here, Susan,' he said. 'Sit at the desk in front of her – no, move your chair back a bit – and look into her eyes. Meg, no matter what happens, I want the two of you to connect.'

Her cheeks were flushed, eyes huge. An embarrassed heat rose in my face; more than anything, I wanted to look away, but Alberic's hand in my hair anchored me to the reality of my lesson. Magic was invasive, yet we must not resist.

Alberic's free hand was stroking the inside of my thigh, playing with the top of my stocking, sliding to the bare skin above. As he drew it up and down my leg, never quite touching my damp panties, he spoke into my ear. 'My connection with you works because, on a deep level of which you're not aware, you know that magic feels good. Even so, every time you try it, you will have to work through resistance. Learn to connect to each other. To others. To objects around you.'

His warm palm cupped my sex, fingers pressing gently against the sweet centre. I swallowed a moan, and closed my eyes; finally, finally. The fingers gave me a little smack right on my lips:

'Look at Susan, girl, this is how it needs to work. No matter what happens. Susan, help her.'

I had hated that her face was so smooth and perfect, but now I was glad; its lovely symmetry helped me hold my gaze. Ever the diligent student, she looked straight at me with her huge eyes, chewing her lip, yet not flinching. With a forceful tug, Alberic's fingers grasped and ripped away the slippery silk of my panties; the hem of my skirt slid up and settled around my waist. With the backs of my thighs, I could feel his jeans obediently slither downwards, to leave his bare flesh pressed against mine. A firm hot presence pushed itself between my thighs, glided lightly along my slick lips, back and forth, and back. My eyes watered, but I looked at Susan.

'Engage,' whispered Alberic, and thrust himself inside me.

The connection was immediate. She was frozen on the spot, but I could feel her warmth, the throb of her heartbeat. Alberic began to ride me with a measured rhythm; his hand left my hair, and instead he grasped the sides of my waist, driving himself inside me. Tears rolled down Susan's cheeks; I couldn't tell whether the tears were a reflection of my joy.

'Very good,' said our master, only slightly out of breath. 'Feel it, Susan. Can you feel the friction inside her? My skin against her cheeks? Meg, let her feel it; keep yourself open.'

I was open; split like an oyster, exposing my warm centre. Alberic raked a nail over my skin, and Susan twitched. He thrust deeper; she and I gasped in a single voice. I tried to sneak my hand between my thighs to bring relief to the sweet tension, but he slapped it away. 'Not yet. Not you. Susan, what am I doing?'

Her voice was breathless, as though it was her and not me he was shoving into the desk with his quick thrusts.

'You're – oh! – you're squeezing her cheeks and spreading them wider and – oh my God.'

We shouted out together as Alberic changed the angle, jabbing a sensitive spot inside me and burying himself in my heat to the hilt.

'Good girl. Keep yourself open, Meg, my girl, you're doing well. Susan, tell me how turned on you are.'

'Sir, I . . .' She opened her mouth and closed it again. I could feel her embarrassment as keenly as the heat of my desire.

'Let go of resistance, girl, follow the magic. Doesn't it feel good to be fucked like this over the desk, Susan?'

'It feels . . .' she sobbed. 'It feels hot, I need it so badly, oh, please, sir, do it again.'

My reflection; her arousal and mine were fused together. I didn't need to keep her gaze any more to feel the tension in her slender thighs, her nails digging hard into her palms as she clenched her fists.

'Susan, touch yourself,' Alberic ordered, tightening his

grip on my waist again. 'You're so close.' He began thrusting in earnest, so quickly and forcefully that my shouts of pleasure came out as a gasping stutter.

Susan gratefully yanked up her expensive skirt. I saw a narrow palm slide between the lacy tops of her stockings; she clenched her thighs together, flooding my senses with the sweetest pleasure. She pushed aside her panties and easily slipped her finger inside her drenched sex, only to draw it out, moistened, and push it against the bud of her clit.

I knew that my own hands were clutching convulsively at the edge of the desk, but the relief of the delicate touch of those cool fingers drew a scream from my throat.

'Yes,' Alberic hissed. 'Meg, yes.'

Full and stretched, I pushed myself back on to Alberic, and I bucked against the silky fingertips, which played around and around my clit, and the intense sweetness turned into a wave of relief, beating inside me, stopping my breath. 'Oh, God,' moaned a voice, Susan's or my own.

Alberic breathed: 'Disengage.'

He slipped out of me with no more warning than that, but I had been ready to let him go. My cheek pressed against the grainy wood of the desk, I closed my eyes, and relaxed against the receding sweet storm. I vowed to find Tom, and fuck him the same night, because he would make me feel good, and it was our magic that mattered.

'Very good,' said Alberic smoothly. 'Now we are getting somewhere, girls; I was beginning to lose all hope. Meg, you have done very well. You can go back to your desk. Susan, would you like to have a go?'

Sweet Dreams A.D.R. Forte

We spend 80 per cent of our waking lives at work. By my count, it's a hell of a lot more than that, and, with that kind of time spent around people, you get to know them well. Real well. When they're nervous or annoyed or lying. Or secretly pleased. What makes them tick. Little things: gestures, tones of voice, catchphrases.

You learn enough to paint a person inside out. Finish their sentences, know what they'd say, know when they'd roll their eyes. You get inside their head and don't even realise it until you find yourself laughing with them for no reason at all.

I got to know him that well. Scary well.

But I didn't think anything of it because I don't like boys. Never have, never wanted to. I didn't try not to; I just never felt that spark travel down my spine and between my legs for a boy. I felt it first for a girl in tenth grade with long pin-straight, blonde hair and small round breasts. She always smelt like plumeria body spray and being around her made my soft bits tingle and my head spin. She was the first, and there were many after.

But no boys. Not for years. Not for all my adult life up until that day in the break room, when he said something utterly stupid and I burst out laughing, almost spitting coffee all over my lap. He sat there grinning at me, with sunlight caught in his hair. I looked at his face and my heart kept on beating hard even after my laughter subsided. I noticed that the sight of the watch on his wrist made me feel hot all over. I noticed his fingers, and I pictured him reaching between my legs. And I looked away.

It didn't do any good.

I went home to the beautiful woman who shared my life and my house and lay beneath her with my eyes closed. Thinking about him fingering me. Kissing me. Easing his hard cock between the lips of my pussy and watching me squirm under him.

I'd never had a fantasy like that before; I didn't know what to do. It was cheating; it was bad. Thinking about it turned me on more than I could imagine.

I stood in the shower the next morning, playing with my nipples and thinking about what he'd look like naked, and wanting him so much it hurt. And I knew what he'd say, just how he'd say it. Knew just the way he'd look at me before he put his mouth over mine. You learn those things even if you've never seen someone actually do it. Instinct tells you.

I'm sure he figured out things were different between us because he changed a little, in subtle ways. His smiles became fewer, but they lasted longer. Especially when no one else was around. His voice when he spoke to me was softer. He always turned up where I did, when I did: the break room, the front desk, the parking garage.

I sometimes caught him playing with his wedding ring, sliding it off his finger and back on. And he would look up and catch my gaze for a few seconds before he looked away again. Just my luck I would decide to want a boy who was as taken as I was.

I thought it would go away; I wanted it to. I told myself it was a passing infatuation that would eventually fizzle, and I tried to act like I always had around him, but something kept intruding. Making me stumble over my sentences and feel much too warm, even in the coldest room. Making me forget what I was going to say every time he smiled at me. After months had gone by, I realised I was hiding from the obvious.

That I should have this little control over myself rankled, but I couldn't shake the need. Craving his touch like a junkie craves a hit. I thought, soon enough, my head is gonna explode and how am I supposed to explain that? Was it normal to want to fuck someone this bad?

The evening I got home frustrated like I'd never been in my life because he'd been wearing a sweater that hugged his chest and arms and outlined their shape to my ravenous gaze, I didn't give a rat's ass about normal.

I needed touch, but I found myself alone. Belatedly, I remembered Casey was gone to her mother's for the weekend. I could've broken something, smashed it with my bare fists just to release the wound-up energy, but it wouldn't have done any good. It was just me with the empty house on a Friday night, and my need for a gorgeous off-limits boy.

So I did the only thing you can do when you feel shitty and don't have a solution: watch TV. I settled into the couch with a pop tart and a frown to stare blankly at the screen. There was someone talking in that wise lofty tone they use for documentaries, and I was half a heartbeat away from changing the channel when the words registered and caught my attention.

Dreams. The gateway into the vast uncharted subconscious where lurks who the hell knows what. Lucid dreaming: the ability to impose control on the subconscious mind and turn its ramblings in whichever direction one chooses. I sat still and listened in spite of my angst. What if I could control the tumble of thoughts when I dreamt of him? Wouldn't *that* be nice.

I grabbed the remote, paused the show and rewound it before I went to find another pop tart. Hooray for DVR.

I lingered at the kitchen table for a moment on my way back, and then picked up a pencil and an empty envelope. Why not? I had to give my fevered brain something to do when it came up with those explicit depraved images late at night. Why not try to teach myself to lucid dream?

I got comfy again and watched the entire show from start to end, and this time I took notes.

It was easier than I'd thought. So easy in fact I got it on my very first try that Friday night, stopping a fascinating dream about remodelling the back porch dead in its tracks and turning it instead to a windswept country lane. Miles eaten up under the wheels of the Mustang, wind in my face. I woke up exhilarated.

That should have maybe clued me in. After all, controlling dreams was supposed to be difficult. But I didn't think anything of it; I've always been able to remember my dreams in full technicolour detail. I used to tell my mother about them and she would look them up in one of her books and tell me what they were supposed to mean.

'Dreams don't just happen at random,' she'd say.

None of the meanings in the dream books ever came close to being right, of course. Sceptic that I've always been, I didn't expect them to. The trick my mother forgot to tell me, or perhaps she left it for me to discover in my own time, was that the real meanings are what we infuse dreams with. What our own subconscious minds give to the tangle of pictures in sleep; that's where the power in dreaming lies.

And I had plenty to fuel the imagination. I took all I knew from watching straight porn and reading dirty romance novels and poured it into the fantasies I created about *him*. Palatial beds and nightclub-restroom stalls and the hood of the Mustang. I made his dream-self pleasure me until I couldn't bear it any more and woke sweating, with my legs and clit still trembling and my panties sticky with my own come.

I would wake Casey sometimes, tugging her nightie off and burying my face in her soft skin and softer curls, and ravage her until my need was finally satiated. She would laugh in the morning and call me a slut, and I would laugh and kiss her. Feeling a little guilty because she had no idea how much of one I really was.

Casey didn't guess at the smutty depths my mind achieved each night, but, if I hadn't known better, I would have bet good money *he* did. During the day, he would catch my gaze and shake his head, smiling as if he knew the fantasy I was replaying in my mind as I looked at him. But he couldn't have; I was sure I'd simply been giving myself away through body language. The odd coincidences on the other hand were harder to explain. Like the day I found him listening to Marvin Gaye when the night before I'd dreamed of fucking him on the leather couch of an apartment I'd had years before while we listened to Motown and got drunk on brandy. He looked at me when I passed his office and looked away while a guilty stain coloured his cheeks. And if I hadn't known better . . .

When he started avoiding me, I told myself it could have nothing to do with those strange little occurrences. It just had to be his guilt over the attraction between us. Or maybe the hectic pace at work when things kicked into high gear and we found our days swamped with meetings and fire drills. The stress of work, the fact I didn't see him every day: that had to be the reason I in turn stopped dreaming of him. Had to.

The trouble with that was I didn't want to stop. I could still turn my dreams any which way I chose; I could still change them like scenes on a DVD, but I couldn't summon the sweet fantasies of him. Not even for a few moments. They faded away and, if I stubbornly held on to the scene, it would be empty. Flat pictures on a screen instead of living breathing 3D.

I didn't want that. I wanted that feeling of being with him, as if I could really smell him and taste his skin. Feel my arms stretch as I put them around him and he pushed my body into his. But the images were hollow, so I stopped trying; I avoided him too.

Not the best idea in the world.

I felt deserted. Cranky. Like I'd lost something. I guess in a way I had. By day I couldn't get my dose of him and by night I avoided REM, fearing the disappointment of half-baked dreams, and it was telling on my nerves. I found myself snapping at random strangers in the checkout line or at the drive-through window and, around the people I knew, the effort to appear normal stretched me thinner than fishing line wound too tight. I was about to snap.

So, since there wasn't a way around his distance at work, I went back to the dreams. I couldn't shake the feeling there was a barrier that, if only I could push through, would let me back to 'normal'; that place in sleep where I could *almost* feel him. I just had to look harder.

As always I wandered in my dreams, but now I wasn't looking for fantasy vistas and landscapes; I wanted real and raw. Here in the present. In my mind's eye, I left my bed, passed through the walls of the house and out into the night to haunt the places I knew from waking hours. Night-time streets, empty office buildings. Cruising the familiar twists of city streets in the Mustang.

And as I would stand on a terrace looking out over the sleeping city, or sit on a damp park bench listening to a homeless guy mutter gibberish, I felt less deserted. I felt *he* was out there, somewhere in this dreamscape; and, if I tried hard enough, if I learnt to fly, eventually I'd find him again.

Then came the night when Casey was travelling for work and I fell asleep longing for him. I'd seen him only briefly that day.

He came up to me and touched my arm with a smile, asking how I'd been; saying that he hadn't seen me around in forever.

'Where've you been hiding?' I asked him, and his smile faded a little.

He looked down and shifted his shoulders. 'I don't know. Things have been crazy around here.'

I nodded.

'But I miss talking to ya,' he added.

His gaze strayed up to mine again and that time I held it, not letting him run away. I looked into his eyes for far longer than I should have before I released him.

'Well, don't be a stranger,' I said.

He nodded, swallowing hard and looking at me as if willing me not to walk off, but I was late for a meeting. I let his gaze go, took a step back and turned, but I heard his voice, compelling me to listen for one moment more.

'I won't,' he said.

Lying in the too-wide king-size bed that night, I tossed and turned, unable to find sleep. What do they say? No rest for the wicked? But I had to sleep; I was powerless awake. I took up the most comfortable position I could find in the middle of the bed, eyes closed tight, refusing to open them or to move, and gradually I slipped into the first fuzzy wave of semi-consciousness. I took my usual route, slipping through brick and cement walls out to where I was free. But tonight I had a purpose and I wouldn't be thwarted. Tonight I was going to find him.

* * *

I stood somewhere not far above him and looked down at him sleeping. I called his name and he turned, restless, but didn't wake. So I touched him, and then pulled my hand back in surprise at the prickle of stubble on his cheek. Wondering at the roughness and how strange it felt ... to feel that in a dream where before all I'd ever known was softness. But as I stood marvelling, he woke and smiled.

He reached up and the bedcovers slipped back from his body. I caught my breath; he was naked as the day he was born, but Holy Mother Mary his body was perfect. He looked like a boy out of those jeans commercials except for the curls of dark hair across his chest, trailing down to his navel and between his legs. And, where the pictures in the jeans commercials stopped, my gaze kept going. Down to that ... thing between his legs that was so not what I had dreamt about before.

I was still staring when he put his hands on my hips and I looked up at him. He didn't say anything, but he didn't have to. The evidence was pressing into the silk of my pyjama bottoms as he unbuttoned my top, button by slow button. His fingers stroked the space between my breasts and, although warmth surrounded us, I shivered. He pushed the pyjama top off my arms and sighed.

'You ...'

It was all he said. But it was all that was needed.

His gaze followed where his fingers moved across my chest and the curve of my belly, caressing, lingering. And then, moving again, down to the waist of my pyjamas, pulling them down. The silk co-operated, eagerly falling to my ankles to leave me bare to his inspection.

While I stood still, not daring to move. Not having a single goddamn clue what to do next; only knowing I wanted him to keep touching me. Keep feeding the need growing in my pussy and my breasts and my arms and my legs and, oh, God, everywhere. He pushed me backwards and I panicked for a moment because I remembered standing somewhere high up when he came to me. But it was my own bed that enfolded us.

The bed that had felt so comfortless and frustrating not so long before, now hot and soft and seductive under me. Like his mouth on my skin leaving wet tingling trails as his tongue moved over my chest. His hands were warm, rough on my flesh that didn't know what to make of this harsh maleness. Except to respond and rise and send pleasure rushing down between my legs.

I ran my hands up his shoulders and arched as his mouth dipped between my thighs. I'd heard the stories from girls who had been with men before. Too rough, too timid, too clumsy. And granted, this was a dream, but his mouth – oh, dear God! Oh, Jesus. I was screaming by the end of it, screaming when I was the type to barely do more than gasp and sigh. My hair was soaked, the sheet beneath me was soaked, and, as I leant on my elbows, trying my best to breathe, he lifted his head and brushed wet hair from his eyes. He smiled and wiped his mouth and then licked his fingers clean one by one, looking at me.

I lay back and covered my eyes with my hands, ran my hands through my hair. I felt like I'd run a mile, my breathing refused to find a rhythm anything like steady, and he was looking at me with that impish smile. Jesus. The night was far from over and I wasn't sure I was going to make it.

He lay next to me, one leg bent at the knee, his hand moving lazily over my torso while he waited for me to catch my breath again. He nuzzled my neck and kissed me and then I felt the sharp pinch of his teeth. Laughing, I batted him away, but I didn't mean it. I loved his strong arms against my back, the way his stubble tickled my neck and made me squirm. He smelt strong and sharp, like soap, and I wrinkled my nose, wondering why my dream sense had come up with something so bizarre and not erotic. And why I liked it so much.

I pushed him off finally when I was back to some semblance of control. He watched me sit up and shake my hair back and stare him down, ready for round two, and he reached downwards. I beat him to it. He looked surprised and then he smiled, pleased and aroused, although his body didn't show it yet, but that part didn't take long, even with my clumsy efforts. He guided my fingers, showing me how to stroke him the right way, and, when I figured it out, he swallowed and closed his eyes. God, I loved being able to do this to him.

I felt dirty and excited like a teenager getting laid for the first time and I laughed because after all I was a virgin. In a sense.

'What?' he asked, smiling.

'You know, technically, you're my first.'

He stared at me. 'What? You mean ... you've never been with ...'

'Nope, not one.'

'Oh shit.' He laughed. And when I lay back he moved over me as if afraid he'd crush me. I didn't know why until his first thrust and then I realised there was a big, big difference between a strap-on covered in lube and the real thing. Not to mention that Casey didn't like dildos that resembled the real thing, preferring bloopy, neon contraptions that were as far from a man's dick as a phallic object could get.

It shouldn't have hurt, not in a dream. But, then, it shouldn't have felt so good either. I shouldn't have been grinding myself against his cock like that. In porn it was always simple: in and out and then 'cut!'

No, this went on and on. And it felt so good that I

forgot about the pain. Maybe straight girls were on to something. Or maybe it was just him. I didn't think any other man could have done this to me.

If any other man had tried to spread my legs in the air and use my cunt like that – because use it he did – I would have fed him his own balls. With béarnaise sauce. But with my boy it was heaven. I lifted my hips for him and fucked him just like a straight girl. I let him roll me over and spoon me while he ground his hips against my ass and came inside of me, crying my name out. And I wasn't ashamed.

I adored every second of it. His roughness, his hardness, the sharp scent of our sex, so unlike what I knew that I wondered again where my subconscious had dredged it up from. I revelled in our fucking.

Because it was just a beautiful dream.

I woke to an empty bed. Ass naked.

I sat up, confused and achy. When had I taken off my PJs? There they were at the side of the bed in a silky blue puddle. And why could I still smell the scent of him from my dream? I stared at my naked body, at my thighs and I gingerly touched my sore nipples. And I told myself it was all psychosomatic. I'd wanted it so badly my body had somehow given me the experience I craved. Right? Right.

Because that was the only logical explanation.

But something in my brain didn't buy it. I stumbled out of the bed, staring at the stained sheets in wonder and thinking that, in all my years, with all the lovers I'd jumped in and out of bed with, I'd never *ever* seen my sheets look like that. But it was me, had to be. Couldn't be anything else.

When I made it to the bathroom and saw the purple love bites on my neck, still tender when I poked at the bruised flesh, I started to doubt my sanity.

I sifted through impossibility after impossibility. An intruder? Not possible. I'd circled the house twice; the alarm was still on. Everything was in place, sealed and unbroken. The only thing that had wandered beyond the confines of the house was my mind. And for all I knew it was still wandering.

I didn't sleep much the next night. I stayed awake for as long as exhaustion would let me and, thankfully, when I did drift off, all that haunted my subconscious were the projects I had due the next day. I didn't dare let my mind go further than that, and truthfully I don't think I had the energy. The dreams had never left me drained before, not until now.

Then came Monday morning. I was almost afraid to go back to work and I thanked my stars Casey was gone all week; it gave the bruises time to fade, and me time to recover. But I still had to face *him*.

And why I did it, I wasn't sure, but I donned a shirt that didn't *quite* hide one bruise on my neck. I wore my hair up so that, if I turned my head and bent a little forwards, the bruise would be visible. It was a test for my own peace of mind. I would be able to prove to myself I had invented that night and everything I felt after it. I would have sanity again.

He wasn't there.

I'd forgotten he was working offsite for the day, and when someone reminded me it was all I could manage not to grind my teeth. I haven't had many days in my life that I prayed would end like that Monday. It was sheer agonising hell. I couldn't think: the wonderful soreness of my body distracted me, my mind skittered. People spoke to me and I watched their lips move but made no sense of their words. I found myself staring out of the window playing the dream over and over in my mind. Running my hand along my neck. And wondering.

* * *

That night he came to me first, almost as I drifted into unconsciousness. He was waiting, sliding into bed beside me and reaching for me under the sheets with a smile.

'I was thinking about this all day,' he whispered as he kissed my cheek and then my lips and then parted my mouth with his. 'And I missed you,' he murmured into our kiss while his hands smoothed the shape of my body under the sheer babydoll nightie. I had worn it on purpose, hoping and dreading. And now I was rewarded.

'Same here. I wanted to talk to you,' I said.

He only murmured assent because his mouth was occupied with the embroidered bra-cups of the nightie, but, after only a second or two, he raised his head and frowned.

'About Saturday? I didn't hurt you, did I?'

He had gone from ardent lover to fierce protector in a flash and it made me smile. My boy, all impetuous charisma and dash.

'No. I wanted ... I wanted to see if you'd dreamt the same I did.'

'Of course, silly girl,' he said, descending again to the scented warmth of my curves. 'I'm here with you.'

Strange how in dreams everything makes sense.

But we had no time to talk. I lay on my stomach and his weight and heat covered me, pressing me into the pillows. His cock moved wet and fast between my thighs, slicking my ass cheeks and legs with our moisture, his balls slapping my clit, teasing it in the lewdest way. I was a she-wolf taken by her mate, my nails digging into the backs of his hands as he held me and drove into me. Hard. Harder. I tore the skin over his knuckles and almost broke my back arching up into him. He slid one hand under me, held me to him and filled me.

We had no breath left to whisper endearments before

we swam away again, back into our own beds and minds. But I left him marked that night; his shoulders and arms and hands. I hadn't meant to, but I wasn't sorry. There, in the dream, I wanted to give him sweet pain and let him know he was mine. Here. Beyond consciousness.

I was exhausted the next day. I felt as if I hadn't slept in days. OK, Sunday. But what about last night? I yawned and poured coffee and slumped into a chair at a table beside the window. My pussy ached delightfully, but I was too tired to try to figure it out. I'd accepted that my overactive imagination was taking its toll on my body, somehow. Maybe next week I'd see a shrink, get my head right. Or maybe I'd just get laid by a guy, see if it cured me . . .

'Hey there!'

I turned immediately, smile at the ready as he pulled out a chair and sat. 'Hi.'

He began to ask how my day was going as he set his breakfast tray down and reached for a bagel. I looked down at his hands, smiling at the memory of what I'd imagined last night.

And then we both saw the mark on his wrist.

Just a small red line left by a sharp fingernail in the heat of passion. A scratch that could have been caused by anything, anywhere: a doorframe, a zipper, a million other objects in the rush of life. But I remembered grabbing his wrist as he reached under my stomach to tease my clit as he brought himself to climax. I remember forcing his hand hard against my body, our combined weight pressing down as he slammed into me.

I reached for his other hand, the one nearest to me and turned it over, palm down. A half-moon cut over the third knuckle, a scratch just above the wrist. I keep my nails long because Casey likes me to tease her with them, trailing them over her breasts and her clit when I tie her up. I keep them sharp.

We looked at the cuts on his hand. And we stared.

Time slowed down and halted while we sat there. Me with my heart pounding, because the impossible – when finally you confront it – is scary. Thrilling. Confusing. I sat afraid to move or breathe or think because God only knew what might happen next, and he pulled his hand away. He reached up, brushed my hair aside and gently pulled the neck of my sweater forwards.

And he found his proof, as I had found mine.

I couldn't drink my coffee, it was choking me. But I sat there, cup in hand as he sat with his barely touched breakfast before him, both of us staring at the TV and seeing none of it until the break room emptied of everyone but us. Then he put one hand over my trembling one and he smiled at me. As if to say it would be OK. That we had nothing to fear because, somehow, some way, our deepest truest wish had come to pass.

Despite reason, despite common sense and logic and all the things we cling to in order to stay sane. We *knew*.

It *had* been real. We did have that power.

He came to me just once more. Three times, a lucky number, he said.

'How do you know?' I whispered in the darkness of my bed as he lay beside me, propped on one elbow, and played with my nipples. Rolling and twisting them between his thumb and fingers. Pinching them and then running his hand down my torso to check that my pussy was getting sufficiently hot and bothered and slippery. Teasing me a little down there so that I wriggled and arched, and then smearing moisture up over my pussy and my stomach, up to my breasts again where he began his maddening playing anew.

'Isn't three times always the charm?'

'Is it? Should you even be here? Should this even be happening?'

He hand stilled, resting on my chest. He looked at me. Serious, but not solemn, and I could hear the calm, assured happiness in his voice when he spoke.'Yes. Yes it should.'

And he kissed me.

Three times and the charm would be wrapped up. So I made the most of it. When he lifted me atop him, I rode him until my thighs would not obey my commands to move any more, and when I fell against him, exhausted, he rolled me over, knelt above me and kept fucking me. Kissing me as his cock pumped furiously, hungrily. One last time I felt the pleasure building like rage, like a storm; and I wrapped my legs over his to drive him further in, drive him to the centre of my pleasure and spill it outwards and all through my body. One last time to feel his body tense and jerk, hear him grunt and then sigh. Feel his wet heat trickling down my legs.

His tongue moved wet and lazy over mine. Saying goodbye; saying 'thank you', and, after the kiss, we let go. He faded past the barriers of my thoughts and it was over. As fast and desperate and amazing as it had begun.

We didn't speak of it, not in everyday words in our everyday world. Only a look sometimes, or a smile. A reminder. I wanted to say to him at least that I would never ever forget, but silence was the understood price and I never said a word. I think he knew all the same.

On the last day I ever saw him, before our lives took us different ways, I bent the rules just a little. Out of context, with no warning, I told him thank you and kissed his cheek. He stared, startled for a few seconds, and then hugged me once, smiling.

'You are like no one else,' he said.

'Did you ever wonder why or how?' I asked. I bit my lip and watched his face as he frowned a little. Thinking.

'I did. I still do. But –' he looked up, found my gaze, and gave me a soft smile '– I figure it's one of those things you don't pry too hard into. You just accept.'

I nodded, and we left it there.

I kept my secret and, I imagine, he kept his. We never tried to bridge the miles or the years between us – by ordinary means or not. But every so often, just before waking, I sometimes think I feel a gentle touch on my arm. Or a kiss on my cheek. And I smile before my eyes open. Because, after all, it's only a sweet dream.

The Girl of His Dreams
Heather Towne

Laura kept smiling at Evelyn, as the woman prattled on about another adorable moment in the life of her one-year-old wonder son. But she wasn't listening; she was staring over her co-worker's shoulder at a man she'd never seen before, walking down the corridor of cubicles into the actuarial department. She brought her 'Kittens for Mittens' coffee cup up to her parted lips, her glasses steaming with the hot beverage, at the sight of the man's tight buttocks twitching beneath his pale-blue suit pants.

'Um, did they hire a new actuary?' she interrupted Evelyn's discourse on her child's diaper contents.

The older woman twisted her head around to look where Laura was looking. 'Oh, yes, that's, oh – what's his name? Oh, yes, Perkin Miller.' Evelyn was a payroll officer and, as such, knew everything about everybody at the medium-sized insurance company – and wasn't afraid to tell it. '*Perkin*. Can you imagine?'

And she was off on another baby Ezekiel tangent. While Laura studied Perkin's short taut physique as he turned around. His brown hair was parted to the right with ruler precision, big blue eyes peering out from behind gold-rimmed corrective lenses, his pale face lean and bony. She played with the possibilities – Laura Miller, Laura Litt-Miller, Perkin Miller-Litt (wasn't that a beer?).

Nerds need lovin' too, she well knew. Laura toiled in

the accounting department checking expense reports and posting journal entries, but she was a girl with a very active imagination. Among other talents.

It was at lunchtime when Laura finally spotted Perkin again. He was sitting all by himself at a table for four in one corner of the company cafeteria.

She swallowed hard and moved boldly, slipping away from the accounting pack and carrying her tray over to Perkin's table. Normally, she was a shy reserved type of girl, but she hadn't had a date in six months, and she was hungry for more than just chocolate and *American Idol*. Not to mention, the batteries were getting low, again.

'Um, is this seat taken?' She gestured at the empty chair across from Perkin.

He looked up from his egg salad sandwich and blinked. 'Uh, no, it isn't.'

Laura smiled and set her tray down, as she slid into the chair. Her long dark hair was loosely braided into twin ponytails tied at the ends by red ribbons, a light dusting of blush and eye shadow and lipstick on her round girlish face. She was wearing a thin pink sweater and a long white skirt. Dressed to thrill? Not exactly, but a girl had to go with what she had.

She bit into her tuna salad sandwich and the two of them watched each other eat for an uncomfortable while. 'So, um, you're an actuary?' Laura finally asked.

'No, not quite,' Perkin replied. He picked up his milk carton and sucked on the straw with a pair of lips fuller and redder than Laura's. 'I still have to complete my exams.'

'It must be fascinating,' she gushed, her brown eyes flashing behind their dark frames. She pouted out her own lips and sealed them around her straw, sucking up milk with a wet throaty slurp. A drop dribbled out of the corner of her mouth, and she scooped it up with her tongue and slowly brought it back home. 'I'm in the second level of the certified general accountant programme, myself.'

'Great.' Perkin brushed a stray hair back into line with a smooth oversized hand.

'Yes, it is,' Laura breathed. She tore into the bread and tuna with her strong white teeth, eyes widened, nostrils flared. 'I don't want to be posting journal entries all my life. Not when I can tell somebody else to do it.'

'Makes sense,' Perkin responded. He licked his lips and swallowed, prominent Adam's apple bobbing up and down above his conservative striped tie.

Laura wagged her legs under the table, face and body flushing. 'Sooo, you ever watch the TV show *Numb3rs*? Last night –'

A buzzer sounded.

Perkin carefully wiped his hands and mouth on a serviette and got to his feet. 'Have to go,' he said, as he lifted his tray off the table and walked away.

A man who takes his responsibilities seriously, Laura thought dreamily, watching the man's pert buttocks disappear into the crowd exiting the institutional eatery.

Laura's first real awareness of her unique ESP abilities didn't come until she was twelve years old, when she attended a pyjama party at a friend's house. As an only child living with her parents in a roomy mansion, she'd never slept in close proximity to anyone before. But, on that night, Ashley Schweinsteiger had bedded down right next to her. And, as Laura lay awake listening to the girl's heavy nasal breathing, a strange image had suddenly flashed across her mind: Ashley riding a unicorn.

And, as Laura concentrated, Ashley's weird dream had unfolded in both their minds. Ashley and her unicorn jumping rainbows and waterfalls and wheeling around a golden meadow to the applause of a crowd of Nickelodeon-cast admirers, accepting a giant red showjumping ribbon from a Freddie Prinze Jr-looking centaur. Laura knew the girl was obsessed with horses. A little too obsessed, she found out, as Ashley hugged the Prinzecentaur, and then ... things got weirder still.

It was when the dot-com bubble burst and softsoaped her father away for a three-year term, forcing Laura and her mother to move into a cramped apartment in a government-subsidised building, that she really discovered and developed the full extent of her telepathic abilities.

She and her mother shared the same one bedroom, and Laura would lie awake at night concentrating on the woman's sleeping mind, receiving her dreams. They were usually about the family in happier times (which made Laura cry), or about the bitchy woman who ran the perfume counter at the department store where her mother worked (which made Laura cry some more).

She determined that she could only read the sleeping mind. But she could also project herself into another person's dream, if she concentrated hard enough.

She first accomplished this when D'arby T. Spoule, part-time artist and full-time parking-lot attendant, moved into the apartment next to theirs. Their bedrooms were separated by only a thin sheet of drywall, and Laura tapped into the man's rich vein of vibrant colourful dreams about painting the sky, sculpting colossal figures and paddling the haughty know-nothing gallery owners and art agents who rejected D'arby's work with rolledup canvases and giant paintbrushes.

She'd lie in her bed and come alive in his spectacular dreams, actually entering his outrageous sleeping scenarios and participating. The two of them and other artists and artist's models embarked on all kinds of wild wonderful adventures in the glorious pursuit of truth and beauty. Fanciful flights of unconscious imagination far removed from the depressing surroundings of apartments 10C and D.

D'arby would stare strangely at Laura and contemplatively stroke his red beard whenever they met for real in the hallway or elevator of the building. Like he recognised her as more than just the girl next door, though he didn't know why, or how. There was more than just paint and clay splashing around in D'arby's artful sensuous dreams.

After a couple more fruitless attempts to arouse Perkin's interest at work, Laura resolved to use her special powers to pique the guy's curiosity. Sure, she could've been using her gifts to preach peace and brotherhood into the dreams of local Jihadists, the need for cheaper bus fares and affordable housing into the dreams of local politicians. But, at twenty years of age and horny as the brass section in a Marine Corps band, the girl had other priorities.

She found out from Evelyn where Perkin lived, and then was lucky enough to snag the apartment directly below the guy. She signed a three-month lease and surreptitiously moved in a fold-out cot, a blanket and a pillow. And put her plan of subliminal seduction into play.

The first night, she clearly heard him walking around overhead (the whole Tudor-style building was as creaky as Granny Moses's rocking chair), heard his TV playing, heard him in the bathroom and then finally heard him walk into the bedroom down the hall. Then she heard nothing. She lay down on the cot and concentrated, her arms rigid at her sides, her body trembling, teeth clenched. She'd never deliberately tried to manipulate a man's dreams before. But she was a woman – as well as a physic – so she knew she was capable. And the call of her wild hormones easily drowned out any dissension.

Unfortunately, Perkin wasn't the type who hit his pillow unconscious because, as she lay there a half-hour and counting, Laura picked up nothing from the guy. But everything from the woman next door. It was straight out of a video game, rated 'P' for Psychos. The woman armed herself like Rambo and then drove through the front of a building like the Terminator, letting loose with enough firepower to clog even the Gears of War, mowing down people like they were dandelions.

Laura watched the mayhem for a while, until it became tiresome, and then she popped out of the dream/nightmare and promptly fell asleep. In the morning, she saw the woman – a petite blonde with a sweet smile and sparkling green eyes – leaving her apartment dressed in the proud uniform of the United States Postal Service.

The second night, Laura and Perkin finally connected. She listened to him wander back and forth between the living room and the bathroom, the kitchen, the living room, the bathroom again, and at last into the bedroom. The floorboards creaked one final time over her head, and then all was quiet.

She clutched the blanket with her damp hands and closed her eyes and concentrated. Men and women in blue screaming and streaming out of a giant warehouse as a maniacal little blonde with a super-gun sprayed lead like water from a firehose. She shook it off, concentrated harder. And there it was. Faint. A black and white world of cubicles and computers and carpeting. Growing stronger now as she concentrated still harder, as Perkin slipped into deeper sleep.

He was seated at his desk, in his cubicle, scrolling

through actuarial tables on his computer screen and leafing through mammoth binders of statistical data and claims reports, making notes, filling electronic spreadsheets. There wasn't even a shade of grey in sight. The man was having a mathematician's wet dream.

Well, dreaming about work wasn't an uncommon occurrence. Laura lay patiently on the cot waiting for the dream to pick up, to take on some life, some colour, something pleasurable to start happening. That would be the perfect time for her to make her entrance, she figured, to make a connection.

But the dream didn't pick up. The guy worked just as hard asleep as he did awake. He was in the midst of amassing the annual actuarial report for the Teacher's Pension Fund, and he was working way beyond overtime. Laura balled up the blanket and cursed, her nose twitching like she was bewitched.

OK, she thought, this can still work. I've got to make it work.

There was a knock on the monochromatic panel of Perkin's cubicle. He glanced up.

And there she was. Dished out in a skintight red dress sporting a thigh-high hemline and a plunging neckline, her long tresses flowing over her bare milky-white shoulders in inky waves, her face blushed to perfection, lashes thickened and lengthened beneath her lenses, lips lacquered a wet crimson. Her plump round breasts heaved almost right out of her designer dress, hard nipples poking almost right through the thin satin. She was backlit in a glowing amber light, her hair ruffled by a gentle backwind. And she'd dream-shopped her waist down a couple of sizes and stuck a mole on her left cheek.

She strolled into Perkin's drab little cubicle on four-inch red spike heels and then bent forwards and placed her hands on the disappearing hem of her dress, flashing a deep warm cleavage and breathing, 'Time for a break, Mr Miller.'

It was a stunning entrance, and it certainly stunned him. His right forefinger jumped up and down on his mouse and his left hand shook a clenched piece of paper like a white flag, as he stared at the bright bold vision of loveliness that had invaded his shabby dream.

Laura straightened up and took his hand. She lifted him out of his dull workaday (and night) existence and led him off down the hall to the elevators. Down in the elevator, his palm wet in her hand, his wide eyes pinballing back and forth between her face and her breasts.

They left the dreary building and she danced down the moon-washed city sidewalk with him trailing after her, her bare legs flashing as she kicked up her heels, attracting the admiration of men in the shadows. She dragged him through the doors of the most exclusive restaurant in town. 'For two tonight, Enrique,' she said, laughing to the maitre d'.

He smiled his suavish charm and ushered them into a candlelit booth.

They held hands across the fine Egyptian linen, Laura puckering flame-licked kisses over the candle at her agog companion. 'The veal is excellent, darling,' she murmured, the Justin Timberlake-esque waiter nodding his approval.

They dined, the Beaujolais flowing freely and expensively. Every chew and swallow was dignified and graceful, the banter witty and urbane, handsome couples at neighbouring tables eyeing them with obvious envy. They devoured desserts both rich and creamy, took dainty sips out of tiny cups of coffee even more so. Then Laura slipped her foot out of her shoe and touched Perkin's shin with her bare toes. The ravishing woman in red had this dream by the short hairs now, and she recklessly pushed it forwards, revelling in her power and purpose.

Perkin spluttered cappuccino. She smiled, hands folded elegantly under her chin, the hunger in her stomach (she'd missed her actual dinner that night) temporarily satisfied, the hunger in her loins insatiable. She rubbed her slender foot up and down his shin, then slid it higher, past his knee, moving smoothly and silkily along his inner thigh. They both jumped when all five of her mischievous toes landed softly in his lap, directly on top of his mounting hardness.

Her eyes flamed like the candle, his glasses and flushed face reflecting the fire. She stroked the swelling length of his desire with her silken ped, as he crumpled a napkin and panted.

'Will you be ... "footing" the bill tonight, madam?' the waiter remarked.

They laughed.

Laura flitted to her feet, light as feather despite the heavy meal, while Perkin slowly and awkwardly unfolded himself. She swept him out of the restaurant and on to the street, into a horse-drawn carriage idling by the kerb. They rode off into the old city, the clop of hooves sounding the cobblestones, moonlight painting the streets and buildings with a silvery sheen. She snuggled up close to Perkin, who wrapped his arm around her while she rested her head on his shoulder, her hand on his stomach.

And, when they entered the dimly lit tunnel linking the old city to the park, the top-hatted driver with the Harrison Ford visage turned around and winked at them. They melted into the darkness, and Laura tilted her head up and pressed her lips into Perkin's. They kissed soft and warm and sensual. Then harder and hotter, Laura sliding her hand over Perkin's erection. He shuddered, squeezing her tightly against him.

She darted her tongue in between his parted lips and entwined it around his tongue, pumping his cock through his pants. His hand slid off her shoulder and slipped under her arm, over her bulging breast. He squeezed the brimming flesh, and she moaned into his mouth.

They were halfway through the tunnel now, the light at the other end becoming brighter. She couldn't wait; she *wouldn't* wait. She broke away from his thrashing tongue and groping hand and quickly and expertly unzipped him, pulled him hard and heavy out into the open. His club throbbed in her hot little hand. She lowered her head.

'Yes, Laura,' he cried, as her wet lips engulfed the mushroomed top of his cock.

She enveloped him in the humid warmth of her mouth, the musky scent of the man, the pulsating hardness of him, driving her wild with want. She took him halfway down and then pulled back. Then went down even further, the tip of his prick bumping against the back of her throat, and beyond.

She bobbed her head, her lips oiling up and down the vein-ridged length of his dong, tongue cushioning shaft, sucking long and hard and deeply. He clawed at her shimmering curtain of hair, ran his hand down the back of her dress and over her electrified skin.

Only when he was bucking with the need to explode, desperately plunging into her sucking mouth, did she finally pull her head back. She quickly straddled his thighs, raising herself up on her knees, lifting her dress and positioning her dripping sex directly over the top of his slathered erection. He gripped his throbbing pole with one hand and her waist with the other, helping lower her down on to his spear. Her moist petals caught on his hood, spread, his stake sinking into . . .

A door slammed somewhere in the building.

Laura's teary eyes blinked wetly open. The dream was gone. Perkin was awake.

She heard floorboards creak as he scurried from his bedroom into the bathroom. She grinned and slipped a hand into her jeans, gripping a breast under her T-shirt at the same time. Maybe it was better this way – get the guy good and hooked, then reel him in.

She watched out of the corner of her eye as Perkin walked by her desk in the accounting department. A half-hour later, he came back the other way, darting a quick glance in her direction. Laura smiled to herself, tingling all over with the memory of the previous night, the anticipation of nights to come.

The third time he stopped, hesitated and then came right up to her desk. She raised her head, enjoying the look of confusion in his big blue eyes. This is it, she thought, the subliminally assisted breakthrough.

'Uh, h-hi, Laura,' he gulped.

'Hello, Perkin,' she murmured.

He flushed, the department becoming a vacuum as all of the girls stared at him, the latest framed photo of Evelyn's little darling spewing mashed carrots into Daddy's face forgotten in her hand.

'I, uh, just wanted to ask you ...'

'Yes?'

He pulled a direct deposit stub out of his shirt pocket. 'Do you know what this deduction is for? The one marked "SF".'

'That's my department,' Evelyn piped up.

She slammed the cot with her fist. Absolutely nothing was coming into Laura's mind that would allow her to get into Perkin's head. He hardly looked at her at work, and now he wasn't dreaming. She couldn't get anywhere with the guy.

She shifted her mental focus from north to east, and picked up the woman-next-door's brainwaves loud and bloody clear. Blondie was on the rampage again, as usual. Laura hid behind a sorting machine and watched, nothing better to do, in that kind of mood herself. Why did all the men dancing to the gunner's tune look exactly the same? Ex-husband, perhaps?

Finally, seven dull days and long dark nights after Laura's first dream date with Perkin, she caught a flicker of unconscious imagination from upstairs. It was weak, at a brainwave frequency so low she could barely pick it up. Like he was being cautious about how he dreamt.

She shut her eyes tight and mustered all her powers of concentration. Perkin was sitting in a colourless conference room at a colourless meeting with ten or twelve other colourless people. They were listening to someone expound on the present value of future benefits payable in the Teacher's Pension Fund. The guy stopped talking, jarring some of his audience awake, and Perkin stood up and started handing out binders as thick as insurance policies to the stony-faced crowd. He actually half-smiled at a pretty young woman wearing a skirt so short he could've folded it up and stuffed it into his suit-jacket pocket.

Which was when Laura entered the picture, blazing technicolour red in her low-cut dress and high heels, skin glistening brown with instant tan, chest sparkling with glitter. Binders thumped to the boardroom floor along with jaws, as she grabbed Perkin by the arm and pulled him out of the stuffy room and building.

A limousine was waiting next to the kerb, the Jason Statham-lookalike driver holding the rear door open. Laura pushed Perkin into the black leather-upholstered back of the stretch-car and then jumped in herself. She slid up next to him, untied the knot in his ever present striped tie and yanked the thing away, before falling laughing into his arms as the limousine sped from the kerb, out of the city and into the country.

They stopped in a flash; the hunky driver opened the door and handed Laura a picnic basket. She sprang out into the bright sunshine and skipped off across a rolling emerald-green meadow, Perkin in tow. They rushed through a forest of tall leafy trees, then burst out on to the loamy banks of a clear babbling brook. Whereupon Laura dropped the picnic basket and all further pretence and flung herself into Perkin's arms, smooshing her mouth up against his.

They kissed for an eternity, Perkin coiling his arms around Laura's vibrating body and holding her tight. She felt his heat, his passion, his hard cock pressing into her stomach, and it set her on fire. They tumbled down on to the soft cool bed of grass, devouring each other's mouth, Laura on top of the guy, all over him.

Perkin slid his hands up under Laura's dress and on to her bare bum cheeks. He kneaded the fleshy mounds to her delight, as she caught his tongue between her teeth and sucked on it, riffling her fingers through his hair, forever mussing up the perfect parting.

They furiously kissed and frenched and fondled one another under the glowing sun, on the banks of the gurgling stream, until, ablaze with desire, Laura arched up over the top of Perkin. She pulled her dress over her head and tossed it away into the water, baring herself to the man. He anxiously reached up and took hold of her hanging breasts, and she tilted her head back and moaned, joyously running her hands through her raven locks.

Perkin grasped and squeezed the soft supple flesh of Laura's burning breasts. Then he crawled his quivering fingers up to her flowered nipples and rolled the rosy-red protuberances, sending twin streaks of lightning arcing through the girl's chest, shimmering all through her body.

She collapsed over the top of him, digging her fingers into the good black earth as he gripped her breasts and licked at her nipples. He twirled his tongue all around her buzzing tips, before finally taking one into the wet hot cauldron of his mouth and sucking on it. She shivered with pleasure, as he licked and sucked and bit into her achingly hard nipples, working her electrified breasts with his hands, until she just couldn't take it any more.

Laura scooched lower down Perkin's body, unbuckled and unzipped his pants, then pulled them down, and his underwear. She gazed at the straining object of her desire, then looked up into his begging eyes and encircled the pulsing shaft with her fingers. He groaned and jerked. She lifted his rigid cock off his stomach and pumped it. He grunted. Then she rose up and pushed the bloated head of his prick in between her slickened pussy lips and lowered herself down, swallowing him up in her hot velvety wetness.

He grabbed on to her shuddering breasts as she undulated her bum, impaling herself on his stake over and over again. She bounced up and down on the man's thighs, the wet smack of their charged flesh melding with the birds twittering rhapsodies and the leaves rustling contentment at the gentle caress of the wind. The brook babbled its delight and the sun beamed down on the heaving dewy lovers, nature in perfect harmony with their erotic efforts.

'God, I'm coming, Laura!' Perkin suddenly bleated, gripping her waist and furiously thrusting his hips up in rhythm to her movements, fucking her with abandon.

Laura dug her dirty fingernails into his chest and cried, 'Yes, yes!' Her body was burning out of control, her pussy gone molten.

He groaned sweet agony, and she felt his hot seed spill into her gushing sex, the two of them bucking and shaking with a fierce fiery ecstasy that went on and . . .

Her eyes shot open. He was awake.

She heard his bed scrape against the floor above a couple more times, and then all was quiet. She closed her eyes again, and slept deeply and blissfully.

Laura wore a red dress and pair of red high heels to work the next day, her face and body done up exactly like they'd been the night before – in dreamland. Evelyn dropped little Ezekiel's latest crayon masterpieces all over the floor, as she and the rest of the accounting gang watched the woman in red strut down the hall and into the actuarial area.

Perkin was standing next to his cubicle, talking to a colleague. She strolled up behind him and tapped him on the shoulder with a red-painted nail. He turned around.

He took one look at her and took off running down the hall.

Laura could see the fear in the guy's eyes, all right, but she couldn't read his wide-awake mind, which was screaming, 'She's out of my league. She's a dream-girl. She's too good for me!'

To Stand between the Wild and the Human

Teresa Noelle Roberts

I stood on the narrow beach and watched as the fishing boat motored away from Torishima, shrinking and finally turning into a speck on a blue-tossed horizon.

The boat had answered my distress call, and was now ferrying Akiko, my Project Albatross partner, off to the nearest hospital, some eighteen hours away.

Thank goodness, she'd only broken her leg when she fell. It looked like a nasty break, but it could have been far worse. She could have broken her back or neck tumbling down that steep rocky slope, or she could just as easily have fallen off one of the many sheer cliffs that protect the albatross-breeding grounds.

I was alone on the island now, just me and most of the world's population of short-tailed albatross.

And I was guiltily relieved Akiko was gone.

Akiko just wasn't cut out for this kind of rough fieldwork. She was smart and she knew her birds. But she was a klutz, and she spent more time watching the sky than the ground under her feet. On a deserted island that features dangerous cliffs, crashing surf, slopes slick with a mix of volcanic ash and bird guano, and an actual live volcano, that's a bad combination. Her stay on Torishima had been a series of small disasters: blundering into a lit Coleman lantern, stumbling and gashing both palms open on sharp volcanic rock, smashing one of the cameras so it looked like a hatched egg, having a few close calls with both her own climbing ropes and mine as we made the steep ascent to the nesting grounds. She was safer at Toho University with her leg in a cast, analysing data, than she was here. Pity she would miss the mating flights, but at least she wouldn't fall off a cliff backwards in her excitement and kill herself.

Right now, standing alone on the beach and staring at the tiny speck of the boat, I felt a bit desolate, but I suspected that I really wouldn't miss her that much. She was a pleasant enough person but, after six weeks alone together, we'd been getting on each other's nerves. Some of that was a problem I'd had with other Japanese acquaintances. As a third-generation Japanese–American, I was a walking mixed signal; I looked Japanese enough and spoke the language well enough that sometimes they'd be taken aback when I didn't get a pop-culture reference or react to something in the way most Japanese people would.

A lot of it, though, came down to differences between Akiko and me. She regarded me as borderline uncivilised, and I could see why; with two naturalist parents, I'd been going on field expeditions since I was an infant, and Torishima was more comfortable for me than Tokyo. For my part, I didn't understand how an ornithologist could be as unconcerned as she was about global conservation issues. As long as it didn't have a direct impact on the albatross, she saw it as someone else's problem. I tried to walk as gently on the earth as I could. She admitted that she simply couldn't be bothered.

For me, the sky, the ocean and the magnificent short-tailed albatross would be better company.

On the other hand, if Project Albatross sent out a gorgeous single man in her place . . .

He'd be married. Or gay. Or, worse yet, he wouldn't

be, we'd have one night of insanely hot sex, then fight and spend the rest of our stay tiptoeing around each other.

That didn't keep me from having a few lovely thoughts about passionate kisses, well-muscled male bodies and hard cocks. About sex in the field of golden-yellow chrysanthemums in the centre of the island, sex under the stars on the 'veranda' (which had been a cannon platform in our research station's original incarnation as a military observation post), sex while we watched the albatross in their beautiful playful courtship rituals.

I swore I could feel a cock inside me, feel hands on my breasts, rolling out my nipples, elongating them, firm pressure but not painfully so . . .

Being alone on the island, I told myself firmly, was getting to me already. That or it was the complete lack of nookie in my life since leaving the States. I'd told myself for over a year that it wasn't important and, compared to my work, it wasn't. I'd been preparing myself to work with Project Albatross since I'd heard of it back in high school and, in the big picture, the fact that finally getting the chance to do so had pretty much derailed my sex life for the time being didn't matter all that much.

But there were times, and this was one of them, where it became damn hard to focus on the big picture over the sheer horniness.

I felt the sexy phantom sensations throughout the steep walk back up to the research station. I was in good shape with all the walking I'd been doing, but trembling legs, a racing pulse and a pussy that was getting wetter with each step made the climb feel more strenuous than it normally was.

By the time I got home, the light was failing. Taking care of Akiko while waiting for the boat to arrive, I'd not got in any fieldwork, but I had notes from the day before to collate and pictures to get off the digital camera and back up. (When you're running your computer off a generator, you back up obsessively.) Dinner to prepare, even.

But, before I did any of that, I needed to release some of the sexual tension flooding my body. There was no way I could focus in my current state, with my nipples so hard I was nonsensically convinced they'd rip my sweater and Gore-Tex pullover and my pussy so twitchy I couldn't think straight and so wet that, if I didn't do something soon, it would soak through to my jeans. Given how inconvenient it was to do laundry out here, that alone was a motivation to peel out of them.

So I did.

Right on the veranda.

Why not? It wasn't like there was anyone to see me, and the view from the veranda was far more appealing than the streaky cement interior of the research station. Fog hung low over the water, but directly overhead the sky was streaked with the last of the sunset and jewelled with a rising full moon. The only sounds were the surf and the cries of birds, my beloved albatross among them. Romantic, even with no one to share it with.

It was cool verging on chilly, but the dusk air caressed my overheated skin. I plopped down on the little table some previous insane researcher had built out of driftwood, lay back and spread my legs.

The cool air on my crotch felt like a lover's touch. I was that sensitive. That wet. That needy, in a way I didn't remember feeling needy when I actually had a lover and was longing for him.

But it was far from enough.

I bit my lip as soon as I began circling my clit, bit back the cries that were threatening to burble out of me.

Then I remembered that I was completely alone, and

let myself whimper encouragement to myself, cries as crazy as those of the albatross. They hadn't started mating yet, but they were getting restless and, with that, noisier.

I pictured a man licking me. Not anyone I knew, but not the usual vague, faceless fantasy fill-in either. I pictured a vividly distinct individual: a handsome long-haired Japanese man with a narrowly triangular face, large but rather close-set almond eyes, a slender hard body I could only guess at under his elegant traditional clothes. His cock, though, I could see, or rather feel, pressing against me as he licked, nipped, took me to the edge of orgasm time and again without letting me slip over. I followed suit with the fantasy, teasing myself into a frenzy, but not letting myself come, letting my need build higher and higher.

I imagined my lover kissing and nipping his way up my body and – in the way of fantasy – slipping his cock into me without any of that awkward fumbling that happens in real life.

As I came, I would have sworn that I was coming around a cock, one that filled me like no other ever had – not because it was so huge, but because it was simply the perfect fit.

When I gave a damn about my surroundings again, it was cold and the blanket of stars you see only in such an incredibly isolated place was coming out.

And a fox was staring at me from the corner of the veranda, cheekiness incarnate in the cock of its head, in the way it held its magnificent tail.

It looked so intent, so interested in what I'd been doing, that I jumped up and tried to cover myself as I would have done for an unexpected human guest. My quick movement startled the beast, which darted off into the darkness.

I followed it for about two steps before I lost it in the shadows.

And I realised I shouldn't have seen what I'd just seen. Foxes were common in rural parts of Japan proper, but not on Torishima. According to everything I knew about the ecology of the island, I should be the only mammal on it.

And yet I was sure I'd seen a fox.

A fox among the world's last breeding population of short-tailed albatross, which had never seen a mammalian predator and had no idea something might try to eat their eggs or chicks.

I couldn't imagine how it got here.

Maybe it was a trick of the fading light, the shadow of a cloud or something, but, if it were here, I was going to track it down and dispose of it.

How, I would think about later. I had no weapons. I was trained to protect wildlife, not to kill it. And I'd always been fond of foxes, with their cocky attitude and beautiful tails. But I couldn't let one maraud through the birds of Torishima.

I stayed up late that night, trying to devise a plan that could kill one mysterious fox and not harm any of the island's other wildlife.

With each minute I spent pondering the creature's death, I felt sicker at heart. Yet I knew it would be far worse to let it roam free, assuming it was actually there and not some bizarre product of hormones and twilight. (But, I reasoned, if I'd imagined anything in the shadows at that moment, it would have been my hot fantasy man, not an animal that had no reason to be there.)

When I finally fell asleep, I tossed and turned in uneasy dreams. A fox, broken and bleeding under my hands, turned into the gorgeous Japanese man of my fantasies, who turned huge sad eyes on me and tried to speak.

I snapped myself from the dream several times, fearing to hear what he'd say, how he'd condemn me. The final time, though, I didn't wake up – and I heard him apologise to me. I didn't understand why he was apologising when I had killed him, but he didn't have time to explain before death took him.

Once I knew to look for signs of a fox, they were laughably easy to find. Scat that never came from a bird. Narrow pathways winding through the sparse undergrowth.

I didn't find broken eggs, though, or the remains of dead juveniles. My count of young albatross was the same as it had been.

The fox might have been going after any of the smaller less threatening-looking seabirds that nested here. Must have been, in fact – it had to eat something. There were no albatross eggs or chicks yet, and the juveniles from last year's mating must be too big to look edible. (No surprise there; the adults have a seven-foot wing span and the juveniles are still impressively large.)

But, still, the day would come when it figured out that, for all their size and magnificence, albatross weren't all that bright and wouldn't know to fight off a fox until it was too late. Newly laid eggs would be extremely vulnerable.

So, to prevent that day, I laid snares on the fox's trails, as far from any bird-nesting sites as I could. They were makeshift, the product of dim memory of having someone show me once how hunters in earlier times would catch rabbit.

I hoped they'd do the job.

And I hoped they wouldn't.

* * *

That evening as the sun set, I gave in again to lust, dreaming of the man I'd dubbed 'my samurai-poet' as I made myself come and come. I'd hoped to wear myself out enough to fend off dreams of dying foxes.

It didn't work.

I woke in the middle of the night in an actual cold sweat, shaking with the conviction of death. It wasn't the dream that woke me, though. It was a voice on the wind, a beautiful voice begging, not for help, but for absolution.

And, once I was awake, I still heard it.

It compelled me out of bed, into my clothes and out into the night, flashlight in hand, looking for God only knew what.

The rational part of me, which was by far the larger part, figured I was still dreaming.

The part of me that had been raised on my grandmother's Japanese folk tales (she was born in America, but she'd learnt them from *her* mother) thought of ghosts – the entire human population of the island, bird-hunters and their families, had been killed in a volcanic explosion in 1902. Thought of demonic *oni*. Thought of all sorts of hideous phantoms that should, by all logic, have kept me cowering in my futon with the covers over my head until morning dispelled them like the nightmares they were.

Instead, I was following that voice as if it were the voice of my lover, and damned if I could make myself stop or turn back.

I didn't have to go far from the station to find what I was looking for. I almost tripped over it despite the flashlight.

I trained the light down to find the fox I'd sought. It wasn't caught in a snare, and under the flashlight's beam I couldn't see any signs of injury, but it was struggling to breathe.

I crouched down next to it, careful to keep back. Despite the threat the fox represented to my birds, I pitied it, wished there was something I could do to help. But I didn't dare. Sick or injured animals might strike out and, while rabies was rare in Japan, that wasn't something I was willing to risk.

And then the fox laboured, turned its head towards me ... and spoke. 'I have wronged you, beautiful lady, and my regret for this is killing me. Please accept my apologies and let me right the wrong I did you.'

At that moment, the talking fox didn't surprise me nearly as much as it should have.

His voice – and the voice was definitely male, and seemingly too large for that small body – was weak but melodious, almost seductive despite his obvious pain.

'You're ... a kitsune,' I stammered. Part of me told me I should be more alarmed than I was, but I was still expecting to wake up any moment and find myself in my futon.

The fox nodded.

Foxes don't nod. But kitsune might.

Kitsune – spirit-foxes, shapeshifters, nature guardians, notorious tricksters and seducers. In most traditional tales, they were females, causing trouble for human men because their human forms were irresistibly lovely, but their ways were too alien for a relationship to last. But, as my grandmother had always said with a wink and a nod, there must have been males, or how would you get little kitsune? Human women were either too smart to be taken in, she reasoned, or too proud to admit they'd fallen for someone who turned out not to be human.

And kitsune, the good ones, at least, could die of regret.

I'd felt bad enough about causing the death of an

ordinary fox. I couldn't risk killing a creature of legend, even if it couldn't possibly be real and talking with me.

'I accept your apology, kitsune-san,' I said in my most formal Japanese. 'But how could you have wronged me?' I felt myself colouring in the dark. 'I didn't mind you watching me last night.'

The fox's voice seemed a little stronger. 'No, not that. That was saying goodbye. I have watched you and your friend since you came here, seen the care you take of my birds and my island. But your friend was so clumsy that sometimes she came close to stumbling into nests. I decided she needed to learn to be more careful and materialised almost under her feet, just to startle her. I didn't mean to do her harm, but she tripped and took a nasty fall. It's my fault she got injured, and I deprived you of your friend, and when I saw you last night I realised how very alone you would be now without her.'

His cadences were formal, some of his words old-fashioned. It took me a while to realise that the word I was mentally translating as *friend* or *companion* was probably more like *lover*.

Despite his solemn tone, I smiled. Then I bowed. 'Master Kitsune,' I said, trying to remember my best formal manners, Japanese-style, 'I accept your apology. I regret that Akiko got hurt, but I also think that you may have saved her life by forcing her to leave here. A clumsy person shouldn't be scaling cliffs and I was scared for her every day. And, if it helps, Akiko was my work partner, but not my lover or even a close friend. I'll miss having someone to talk to, but eventually someone else will come to watch the albatross with me.'

I swore that even under the flashlight's beam I could see the kitsune's breathing become easier, see his form relax.

'But I must make amends,' the kitsune insisted. 'I only

meant to scare her a bit, not to harm her or to leave you without companionship. May I offer you ... conversation?'

My flashlight popped out, and then popped back on, equally mysteriously.

And, when it did, a beautiful man in old-fashioned layered robes stood where the fox had lain. A fox tail peeked out from under his robe. The man I thought I'd invented in my sexual fantasy, only far sexier in the flesh. Far sexier than any human had a right to be.

'I hope my appearance pleases you,' he said. 'I cannot seem to create clothing like that worn today. Ah well.' He shrugged with incredible grace. 'Even if I could, they would not accommodate my tail.'

Then he touched my arm, and I felt heat sear through my awkwardly thrown-on layers.

He drew closer. His eyes weren't brown but a pure gold like a fox's eyes, and he was entirely male yet utterly beautiful and elegant in a way that men usually weren't, at least not 21st-century straight men. More masculine and grown-up than the androgynous *bishonen* boys of anime, but with that silken appeal.

'Conversation?' I said, realising my voice was coy, flirtatious, dripping honey almost as much as my pussy suddenly was. 'I forget ... is that another word with more than one meaning?'

When he kissed me, I did something I'd only read about in particularly bad books: I swooned. Fire and earth and growth and pure animal lust overwhelmed me and for a second I literally couldn't see or breathe.

He caught me as I started to buckle. 'Forgive me yet again,' he said. 'It has been far too long. I must remember how to ... moderate myself. Let me take you to my home.'

It was and was not a cave. That is, I knew where we

were, and I knew that what I was entering was a small cave, a crevice in the lava. But, when we entered, it opened into a lovely home in the antique Japanese style, complete with rice-paper walls that couldn't possibly be there. It was warm, well lit and as elegant as my handsome kitsune friend.

And it should have bothered me immensely that none of this was possible, that I was apparently about to make love with a mythical being in a house that couldn't exist.

I was having a harder time by the second, clinging to the conviction that I was dreaming. It was too vivid, too detailed, too unlike any dream I'd ever had. Either I was going insane or the kitsune was throwing off pheromones my long-deprived body couldn't resist – and, since I was way too busy to become crazy, I was voting for the latter.

He offered me food and, when I accepted, a lovely meal appeared: rice balls, inari and other sushi, beautifully presented on lacquerware, and a steaming bowl of udon soup. 'You will still be hungry in the morning,' he explained, his face merry. 'But it will taste good. We so crave human food that we've learnt to create its likeness from air and will, although we have little need for nourishment.'

'No problem there. What woman wouldn't love a great dinner with no calories?'

He laughed, although his face showed he was puzzled. Then again, he probably hadn't interacted much with humans since the volcano erupted, and, in 1902, people in such a remote place would be more worried about keeping weight on than taking it off.

We ate and chatted, and the food (though it might have been an illusion) was delicious, and his conversation quirky and poetic and charming, although some of it didn't make a lot of sense to me because his vocabulary was archaic. And all the while, as we spoke, I felt my lust building.

Dream, hallucination or creature of the spirit world – whatever he might be, I had to have him.

I kept shifting my seat, feeling the weight of my desire in my pussy, in my hard eager nipples. The conversation was light, layered in innuendo and double meaning, but I couldn't figure out the right way to say what I wanted.

Luckily, I didn't have to. We reached at the same time for a rice ball. When our skin touched, my breath hissed in and I could feel my eyes widening. I strained forwards.

He brushed the remains of dinner aside with one grand gesture (they turned to twigs of heather and bright chrysanthemum flowers as they hit the tatami mat, the lacquered plates to large shells), grabbed my shoulders and pulled me bodily towards him. He was strong for all his sleek elegance, strong and graceful like the predator he was.

When he kissed me, I swore the island shuddered, like it did occasionally when the volcano grumbled and threatened. I half-expected his breath to be fetid, like a dog's, but it smelt of sweetgrass and green tea, and he wore an elusive perfume, amber and cherry blossoms, that lay lightly on top of a natural scent that was half sexy man, half warm animal musk.

My clothing – sweatpants, T-shirt, fleece, Gore-Tex jacket – moved aside for him as gracefully as if he were peeling back layers of brightly coloured and patterned kimono to reveal the red silk hakima underneath.

My underwear wasn't nearly as elegant as that, but he made it melt away.

Damn, I had to sleep with more supernatural beings.

I delved through layers of silk, enjoying the journey,

but eager to get to the goal. His skin was as silken as his clothes, but hot, hotter than a human, and his chest was downy with fine red hair – no, fur that extended in a vee to his cock.

He whimpered when I toyed with his nipples, a puzzled, but pleased sound. When I dropped to my knees (wishing as I did that I had a modicum of his animal grace) and kissed my way down to his cock, his reaction was an amused aroused chuckle. 'So bold! Are all women of this era like you?'

I looked up into his golden eyes. 'Some are much wilder than I am. I'm kind of out of practice.'

His cock was shaped a bit differently from a human's, and the way it emerged from the foreskin seemed different as well, not that I'd had a lot of experience with uncut cocks. And, when his tail swished forwards and brushed against me, I briefly had second thoughts.

If he were just my fantasy, my dream, he'd have been human inside his clothes – but he was definitely not. His differences were beautiful, even erotic, but at the same time startling.

Not an animal, but not a man either. A kitsune.

Alien. Wild. Supernatural, or perhaps *extra-natural*, an incarnation of nature. Not a safe partner for a human, if I were to believe my grandmother's stories – not because he was evil, but because he was simply other.

Then the tail swept forwards again and very deliberately brushed between my legs, flicking at my clit.

Soft. The very definition of sensuality. But the rest of him was deliciously hard, and the contrast made me crazy.

I've never feared adventure. I'd come halfway around the world to pursue my dream, then planted myself on a deserted island.

This was just another adventure, or so my overheated body and mind assured me.

I took him in my mouth. He tasted of male musk, but not much more so than a turned-on man would at the end of a long day outdoors.

But, under that, he tasted of sunlight playing on the water, of the albatross dancing over the island, of the scruffy shrubs and the chrysanthemums, of salt and stars and volcanic ash. I could taste all of Torishima on his cock, and I wanted more, wanted him to spill the essence of the island into my throat.

He buried his fingers in my hair, began moving in opposition to my movements, letting his length fuck my mouth. I let one hand slip between my legs, stirred at my cunt to slick my fingers, began to circle my clit.

'No!' he cried. 'Not like this!' He tore away from me, leaving my mouth bereft. Then he pushed me back on to the low table.

'Such lovely human skin,' he murmured, as he kissed and licked my throat, kissed my collarbone. He suckled my breasts, first one, then the other, taking them further into his mouth than I would have thought possible, and I could tell he was tasting my world on my skin as I had tasted his world on his.

And, when he worked his way between my legs, he lapped at me eagerly, delicately, his hands working in concert, almost pushing me over, then pulling back at the last second and letting it build again.

'You taste of art I've never seen, poems I've never heard,' he said. 'You taste of cities and, yet, of caring for what is not human.'

That so struck me that, even though my brain should have been non-functional by that point, I asked, 'You know cities? I thought you were a wild thing.'

'My kind is between the wild and the human, guarding each from the other. I have been in cities, before I followed the first humans here a century and more ago. They needed more kitsune here,' he added sadly. 'One was not enough for the balance to be preserved. But now there are humans like you to help.'

Then, without warning, as if to force his mind away from melancholy thoughts, he pulled back. 'Turn over,' he said and, when I didn't arrange myself in quite the position he'd had in mind, he roughly positioned me on hands and knees on the mat, ass high, head down.

He knelt behind me, teased at my pussy with his cock. When I pushed back towards him, he growled and put one hand on the scruff of my neck, pinning me into place.

I've never been submissive in bed and I wasn't submissive then – I growled back at him, pushed against his cock – but, still, the show of dominance made me shudder, made me open for him even more than I already was.

'Now!' I'd meant it as a plea, but it came out as a snarl.

And apparently he liked that, because he drove into me. None of this inching in, teasing, that I'd expected after his delight in foreplay, but a claiming.

And I gave it right back, shaking his hand off my neck, driving back on to his cock, thrusting on to his thrusts.

I'd been rippling at the edge of orgasm so long that when the wave broke it was a tsunami, or maybe more like the volcano blowing the top off my world, sending wave after wave of white-hot lava over me. I clenched around him, working his cock without even trying to.

But he kept going.

Another series of waves threatened to drown me.

But he kept going, slowing down a bit to let me catch my breath, let the tension build again. This time, I sensed, he would let himself come with me.

'Not so fast,' I said. 'This time I want to look at you. I want to watch your face while you come.'

'But my tail ... and my face ... I might not look ...'

I understood what he couldn't say. As he lost control, he might also lose control of his shape, lose his gorgeous human mask.

'Will it be your true face I see?'

'Yes.'

'Then please ...'

I think he expected me to lie under him. In any event, he seemed surprised when I urged him on to his back and straddled him – surprised, but pleased.

'Good,' he said. 'I get to watch you. You are so beautiful.'

I wondered at that for a second. I'm not unattractive, but not beautiful by either Japanese or American standards: too sturdy for the one, too small-breasted and short-waisted for the other, with the broad nose and flat cheekbones of someone from Japanese peasant stock.

And then I sank on to his cock and began to move, deciding that, if a glorious supernatural creature thought I was beautiful, I was damn well going to believe him for the moment. Especially when his clever hands began to play with my clit, coaxing me towards another climax.

Heat filled me, blinding me. I had to close my eyes against the surge of pleasure. Closed my eyes and saw Torishima below me, a tiny rugged jewel in the ocean, as an albatross saw it, then saw it as obsidian and shale and plants and nests and feathers and guano, a fox's-eye view.

But I wasn't going to be cheated. I reached back, began tickling his balls, felt them shift and clench under my touch. When I felt his muscles tighten and ripple, I forced my eyes open, forced myself away from the vision to watch his face.

Or rather his faces, morphing back and forth.

The handsome man. A woman lovely in the old

Japanese style, with fragile features and a cloud of black hair. An ordinary red fox. A black fox with nine tails. An old man with wise merry eyes.

A being not clearly male or female, not clearly fox or human. Fox ears and whiskers and human eyes and lips. Stunning.

That face was the one he settled into as his climax claimed him.

His back arched like someone had fed him strychnine, and the sound he made was high and surreal, as much a fox's yips as a human's cries.

And as he poured hot as lava into me, I came again, even more violently than before.

I ended up curled in his chest. He was a human man again, or as much of one as he ever had been – his tail, as well as his arms, were curled possessively around me – and we were floating on a cloud of his long black hair.

'I am of the night,' he whispered. 'In the morning, you'll be in your own bed, alone, but you'll see me again.' He sniffed at my hair like a cat might, an endearingly animal gesture. 'I won't stay away. I can't. You are far too beautiful.'

This time, he used a different word for *you*, one that roughly translated means 'all of you honourable people'. This time he definitely meant not me as an individual, but human women, or humans in general.

Well, that worked for me. He was beautiful in his own right, but all wild things were beautiful in their wildness.

And, from what I could tell, we both had the job of maintaining a balance between the wild and the human.

Perhaps we had more of a chance to make things work than the human–kitsune couples in traditional tales, more common ground to build on.

And, if not, I had had an experience even rarer and more marvellous than observing the albatross.

The albatross! I'd almost forgotten them. How much time had passed in this world between worlds? In some old tales, visiting a kitsune could distort your sense of time horribly. A day could be a year; a year could be a day. Was I reckoned to be missing, lost somewhere on Torishima? Worse yet, had I missed the mating flights?

'Don't fret,' he said. 'When the sun comes up, only one night will have passed, and it will be time for the albatross to dance.'

I had been too sleepy by then, worn by great sex and sheer strangeness, to parse that.

But, when I took my weary, but still blissful body to the cliffs in the morning, still bemusedly brushing fox fur from my clothes, the air was filled with wings tinted rose by sunrise, meeting and courting in a dance older than anything human.

Somewhere in the distance, although he'd said he was night's creature, I heard a fox's bark, sounding for all the world like a man's sated laughter.

I turned to the direction from which it came and whispered on to the wind, 'Tonight I want you in your true form.'

And the wind caressed me like a hand, like fur.

Watching the Detective
Portia Da Costa

Uh oh, here we go! How many times have I heard this theme tune tonight? How many times have I pressed my hand to my heart as if I could stop it pounding fifteen to the dozen? I always get a little tingle when I hear this heavy plinkety-plunking intro. A fluttery tingle in my mid-section and a big fat horny twinge way down low, because I know I'm going to see *him* any second!

Or at least I'll see him if we don't get struck by lightning in the meantime. There's a classic Hammer Horror thunderstorm raging outside and the power's been fluctuating and even gone out momentarily once or twice. It's not all that long since we moved into this old house that my uncle Edgar left me and, frankly, it's a bit of a death-trap. The electric wiring is rudimentary in places – and the plumbing and the heating aren't much better either.

We're warm and cosy at the moment, though, in spite of the crashing thunder, the pouring rain and temperatures outside that feel more like midwinter than 23 June. Our big old bed is like the warren of some animal tonight, a sweaty sexy burrow of tangled sheets and a moth-eaten duvet, all garnished with a liberal smattering of crumbs and crisp bits from our usual television snacking.

Normally, at midnight, I'd be fast asleep, snuggled up against my honey, breathing in his familiar raunchy man-smell and probably smiling in my slumbers.

But tonight isn't a normal night. It's the Midsummer's Eve twelve-hour marathon of my all-time favourite cop show, and my boyfriend Sam and I have decided to watch the whole thing here in bed.

Well, *I'm* watching.

Sam's not the rabid fan of the show that I am, but he's an easy-going soul – bless his heart – so he indulges me in my televisual obsession. He's been passing most of his time catching up on his newspaper reading, and poring over back issues of his beloved car magazines while I worship at the shrine of The Detective.

Oh, The Detective! He's a bit like the chocolate biscuits I've been scoffing far too many of – irresistibly delicious, but detrimental in unrestrained excess. I ought to feel guilty but I couldn't give a monkey's!

It's terrible of me really.

Here I lie, ogling my god while my real sweet long-suffering bloke lies ignored beside me, making his own amusement. Not many other men would stand for such offhand treatment so amiably, so, in a spirit of fairness, and because I'm *very* turned on, I start feeling Sam up during the adverts. There's a less than brilliant episode on just now, so I decide that I can spare some of my attention in order to rub my pelvis provocatively against the man who's actually in my bed. He deserves a treat for putting up with my foibles, and pretty soon he takes notice. I've surreptitiously slipped off my panties and kicked them away down amongst the mangled covers. And when The Detective makes his big entrance, scoping out the scene of the crime, *I* notice that Sam starts touching me and naughtily flicking my clit. I've got a sneaking feeling this is something of a sly competitive tactic on his part, to see if he can completely wrest my attention from the screen, but who cares what it is when it feels so wicked and so good. Pretty soon, I'm wriggling and pulling at him, Detective or no Detective, and Sam complies obligingly by climbing on top, slotting himself into me and starting to pump.

Mmm ... that feels so good ... so familiar, yet also new ... because I'm still following the course of the investigation ... oh, bad me!

From time to time, I grapple with my concentration, and attempt to focus on Sam, who I think the world of, and who is undeniably very cute and lovable. But, as my cunt ripples, he drifts inevitably from my consciousness. All of a sudden it's The Mighty Detective between my legs, shagging me senseless.

My Detective, oh my Detective, how can I describe thee? You're so tall and broad and handsome, with your angelic face, your naughty mouth and your bitter-chocolate eyes full of mischief and wisdom. It might actually be Sam putting his back into it between my legs, but it's *your* passionate lips that I'm kissing and *your* huge delicious dick that's surging inside me. And *your* name I moan deliriously as I come.

Oh my God, what a selfish bitch I am! The instant I've stopped fluttering and glowing and I'm back in my body again, a great weight of lip-gnawing guilt descends upon me. It's one thing to have a crush on a television character and fantasise about him during sex – but it's well out of order to let your partner know you're actually doing it at the time!

How could I do that? Isn't it bad enough that I'm subjecting Sam to twelve hours of the big guy on the television?

But my Sam is a saint and, now that's he's huffed and puffed and shot his load, he's feeling more than mellow. He just chuckles and gives me a sloppy affectionate kiss.

'I knew you were pretending I was him,' he growls, mock fierce, and beneath the covers he slaps me playfully on the thigh 'But don't worry, it was *me* you were fucking, and not Sherlock, so I'm still the winner.' Rolling over, he squeezes my bottom, and gives that a little play tap too. Well, slightly more than a tap ... It's a second slap that stings in a mild but interesting way. 'And you can always make it up to me by giving me a nice blow job when the next lot of news comes on!'

'Um ... OK.' I feel strangely shaken by those slaps, especially because all of a sudden they make me want to fuck again. We've never actually played spanking games but it's something I've always thought of suggesting.

A few pretty half-baked scenarios flit through my mind during the next adverts, but, after a few minutes of car insurance, teeth whiteners and Andie MacDowell's hair, it's time to commune with my glorious hero again. There's one of my very favourite episodes coming up next but a part of me *still* can't help thinking about those slaps. Sam was only fooling about, but to me they suddenly seem quite deadly serious. God knows, I deserve to be punished after my faux pas over The Great Detective's name!

As the channel ident flashes, I steal a split-second glance at Sam, but he's fast asleep already, mouth open, mad black curly hair sticking up at all angles and a tea stain down the front of his muscle vest. What a contrast to the sartorial *GQ* treat that lies ahead of me.

The story preamble begins. Some nasty perp up to no good as usual, but I'm not yet paying full attention due to The Detective not appearing until after the credits. Then the credits begin ... thunder rolls ... and the room goes black!

'Fucking, fuckety fuck!' I shout, regardless of Sam's slumbers, and, like an idiot, I start stabbing buttons on the remote still in my hand. As if *that'll* restore the electricity.

And yet, against the odds, it does do something.

Thunder cracks again and the lights flicker faintly but only for a second. They go out again, but, astonishingly, the television springs back to life. The screen looks slightly blue tinted, but not too badly. It's still perfectly watchable.

And the credits of my beloved cop show are still rolling.

At least it *seems* to be my cop show. My heart leaps again with bubbling excitement. It must be a special episode or something – maybe recorded just for this marathon – because the sequence of images isn't one I've ever seen before. The frames are sharp, ultra clear, almost 3D, and, as they fade from one to the other, each one of the hairs on the back of my neck seem to prickle and rise individually. And, even though it's the same familiar music, and the same graphic styling, there's only the one character featured in the montage.

It's just The Detective with no sign whatsoever of the rest of the team.

And at the end, he seems to walk towards the camera, my guy, tall and intent, dressed in an immaculate thousand-dollar suit of bluish grey. His long stride eats up the ground and, as he approaches, he just keeps on coming ... and coming ... and coming ...

'Vicky Sheridan?' he enquires imperiously when he reaches me, flipping out his handcuffs from the clip at his belt.

But, before I can answer, he grabs me by the shoulder, hauls me from the bed and snaps the cuffs on me while I'm still wondering what's happening and trying to catch my breath.

What?

'You have the right to remain silent. Anything you say can and will be used against you in a court of law.' He grips my shoulder again, and propels me forwards, parroting out the Miranda as if I'm the lowest of low-life scuzz-buckets he's just apprehended. 'You have the right to speak to an attorney, and to have an attorney present during any questioning. If you cannot afford an attorney, one will be provided for you at government expense. Do you understand the rights I have just read to you? With these rights in mind, do you wish to speak to me?'

By now, he's manhandling me through a familiar door into a familiar room, and I'm so gob-smacked I don't have a breath of resistance in me.

It's the interrogation room. We're in a familiar chilly grey box with the mirror and the metal table and chairs that I've seen in scores of episodes. And it's just as soulless and intimidating in real life as it is on the television.

Real life? What the hell am I talking about 'real life' for? My heart's bouncing around as if it's on a bungee and my skin is a pointillist fresco of painful goose-bumps. This *isn't* real. How can I *be* here? This place is just a film set really.

It's all got to be a dream but, despite that, I can touch and I can feel.

Especially The Detective.

He still has me by the arm and his fingers are like points of fire against my bare arm while I just stand like a lemon in the middle of this cold claustrophobic room, letting him loom over me like a dark imposing nemesis. All these months – years even – of adoring him, and now I'm too afraid to even lift my eyes and look up into his face. I just stare in awe at the shiny polished toes of his great size-thirteen shoes.

I shiver violently, but it's not just from the refrigerator cold in this oh-so-impossible room.

'Please, take a seat, Vicky,' he says, sort of all polite business and sharp sardonic mockery at the same time.

With feigned courtesy he pulls out a chair and pushes me into it.

Is he playing bad cop? Or good cop? Or a bit of both?

As The Detective releases my arm, I shuffle into place. The floor is some sort of shiny institutional vinyl stuff, and my bare feet adhere to it, but far worse is the cold unforgiving metal of the chair itself. I'm reminded with a shock and a gasp that I dispensed with my knickers to fuck Sam. My post-sex stickiness almost audibly squelches against the slick surface of the seat as I inch towards the edge, trying to accommodate my still-cuffed hands behind me.

Despite the burning urge to look, I simply can't bring myself to lift my face, but I hear The Detective pull up a chair of his own and settle his large magnificent body into it.

'So, Vicky, do you know why I've brought you here?'

Oh that voice! It's like the vocal equivalent of velvet, so seductive, so smooth and so challenging. It's the same voice from the show, but somehow it's never sounded quite like this before. Never so intimate, never so sexy, despite my crush on him.

My eyes are still glued to anything but him, and my attention flits from the stark smudged surface of the functional table to the leather binder stuffed with documents that he has open before him. As I watch, he picks up a pen in his left hand and makes a small notation on a yellow legal pad. I've no idea what he's just written, but I sense it's not a plaudit for my good behaviour. All I can do is ogle those fingers, imagining, imagining . . .

'Nothing to say, Vicky?'

I'm just about to shake my head, when a huge mitt of a hand shoots out across the table and lifts my chin, forcing me to look at him.

Oh, God! Oh, God! Am I drowning? I feel as if I'm

spiralling down a time tunnel, yet, at the same time, I catalogue each detail of the heartbreak-handsome face before me.

He's smiling. It's a warm wide white smile, but it's tricky. His broad but subtle face is full of secret teasing. We're playing games, I realise, and that makes me relax. My belly warms as his pink tongue suddenly peeks out and sweeps his sexy lower lip.

'Well, no . . . I don't really know what to say . . . I don't know *why* I'm here and I've no idea *how* I got here either.'

The Detective cocks his head on one side and regards me archly. I notice that, in the blue-toned room, his deep-brown eyes look redder than usual and, as I wait for him to say something, they light from within and seem to dance with ruddy sparks.

'We don't bring people here without a reason, Vicky,' he purrs, his fingertip still lifting up my chin. It's just a minuscule contact but it's as solid and secure as the handcuffs. 'This is an interrogation room, so that makes you a suspect. Are you seriously expecting me to believe that you're totally innocent of any misdemeanour?'

Guilt floods me. Heat floods me. Arousal floods me. Literally. My bare sex oozes anew against the cold cheap chair.

I've perpetrated a heinous crime. One that's deeply shameful and reprehensible. At least it feels like it. I thought about this man, and imagined him in me, while fucking my Sam. That's just got to be on some statute book somewhere, hasn't it?

The Detective nods, and his hand slides lightly up and down the side of my face, before stilling again. He cradles my jaw, holding it delicately with just the tips of his very large fingers. 'That's better,' he observes, his thick lashes drifting down. They give him a hooded look that's deceptively sleepy eyed and sultry. 'Now we're getting somewhere ... Now we can negotiate a just retribution.'

It's like being hypnotised. In fact, it's possible that I *am* being hypnotised. Those beautiful eyes are like two hot coals and I can't avoid them.

'I ... um ... er ... shouldn't you be sending for the DA or something?' I stammer, grasping for shreds of the reality of the show I love so much. I don't know what's happening here, but the show is where it started.

The Detective laughs, and it echoes around the grey box we're in like strange deep music. He moves in closer, rising out of his seat and leaning right over the table to get in my face, and it's as if I'm paralysed yet at the same time also in motion. Violent motion on the deepest level, as every cell in my body furiously vibrates with wild desire.

I'm making a pool of lubrication on the metal of my chair, and my nipples are like stones of lust beneath the thin cotton T-shirt.

'Oh, I don't think there's any need to involve the District Attorney's Department at this stage, is there?' He does the head-tilt thing again, ever so slightly, his eyes still locked on me, swivelling in their sockets as his face moves. 'Better to cut a deal between the two of us for now, don't you think?'

'B– but surely it's not legal or regulation or whatever ... And where's your partner? And the captain? You can't just – just –'

'Just what?' he demands, releasing me, before spinning away like a dancer. He ends up leaning with his back to the great big mirror that covers almost half of the opposite wall. I know from the show that this is a two-way, allowing observation from another room beyond.

But who's watching us? And, if it's the captain or the DA, why hasn't anyone rushed into the room to put a stop to this completely non-regulation interview? I peer at the mirror. I suppose The Detective, with his preternatural powers, could tell me who's behind it, even if he didn't already know. But, to me, the mirror is impenetrable, reflecting only his magnificent back, his dark crisply cut hair and me, trembling behind the table in my T-shirt.

And then he does something. Something that seems to confirm that this is indeed a dream.

Still staring at me, he makes a strange elegant magician's pass with his fingers against the glass . . . and then it ripples and becomes partially transparent like a sheet of water.

The scene that it reveals makes me gasp.

Lit by the flickering illumination of what must be our own television, I'm staring into a familiar room. It's my own bedroom. The one I share with Sam. And there he is too, my tolerant easy-going boyfriend. He's propped up against the pillows, staring avidly back towards the screen. The light is poor, but I can see the flush high on his cheeks and the hot hunger in his hugely dilated eyes. Not only that, he's kicked back the mountain of covers and exposed the fact that he's touching himself, stroking his penis where it protrudes like a fat red bar beneath the hem of his grungy vest.

He licks his lips as if he's keen to see more of what he's watching.

'So, shall we continue?' The Detective pushes himself away from the mirror and returns to the table.

Prowling round to my side, he sits on the table, just next to me, unashamedly staring down the loose neckline of my T-shirt. With his left hand, he reaches casually to one side and touches a fingertip to my nipple – and I leap two inches into the air as if he's goosed it with an electrode. He laughs softly and shakes his great head, then takes a hold of the little bump of stiffened flesh.

'You're quite something, Vicky, aren't you? A real piece of work...' He tightens his grip and twists a little, making me gulp and moan and groan like a total slut. 'Mostly when people come into this room, they're nervous and afraid and on edge.'

He tweaks again, and my hips start moving of their own accord, rubbing my slithery sex against the chair. I find myself trying to spread my legs, and sit down harder to open myself. The Detective notes this immediately, and his moist pink tongue sweeps across his upper lip as if he relishes my helplessness.

'But you, Vicky, you're just horny, aren't you?' He grins, his teeth glinting and predatory. 'You're in the biggest trouble, but all you want – all you *really* want – is to get laid.'

Ah ha, Mr Clever Detective! You've slipped up ... you've got it wrong ... I don't want to get laid, as such, I realise in a sudden blinding flash. I want something else, sort of similar, but different.

His sparkling demonic eyes widen as if he's read my thoughts. Maybe he has. This is a dream, isn't it? Anything can happen ... and he's me, isn't he, really? He's from my mind ...

'So that's the way it is.' He pulls at my nipple. Quite hard. I wrench against the cuffs as sensation streaks from my breast to my pussy, but I can't for the life of me tell whether it's really pain or just a twisted form of pleasure. 'I *knew* I was right about you.'

Inclining sideways, he surprises me with a kiss. He presses his firm lips against mine, and then tickles them with his tongue as if asking for entrance. As I open my mouth, my glance flicks to the glass again, but the surface seems to swim, and I can't see any image but the incriminating one of us.

Is Sam still watching? Was he ever watching? To my shame, sucking on The Detective's warm mobile peppermint-scented tongue, I can't seem to care or worry about Sam's feelings for the moment.

And, for that alone, I know I must invite my fate.

I duel with The Detective's tongue. I press my body against his hand. I part my thighs, press my cunt against the chair and rock and wriggle lewdly.

The Detective laughs joyfully into my mouth as he grips the back of my head with one hand and lets the other slide from my breast down to my belly. His mighty form seems to weigh down on me as he thrusts hard and ruthlessly with his tongue and slips two fingers down between my legs – and then in between my sex lips.

A cry bubbles up from my chest, but he suppresses with his mouth and his sheer force of will. Down at my core, he rubs ferociously, working my clit. My body jerks like a fish on a line, thrashing against his caress and his presence, making the flimsy metal chair clatter and shake. I can't break free of him, but I can't see why I'd want to. All my struggling and writhing is a pure reflex action, more incitement than any kind of escape attempt.

When I come, I feel as if I'm going to choke for a moment, but still he won't free me. He subjects me to more and more tongue, and more and more fingering, without an instant of respite. My head starts to swim and I smell my sweat and my foxy juices – and his cologne, sublime and expensive.

'Naughty, naughty,' he whispers when he finally releases me. He takes out a large monogrammed hand-kerchief, wipes his fingers, then refolds the white square meticulously and pushes it back into his pocket. 'You just failed your endurance test, and now you really need a lesson.'

Suddenly on his feet again, he drags me to mine, then kicks away the chair. I sway precariously, my head like cotton wool from all the onslaughts on my senses. He holds me by my shoulders, his grip firm and unyielding, and I almost imagine that my feet have left the floor.

'Over you go,' he instructs me, manipulating me in space as if I were a doll made of papier-mâché or some other super-light material.

Before I can protest, I'm face down across the grimy metal table, its hard edge pressing sharply against my crotch. The room's chilly air wafts like a breeze across my labia.

It's very uncomfortable, pressed face down across the table like this, with my hands fastened so I can't adjust my position. My warm cheek is squished sideways against the unfriendly grey surface and my breasts ache where they're flattened by own weight.

I'm vulnerable. Exposed. Hugely excited. Silky fluid slides down the inside of my thigh.

I imagine The Detective's eagle eyes watching its progress. I wait for a sardonic comment but he remains tantalisingly silent. The only sound is a slight rustle from his clothing.

What the hell is he doing? I twist and strain to see him, unconsciously aware that I must not lift my head. Across the desk, I see him drop his jacket neatly over the back of his chair, and then there are faint noises like fine fabric being folded.

The bastard's rolling up his sleeves, ready for action!

It's a shock when I feel his hand slide beneath my T-shirt and touch my bottom.

'I could have you now, couldn't I?' he whispers, leaning right over me, fingertips skittering and flickering over the nervous surface of my buttocks.

I purse my lips, determined to resist him for the sheer devilment of testing our limits. I want him. I think … But it's different now. Lusting from afar isn't dangerous … and this is.

His fingers slip into the groove of my bottom, sliding

downwards, delicately disturbing my slippery folds. I bite my lip, trying not to whine like a horny bitch.

'I could have you ... but I don't think I will.'

I wait for my own wail of disappointment but it doesn't materialise. Touch is enough, touch and something more assertive.

'I know what you need, Vicky. I know what you want ... I know what's best for a naughty girl like you.'

Slowly, with what feels suspiciously like reverence, he raises my grungy T-shirt, tucks it beneath my cuffed hands and exposes the trembling cheeks of my naked backside. He steps to my right side and places the points of his fingers on first one buttock, then the other. The whine gets away from me this time and I lift my hips to meet his touch.

'Patience, little girl, patience,' he says steadily, then begins to slowly pat my cheeks, first one, then the other, as before.

It's so measured, so detailed, so leisurely.

The pats become taps. The taps become more forceful. The forceful taps gain momentum, becoming slaps.

And they hurt!

They hurt like hell! Like fire! Like burning, biting flames!

A little bonfire that seeps and flows into my pussy.

I'm making all sorts of noise now. Grunts, whines, groans and whimpers ... the sound of my own voice turns me on even more. There's something thrilling about being reduced to a giant hormone. A drooling, needing creature of submissive lust ...

The Detective laughs with delight.

'Now you know,' he announces exultantly. 'Now you know what you really want and really need.' His hand stills on my right bottom cheek, squeezing lightly and making it hard for me to breathe. 'And now we need to resolve the situation.' His voice is brisk. He's still pleased with himself. And he's smiling as he turns me over, sits me on the edge of the desk and induces another groan as my reddened bottom takes my weight.

But what he does next is a total surprise.

With a grace that belies his towering height and his muscular girth, he sinks to his knees, grabs me by the thighs . . . and gives me head.

I sway, I almost topple over, but I manage to rest myself awkwardly on my elbows and my shackled wrists.

The pleasure is exquisite. His tongue is nimble beyond imagining. I shout out loud, my bare thighs clamping round his head.

Within a few heartbeats, he laps me cleverly to my climax and, as I flail about, I feel myself begin to fall . . .

'Wake up, love! You're missing your favourite episode. It's nearly finished.'

Someone's gently shaking my arm and I lurch back into consciousness. It's a bit like that horrible jolting 'stepping into a lift shaft' sensation that occasionally wakes you from a dream of suddenly falling. Flying bolt upright, I try and catch my breath.

The bedside lamp and the television are back on, and The Detective is just about to pull the old bait and switch on some crafty criminal who thinks he's very clever, but is just a microbe compared to the intellect he's up against.

He's on the case, totally focused and playing out his role, just as normal.

He's a million miles away from the demon sex fiend who just licked my cunt.

There's a funny noise and I suddenly realise that it's my teeth chattering.

A warm familiar arm comes around my shoulder and I turn to Sam, who's looking rather worried with a slight side order of guiltiness.

'Are you OK, sweetheart?' He gives me a squeeze. 'I'm sorry about not waking you up sooner, but I was dozing myself and when I opened my eyes I realised this one is nearly over.' He nods to the screen, where The Detective is leaning against the wall of the interrogation room, his arms folded and an arch slightly pitying expression on his handsome face. The miserable perp has just this moment realised that he's been tricked.

'Don't worry, love . . . I've seen it before. I know what happens,' I find myself saying.

Sam is so sweet. I never realised that he knew what my favourite episodes were, and it was so thoughtful of him to actually worry that I was missing one.

I make a decision, reach for the remote and snap off the telly.

'What on earth are you doing?' Sam demands, but he's smiling. 'You've been looking forwards to this for weeks. Aren't you going to watch it all?'

'Nah . . . I've seen enough for tonight.' I wriggle out of his arms, touch his dear face and then push on his shoulders to encourage him to lie back on the bed. 'I promised you a blow job, didn't I?' I tug down the covers and find a pleasing erection springing eagerly from his groin.

What on earth has he been dreaming about? It couldn't be as vivid as mine, surely, but something's got him up and at the ready.

'Nice . . .' I murmur, letting my fingers walk up his thigh until they reach the cradle of his groin. He lets out a gasp as I make a circle around his cockhead. 'But what's brought this on?' I punctuate the question, by leaning forwards to give him a nice but naughty licking.

Sam puffs out his lips and starts to wriggle a little.

He tosses his curly head on the pillow when I point my tongue and start to probe.

'I had this dream ... this weird dream ...' he pants. 'It was about you and him ...'

When I open my eyes and glance sideways at his face, he's nodding towards the television.

A strange unease stirs in me, but it's not fair to break off from my task now, so I continue.

'You were in the interrogation room with him, and he had you handcuffed, and it all got a bit fruity.'

I pop up.

'What happened?'

'He was touching you ... and he spanked you ... and then he gave you head.'

The room starts to revolve a little, and I'm back there ... cowering, ready and yearning, before my hero.

'God, it was hot,' goes on Sam, still moving uneasily against the pillows, his eyes closed, and licking his lips. 'Really horny ... we shall have to do that spanking thing one of these days, I think ... Would you like that?'

'Yeah, it'd be fun,' I whisper, feeling wildly turned on again but, at the same time, slightly terrified.

'Hey, don't leave me high and dry, babe!' Sam protests, reaching out towards me and pulling me back in the direction of his dick again.

I comply, and begin to suck him slowly and industriously in the lamplight, but the hairs on the back of my neck are prickling and crawling.

How can Sam have had the same dream as I did? How can he have seen what I dreamt he was seeing through the glass?

My mouth still full of my boyfriend, I can't help glancing sideways towards the television, and I nearly do him a mischief when I see the screen all aglow again.

And there, bathed in the same blue-toned eldritch radiance as before, is The Detective. He's sitting on the edge of his metal table, his suited arms crossed and a silky smirk on his broad handsome face.

What are you doing? You're not real! You're a dream! Sod off!

I close my eyes and apply myself to my delicious task, but, when I weaken a moment later, I sneak a sideways peek at the screen and find him still there and smirking...

And, as he reaches for his zip, his familiar eyes gleam red as coals.

All I Want for Christmas
Mae Nixon

Frank Kapra had a lot to answer for. There was Jimmy Stewart, in his handsome wholesome prime, pumping out seasonal goodwill from every TV set in the nation while I was standing at the top of a rickety step-ladder, wiping the dust off DVD boxes.

No handsome hubby and cute kiddies waiting at home to trim the Christmas tree and no thoughtful and tastefully expensive gift waiting underneath it for me. Just the cats for company and a couple of old films to watch on DVD.

I should have known that volunteering to clean up after the shop closed on Christmas Eve would depress me. It had been a slow day and a long one – only sad lonely people wanted to rent films at Christmastime. I could spot them the minute they came into the shop – even before sometimes. The women were usually neat and organised. They talked too much and too loudly, like they weren't used to the sound of their own voices. They rented musicals and sloppy romances, having no doubt popped into the chemist's next door to buy a box of tissues especially for the occasion. They'd hand over the exact money in small change, which they dug out of their wallets a coin at a time, all the while smiling and anxious to please.

The men always seemed to need a good haircut and they wore unfashionable shirts, badly in need of ironing. They chose action movies with muscular heroes and violent endings. Sometimes they'd slip in something from our 'adult selection' and bring them to the counter red-faced and sheepish, hoping I wouldn't comment. I never did, I felt far too much empathy for that. I expect they also found a use for some tissues at the end of their evening's viewing.

When I closed the shop at eight, there hadn't been a customer for an hour and a half. I locked the door, got out the step-ladder and cleaning stuff and went to work, having first put Kapra's *It's a Wonderful Life* in the shop's player.

In the street outside, the night people slowly began to appear. Young lads loitering outside the offie, not really old enough to drink but laughing loudly and quaffing their illicit lager ostentatiously out of cans. In the doorway of the department store across the way, two down-and-outs hunched sullenly inside their cardboard boxes, hoping not to be moved on.

I worked methodically, emptying and cleaning each shelf in turn and putting the DVDs back in the right order. The Kapra movie was obviously a bad choice. The only Christmas spirit in me it appealed to was the kind the lager louts outside the off-licence were enjoying. When it came to the part when Clarence the trainee angel lets James Stewart see what the world would be like if he had never been born, I came down that ladder so fast I almost got my feet tangled in the rungs. I leant over the counter and thumped the eject button on the player as hard as I could. The disk plopped out and I resisted the urge to fling it through the plate glass of the shop's front window.

That was typical of me. I'd been resisting temptation all my life. The temptation to say what I thought, share what I felt, have fun, have sex, be happy. It struck me that what I'd been resisting was the temptation to live and I picked up the disk and hurled it straight at the window like a gleaming silver frisbee.

It hit the window with a surprisingly loud metallic tinging noise, which made the lads outside the off-licence laugh and instantly sent my face as red as Santa's hat. To make matters worse, it ricocheted off the glass and disappeared into a tiny gap between two display cases.

I got on my hands and knees to retrieve it but I couldn't reach it. Still red-faced and now angrier than ever, I tried to squeeze a finger in behind the disk so that I could pull it out. But it was no good; my finger wasn't long enough.

I was pissed off now and tired and hungry. The cats should have been fed two hours ago. But I said I'd clean up the shop and I was far too polite and eager to please to go back on my word. And now I'd somehow managed to get one of our valuable pieces of stock (and a classic of the modern cinema to boot) stuck between two display cases and I had to get it out. So, swearing quietly to myself and generally venting my anger in the most explicit terms against first my employer, then James Stewart, then Frank Kapra and finally Christianity for inventing Christmas, I went back to the counter to find a pen.

After pushing the pen down behind the far edge of the disk, I eventually managed to slide enough of it out of its hiding place to take hold of it and pull it out. It was pretty dusty and knocked about, probably unwatchable, but what did I care? Anyone who wanted to watch that sugar-coated unrealistic kitsch ought to have their head examined anyway.

I was just about to get up off my hands and knees when I noticed that a video-cassette, still in its box, was wedged much further back in the space between the two cases. I wiggled my biro into the gap and slowly and painstakingly edged it towards me. It was hard work because it'd been there a long time and it was wedged tight.

'Come on, you bastard,' I said aloud, grunting with the effort of trying to ease the trapped tape out of its hidey-hole. 'Don't fuck me about – come out of there!' I swore a lot when I was alone, though you'd never have thought it to look at me. But a girl had to have some vices and that was mine.

I was hot and dusty, I had broken a nail and there was a hole in my tights. I was about as angry as it was possible to be and the only thing I had to vent my rage on was this little plastic box. I managed to manoeuvre it so that about an inch was sticking out between the two cases. I was squatting down, gripping the slippery plastic box tight in both hands, struggling to keep a grip. I leant backwards and used all my strength to get it free. I felt like King Arthur trying to pull Excalibur out of the stone.

I grunted, gritting my teeth and straining with the exertion and the bloody thing didn't budge. I decided to give it one last effort before calling it a day. If it wouldn't come out, it could stay there. After all, it could have been there for years and hardly anyone rented videos these days, it was all DVDs.

Gripping the free corner of the box with all my strength, I pulled hard using my body weight as a lever. 'Come out now!' I shouted.

Without warning, the box came loose and slid out from between the cases and, because I wasn't expecting it, I tumbled backwards and landed flat on the floor, my legs in the air and my skirt around my waist. I heard laughter and hooting from over the road. The dossers and drinkers were certainly getting a free cabaret tonight. I resolved to leave by the rear entrance to avoid any further embarrassment.

Brushing away the thick layer of dust and cobwebs from the box, I uncovered a gaudy photograph of a partially clad young woman with improbable breasts and buttocks so pert she could have balanced a tea tray on them. The title *Succubus Sluts* proclaimed itself proudly from the spine of the box. 'A fuck flick,' I said aloud, though the shop's manager preferred to call that sort of thing 'our adult selection'.

I'd had enough for the night. Every item of stock and surface was dust free and gleaming; I'd recatalogued the cartoon section and balanced the till. Time to go home and spend the next few days without having to worry about the shop. Just three days alone with the TV, the cats and as much Christmas chocolate as I could eat. Bliss.

I got my coat, scarf and gloves and picked up my shopping bag from behind the counter. On the spur of the moment, I stuffed *Succubus Sluts* into my bag. After all, it was Christmas and, if I couldn't let myself go then, when could I?

As I let myself into my house, my two cats ran up the hall to greet me. 'Cupboard love,' I mumbled as they rubbed their sleek bodies against my legs, snaking in and out of my feet as I approached the kitchen. Having fed them, I started the bath running and headed for my bedroom where I undressed. Before long, I was languishing in a steaming hot bath, a glass of Australian champagne in hand, soft music on the CD player and relaxing, fragrant oils in the water.

I sighed. I felt cosy, languid and comfortable. Fuck it, I felt sexy. I considered having a nice slippery warm wank in the tub. I had learnt the pleasures of solitary sex early in life. People said it wasn't as good as the real thing and I took their word for it, but it was always available and it was a lot less complicated. I didn't have to wash anyone's dirty socks, for a start, and I never cheated on myself or had too much to drink. And I never ever turned over and fell asleep before I'd come.

I slid a wet hand between my thighs, then I remembered *Succubus Sluts* still in my shopping bag and decided that a little external stimulation might heighten the experience. So I dried off, applied body lotion, wrapped myself in a cosy towelling robe and settled down in front of the TV – chocolates, wine and remote control all to hand.

As I pressed the button to start the tape, the bells of the parish church started to chime midnight. The church bells sounded eerie and echoing in the otherwise silent night air.

'Merry Christmas, Carole,' I said, bringing my wineglass to my lips.

The tape began to play and the TV fluttered to life. Static buzzed across the screen and, when the picture began to clear, I gasped and dropped my wineglass, the spilt liquid leaving a dark spreading stain on the carpet.

'Oh, shit,' I whispered, my voice trembling with fear. I must have been putting away the Aussie champers much quicker than I'd realised. Either that or I'd borrowed one too many horror movies from the shop. I should have known that bringing work home would lead to no good.

My body was suffused with adrenaline, my heart beat loudly, I was panting. I rose to my feet and shuffled about aimlessly, my eyes riveted on the TV screen – the screen on which I could see a smaller, yet identical, version of myself performing the same actions.

'Too much wine,' I said, making a mental note to give up drink and make an appointment to have my eyes tested as soon as the holiday was over. I shuddered in surprise as my TV version uttered the same words. I sat down in panic, rummaged around under the sofa cushions for the remote control and pointed it at the TV, my extended arm trembling as the woman on the screen mirrored my actions. I pressed the off button and the image was replaced by the familiar grey-green eye of the blank screen. Tentatively, I turned the TV back on and the picture that flickered to life was my own face, the eyes eloquent with panic, confusion and indecision. My legs gave way.

I didn't understand what was happening and I didn't want to. I must be losing my mind – nothing else made sense. I slumped on to the sofa and stared at my own bewildered eyes on the screen, contemplating the prospect of spending the next thirty years as a crazy old maid. It would probably only be a matter of time before I started peeing in my pants.

A shadow appeared behind my image on TV. Grey and formless at first, it slowly became more defined until after a few seconds a tall shapely incredibly beautiful woman wearing a sort of toga was standing behind my mirror image. I got goose-pimples. The hair on the back of my neck stood up.

Fuck it. I was so scared I wouldn't have been surprised if the hair on my head stood up. I wasn't alone and I realised gradually and unwillingly that if there was someone in the room with my TV reflection there was almost certainly someone in this room with me.

I held my breath and steeled myself to turn around and check, but before I could summon up the courage she spoke. The sound of her voice intruding on the silent room was so shocking and unexpected that I leapt to my feet ready to flee. Only there was nowhere to run. Suddenly, the prospect of peeing in my pants didn't seem quite so improbable.

'Stay calm, honey, I'm not here to hurt you. Quite

the reverse, in fact.' She put out a hand and stroked my hair.

It was a soothing gesture, a reassuring one and I felt the heat of her palm, the gentleness of her touch, as I watched her make the identical movements on TV. There was something about her voice, soft and deep and bubbling like running water over pebbles in a brook, that calmed me. I felt my breathing slow down, my heartbeat return to normal and the tightness in my chest relax. She walked round the couch, sat down and switched off the TV.

Only she didn't use the remote control. She just snapped her fingers and the picture disappeared. I ought to have been scared, but I wasn't. I was just curious, my earlier fears having melted away miraculously when she touched me.

'Who are you?' I asked.

'You can call me Joy,' she murmured, stroking the short blonde hairs on my arm. It felt good and I looked down at her warm and gentle fingers caressing me.

'But what –?' I began to ask, but stopped when I realised that, although I had a million questions, I didn't know how to ask any of them. I wasn't sure I wanted the answers anyway. Either I was crazy or she was a spook of some kind and it was a toss-up which solution I liked least.

There was a beautiful – dare I say sexy – and obviously friendly woman sitting beside me on the couch. She was touching me and making me feel better than I ever had but I didn't know who she was, where she came from or how she got there. I did know, however, that I liked the way she was fondling me. She was now trailing her fingers up my forearm, on the inside of my elbow. The sensation was so pleasant and comfortable that I noticed, to my embarrassment, that I was beginning to get wet.

'Do you know what an incubus is Carole? Or a succubus?' she asked me, her soft voice seducing me.

'Sure,' I replied, glad she had asked me something I could answer. 'I've always been interested in mythology. Incubi are male spirits who visit women in the night and have sex with them. Succubi do the same with men.'

'Right,' she whispered.

By this time, she was right alongside me, her mouth up close to my ear, her fingers caressing my neck, my cheek, my lips. I could feel that familiar moisture between my legs; I could smell her sweet breath and the perfume rising from her skin. God, I was horny.

'I am a succubus, Carole, and I've come to give you the best sex you have ever had,' she said quietly, looking directly at me.

I swallowed hard, trying to take in the fact that I had a beautiful sexy spirit sitting alongside me who by now had my robe open and was caressing my thigh. The sensation of flesh on flesh made me tingle.

'The *only* sex I have ever had,' I mumbled, embarrassed by having to explain my pathetic condition to a sexually supercharged supernatural being.

'I know that,' she reassured me. 'Only a virgin can create the spell, by watching the video and drinking wine at midnight on Christmas Eve to the sound of church bells. You did that and here I am, large as life and twice as horny. Aren't you lucky?'

By now, she had her hand between my legs, cupping my slit; her mouth was right next to mine and before I had time to answer she kissed me on the lips. It was deep and hot and wet, I could feel her tongue, exploring my mouth. She nibbled my lips and caressed the back of my neck with her free hand. All the time I could feel the heat of her palm up against my pussy, which by now was so wet I felt like I was sitting in a puddle.

Joy rose and took my hand; she led me to my bedroom, pausing only to pick up my empty wineglass and the bottle of fizz. I trailed along beside her, obedient and willing. Once inside my room, she quickly slid my robe off my shoulders and let it fall to the floor. With one movement, she loosened the shoulder of her toga and she too was naked. I'd never seen anything so beautiful. She was tall, maybe six feet, and her blonde hair tumbled in curls down to her waist. Her skin was the colour of clotted cream; her body was curvy, womanly, ripe and inviting. Big round breasts with brownish nipples which, like my own, were erect. A soft full belly beneath which nestled golden curly hair.

In none of my wildest fantasies had I ever considered getting down and dirty with a member of my own sex. But here I was, staring at the body of the most perfect creature I had ever set eyes on and I wanted her. I held out my arms and called her name and she walked over to me slowly, sinuously, all that delicious creamy flesh undulating as she moved.

Next thing I knew, I was lying on my bed with Joy's delightful, soft and perfect body on top of mine. My heart was thumping in my chest so loud I could hear it. My head was spinning. Her mouth was near mine, her breath gently touching my skin. Her hands were on my shoulders. She kissed me softly, tenderly, lightly on the mouth, then behind my left ear. My body was rigid, tense with anticipation. I could feel the heat from her, feel her heart beating against mine, its rhythm an echo of my own excitement.

'Shouldn't I get an incubus, because I'm a woman?' I asked. My voice sounded soft and throaty.

'This particular spell invokes a succubus, sorry if you're disappointed. But, if you ask me, I'm a lot hotter than any incubus you are ever likely to meet. Do you mind?'

I looked down at her body, trying to make up my mind. I'd spent the past 25 years waiting to have sex. By some unrepeatable chance, I had managed to invoke the sexiest being that ever walked the earth and she was ready, willing and able to give me the time of my life. Could I pass up the opportunity just because we both happened to be women?

'Do I have a choice?' I leant forwards and inhaled, drinking in the honeyed heady scent of her skin.

'Actually you do. If you really want a male spirit I can change for you.' Joy sounded a little sulky and disappointed. 'But I can't see what all the fuss is about. Pleasure is still pleasure, does it really matter how your body is arranged?' She ran the tip of her finger along the front of my torso from my belly button up to my throat, leaving a trail of shivery sparks in its wake.

'But it will still be you? You'll just have a male body?'

Joy nodded. 'That's right, only the anatomy changes.'

My eyes made a slow inventory of her body. From the soft golden curve of her shoulders across to the twin hollows where her collarbones met, from the heavy globes of her breasts with their chocolatey dark nipples down to the froth of golden hair at her crotch. When I looked back up at her face, she was smiling.

'You're beautiful but, if you don't mind, I think I'd prefer you to be male.'

Joy laughed, a rich trill of musical notes that hardened my nipples and made my crotch tingle. She clicked her fingers and the sound of her laughter slowly began to deepen. I watched as her hair shortened and her face changed shape. Her jaw remodelled itself before my eyes, becoming more square and masculine. I could see dark beard stubble forming and a shallow dimple gradually appeared in the centre of her – *his* – chin.

Her breasts shrank and reshaped themselves into manly pectoral muscles covered in a mat of fine golden hairs. Her hips narrowed, her thighs lengthened and her feet grew before my eyes. Feminine curves were replaced with hard muscle. Joy even smelt different, her honeyed citrus perfume seemed to transform into something musky and masculine.

Only the sparkly blue eyes remained the same, gazing at me with an unmistakable expression of lust. I looked down at Joy's crotch and now there was a long thick cock, already half hard, standing out from the curly blond hairs.

'I hope you like it.' Joy spoke with a deeper version of her old voice. 'I made it extra fat, just for you.' He wriggled his hips and his cock bobbed and wobbled.

'I love it. You're really handsome. What should I call you now? Joy doesn't seem to fit any more.'

Joy laughed and a slow shiver of excitement slid along my spine. 'Joy is what I *bring*. It's a title rather than a name. You can call me whatever you like.'

I ran the flat of my hand down the front of his body, over his rippling six-pack and the hard plane of his belly. He gasped.

'In that case I think I'll call you Joe.'

Joe put his mouth near my ear and whispered so softly that I sensed it rather than heard the words. 'Are you ready, Carole? Are you ready to take the risk, to taste passion, to give yourself up to it, to live?'

I nodded my head in silent agreement, momentarily struck dumb by the strength of my emotions.

'Say it,' he whispered, nuzzling my ear. 'Say it out loud.'

'I want you, Joe,' I managed to gasp, as the sensation of his tongue and teeth on my neck took me to a new plane of pleasure. 'God, how I want you!'

He smiled, holding my head in his hands and looking into my eyes so deeply I swore he was staring into my soul. Wet tongues intertwined, flesh slid against flesh, fingers caressed, stroked, pinched and probed. He stroked my nipples, his mouth still on my neck. I groaned under him, my body trembling and sensitive.

His mouth was on my collarbone, then a little lower, getting closer and closer to the hard, hot buttons I so wanted him to suck. His warm wet tongue dipped down my cleavage, trailed over the swell of my left breast and flicked over my tight swollen nipple. He took it in his mouth. It felt like nothing on earth, more intense than anything I had ever imagined.

Joe glanced up at me, a look of amusement in his deep-blue eyes, and then went back to working on my nipple. He sucked, nibbled, tongued it, creating incredible sensations that radiated through my by now writhing body. My other nipple was receiving the same treatment from his fingers and the tremors of delight that ran through me caused me to moan out loud. My hot hungry pussy was producing so much juice that we were in danger of drowning.

I couldn't keep my hands off his body. I stroked his shoulders, his face and the nape of his neck. I laced my fingers through his silky perfumed hair. He felt so warm against me, his skin so soft. By now, I was on the edge. I was breathing hard in short little gasps, my face and chest were burning and I knew they must be flushed and red.

Sensing my growing excitement, he lowered a hand between my parted thighs and dipped a finger into my wet slippery pussy. I gasped in delight, throwing my head back and arching my back. He began to rub his fingertips lightly across the hardening bud of my clit.

It didn't take long. My thighs started to quiver and I felt the first contractions begin deep inside my cunt. My clit tightened and retreated under his fingers as the first throb of orgasm began to grip me. Body shuddering, legs wide open, fingers tangled in his wild soft hair, I gave myself up to the overpowering sensation of the best orgasm I had ever experienced, and the first I ever got from someone else. It felt good.

Before I could recover, he moved, sliding down my body, repositioning himself, getting himself comfortable, and suddenly he was between my legs, the wet tip of his cock pressed up against my hole. He slid it up and down, parting my lips and sliding it across the hard button of my clit.

I looked up into his eyes as he tensed his hips and pushed slowly forwards. I sighed as his meat began to slide inside me. Nerve endings buzzed and tingled with pleasure and excitement. I felt my muscles stretching to accommodate him and the delicious feeling of him slowly slipping inside.

I gave myself up to the sensations he was creating. I opened my legs wider, and I reached behind him to cup his hard buttocks. I pushed my groin up towards him, my breathing quickening now, sweat glistening on my aroused body. Damp hair clung to the nape of my neck, my brow.

I tightened my grip on his buttocks, digging in my fingers and moving my pelvis to a rhythm of my own, grinding myself against him. He moved inside me – arousing, exciting, tantalising me. I was moving wantonly now, lost in the sensations of my own body. I was grinding myself against him, panting and moaning, my breathing ragged and fast. My sensitive crotch rubbed against his wiry hairs on every stroke, exciting my clit and making it tingle.

I gasped as he jabbed his hips hard and deep. Muscles tightened and throbbed, squeezing his thick hot cock. Tension built, aching for release. My whole body was tense, taut, quivering.

I was deaf, I was blind. I felt nothing but the exquisite sensations coursing through my excited body. Every nerve ending was transmitting pleasure and excitement, keeping me on the edge of fulfilment. My clit rubbed against his pubes, providing delicious friction, as a wave of contractions began in my crotch. It spread through me, filling me with heat and pleasure. I shuddered, my movements abandoned. Gasps, moans, cries, wild breathing shattered the silence, piercing the air in the room.

My muscles gripped his cock, and tightened around him. I quivered with pleasure as I reached my peak. He held me tight, pulled me on to his cock, rotating inside me as I shuddered, rocked and throbbed to orgasm.

Joe looked down at me, his eyes blazing with intensity and excitement, his hard body gleaming in the light. He circled his hips, moving his erection inside me, wringing out the last shreds of orgasm. It came in waves, knocking the breath out of me. My body twisted and bucked, as the bed creaked and shook beneath us. I was gasping, almost screaming as pleasure and release washed over me.

When it was finally over, Joe rolled off and lay down alongside me, as satisfied and excited as a puppy after its first walk in the park. Without a word, he gently cradled my head and gave me a deep, passionate, lingering kiss.

'That was wonderful.' I smiled at him. 'Did you come?'

He shook his head.

'Teach me how to make you come,' I asked, eager to give him as much pleasure as he had given me.

'You don't need teaching, Carole — you're a natural. Just do what feels good and I guarantee I'll enjoy it. It's been centuries since I've met a mortal as hot as you.'

Touching a man's body was a new experience for me. Joe was hard and flat where I was full, round and soft. He had inviting slopes and hollows and smooth skin, all of it the colour of my favourite vanilla ice cream. I climbed on top of him, my long hair falling over his face and mingling with his own golden curls, my pale skin contrasting with his creamy complexion.

He felt warm, soft and comfortable. I kissed his neck, breathing in the strong manly scent. I ran my hands up and down his sides, feeling his flesh tighten and contract into goose-pimples under my fingers.

He was as excited as I was. The air in the room was heavy with the scent of arousal. The only sound was the gentle metallic click of my alarm clock and our own frenzied breathing. I wanted to taste him, to explore him, to possess him as he had already taken me. I found his stiff brown nipples first with my fingers then my mouth. He tasted salty. Moans and gasps erupted from his mouth as I teased his erect buds. He writhed under me.

I lost myself in the sensations of his body. His nipple in my mouth was hard and rubbery; he wriggled as I nibbled it. His chest heaved, breath coming fast and short as his arousal increased. The warmth of his body engulfed me. I slithered downwards, kissing as I went until I found myself kneeling between his beautiful spread thighs. His cock stood up, hard and proud, pointing at the ceiling. I could see the tip of his cock glistening with pre-come.

I fastened my mouth over his erection, wrapped my arms round his spread thighs and started to suck. I was anxious to do it right but I needn't have worried. The urgent writhing and thrusting movements let me know that my efforts were having the desired effect. I lapped at his helmet, sucked it, even nibbled on it. I slid my tongue up and down the full length of his shaft, pushed it against the single eye. He was wet and slippery, hard and hot.

I pulled him closer as I sensed his responses becoming more frenzied, more urgent. Tongue darting and probing, lips sucking, I tried to give him as much pleasure as he had given me. It was getting harder for me to keep up with his movements as he thrust his whole pelvis into my face and tried to grind it against my mouth. Moans, groans and sighs escaped his throat. His hands snaked down to join mine and clasp them.

I felt his muscles contract in my mouth. I freed a hand and slipped it between my face and his body. Quickly I curled my hand around the base of his cock, just in time to feel the first throbbing earthquake of his orgasm. He began to cry out then, wailing almost, like the kind of sound Muslim women make at funerals. I guessed it felt good. He began shuddering all over, rocking to and fro with the rhythm of my mouth and hand. He twitched in my mouth and began to pump out spunk. I swallowed it eagerly down.

I thought it would never end but, eventually, the cries faded, the throbbing slowed, then stopped and his breathing returned to normal. Joe smiled and raised his head weakly, his beautiful face surrounded by its halo of sweat-soaked curls and smiled down at me.

We spent the night, all of the next day and the other eleven days of Christmas doing what comes naturally and, let me tell you, when an incubus comes, the whole of the neighbourhood knows about it.

That was a year ago and I never did go back to the video shop. I opened my own florists with the money I'd inherited from my mum and dad and the nest egg I'd always been afraid to touch because it was meant for my old age. Well, I don't intend to get old for a very long time yet and in the meantime I intend to live life to the full.

Joe works with me in the shop during the daytime and we're doing pretty well. With my artistic flair and his knack for charming the customers, we seem to be making a go of it. 'Blooms' the shop is called – it was

Joe's suggestion. He says that's what happened to me, I've bloomed. Maybe he's right, I certainly know I'm alive these days.

It didn't take a trainee angel showing me what life would be like if I'd never been born to bring about the transformation. A beautiful sexy spirit did the trick for me, by helping me to unlock the passion, love, power and joy that lives inside us all. Maybe Frank Kapra knew a thing or two after all.

The End of the Pier
Angel Blake

'I was beautiful – once.'

Steve leant back in his chair, letting his fingers wind through the phone cord, and stared at the photos of her arrayed before his desk, trying to imagine how she might look now. He'd selected the prints specially, out of hundreds he'd collected, as his personal favourites: Lisette bound with ropes around her arms, midriff and legs, gagged, her eyes staring up at the camera in mute supplication; Lisette and another girl, both in leopard-print bikinis, clawing at each other, their hair wild over their faces, eyes sparkling with feigned rage; and his absolute favourite: Lisette modelling a training corset, an impossibly tight belt around her waist and a choker around her neck, gazing into the camera, eyes suggestively heavy lidded, glossy black hair tumbling down over one shoulder, her full lips parted just a little to show the promise of the dark warm mouth within.

If she'd been in her early twenties then, and all his researches for the fan club indicated that she had been, she'd be in her seventies now, and he shuddered a little at the thought of her wizened frame, so far from the voluptuous figure he'd seen so often, fantasised about so much. Yet still her voice held a husky promise, a hint of something forbidden, something more . . . *refined* than the young women Steve saw around him today, mincing their stick-insect legs and swinging the ever-present shopping bags, brash and brittle.

'I'm sure you look just as stunning today,' he offered, still barely able to believe that he was finally speaking to her. She didn't seem to be aware of the lengths he'd gone to to get her number; she'd just picked up the phone with a dusky 'hello?', and had listened to him rattle off his prepared spiel with hardly any comment, nothing but a whispered 'oh?' when he'd revealed, unable to keep a note of pride out of his voice, that he was the president of her fan club; nor had she responded as he'd expected and hoped she would, with delight, or at least gratitude, when he'd explained that he'd tracked her down to make sure she received some of the royalties from people who were still making money out of her image. Surely she'd known she was a cult icon, her picture on the covers of countless fanzines, Camden market badges and rockabilly T-shirts?

Most people seemed to assume she was already dead, although he wasn't about to tell her that. He'd put more effort into finding this number than anything else he'd done in his life, chasing forever-vanishing hints of it, always elusive, always just out of reach, disappearing like the tail of the rabbit down the hole. After what seemed an eternity of dead ends, bad calls and rumours, he'd finally tracked it down to a second-hand magazine dealer in LA, an individual specialising in the fifties cheesecake industry of which Lisette was such an important part. The man had oozed sleaze on the phone, and had only agreed to part with the number – had only acknowledged that it even existed – when Steve had sent him a signed original of one of John Willie's Gwendoline paintings, a pony-girl image that it broke his heart to lose; but he wasn't about to miss out on this opportunity.

The first shock had come when he'd finally received the number. It was a UK number, which wasn't too much of a surprise – she was British, after all, and, even though she'd modelled for some American photographers, he knew she'd returned home after her star had begun to fade in the US. What *was* surprising was, when he checked the area code, he found that it belonged to a tatty seaside town in the West Country. He could have understood her ending up in one of the fishing villages in Devon or Cornwall, remote retreats with a genuine beauty outside the summer months, when they were swamped by ice-cream-guzzling tourists; but this was further north, not far from Bristol, and while Steve had never been there he'd heard of it and knew it had a reputation for casual violence and drug problems. A dead town, like so many littering the coast.

Her voice broke into his thoughts with an unexpected question.

'Would you like to come and see me?'

There was a coquettish tone to the voice that startled him almost as much as the invitation itself. This was what – although he hadn't dared admit it to himself – he'd hoped she'd ask. The chance to meet her, finally; to be the first, and perhaps only, of the current base of fans, an exclusive treat, and maybe even to see some of her older photos she'd never released. There must be some; surely she'd reward him if he went to visit her?

'Yes –' His voice was a croak, and he had to clear his throat before going on. 'Yes,' he continued more firmly. 'I'd love to come and see you. What's the address?'

'Seventy-eight Pier Road. I don't have many visitors, and I always used to enjoy meeting my fans.' She chuckled, a low throaty tone.

Steve's heart was pounding, and he was aware that he'd broken out into a slight sweat, staring at her face in the photo of her wearing the corset. 'When – when's good for you?'

'Any time. But, perhaps, if you could come down this weekend? Saturday?'

Steve would have missed his own wedding to meet her, and as it was he had nothing on for the weekend. 'I'll see you then,' he managed, then stared dumbly at the receiver, as though trying to wring an explanation for the situation he'd suddenly, unexpectedly found himself in from the disconnected tone.

Since his mid-teens, Steve had tried to mould every girl who'd shown an interest in him into the image of Lisette. Some were more amenable than others: a couple of fellow students when he'd been at college, bonding through a shared love of psychotic rock'n'roll and cheap sulphate, had humoured him enough to allow themselves to be tied up in Lisette's signature poses and outfits, gear that Steve had blown most of his student loans tracking down.

Later girlfriends had tended to be both more involved sexually and more detached emotionally, regarding his obsession with a wry amusement that invariably soured when they realised they could never be, for him, anything more than second-rate copies of an original that had never really existed. Patricia, who'd drawn him in by her evident embarrassment at her voluptuous over-spilling curves, had been the most memorable of these partners, able with judicious application of makeup to pass as a reasonable facsimile of Lisette and throwing herself into the role with a passion that had surprised him.

Shy and prone to blushing in her everyday guise, she'd become a different person entirely when dressed up, demanding to be spanked and fucked hard with the foulest language Steve had heard from anyone, as well as displaying a taste for anal play a million miles away from Lisette's own tastes, Steve was sure; but even she had tired finally of his inability to acknowledge her as a person in her own right.

He knew his obsession must seem finally like an

insult to the girls who were attracted to him, but even approaching his fortieth birthday he couldn't help himself. And now it hardly seemed to matter: he was going to meet his idol in the flesh.

Steve kicked the wet sand from his leopard-print brothel creepers as he squinted at the corroded street sign. Pier Road. This was it all right. Hunching the shoulders of his black leather jacket against the wind and hugging his bag tightly to his side, part of him wishing he'd worn something more substantial underneath than a Cramps T-shirt, he looked at the house numbers.

One, Two, Three: the numbers ran sequentially down one side of the road, with no houses opposite, just the low sea wall overlooking the bay's vast expanse of muddy beach. As he walked down the street, he felt a familiar nervous anticipation and took a few deep breaths to calm himself down. It's OK, he reassured himself: he was about to meet Lisette. It was only natural that he should be feeling nervous.

He approached the end of the road, where it swelled out to a broader area before the gates leading on to the town's second derelict pier, an abandoned hulk he'd noticed as soon as he reached the seafront. He anxiously counted down the houses, staring at the rusty metal numerals on walls and gateposts, the swell of nervous excitement building to fever pitch, until he reached the final house. Number 75.

He looked around, puzzled, checking again to make sure there were no buildings on the other side of the road. He peered at the number again, then at the two before: 73, 74. He took out the scrap of wrinkled paper from his back pocket and checked that he was looking for the right address, spun round and looked at the gates to the pier, then turned back to the house. He was half-tempted to ring on the bell and ask, but his stomach lurched at the idea. Maybe she didn't want people to know she was living there – he didn't want to attract undue attention. He moved towards the pier gates. Maybe there were more properties on the other side.

Closer now, he could see loose trestles hanging down, and holes in the roof of the pavilion at its end of the pier, a rotting pile without even the faded grandeur of the town's candyfloss and slot machine showcase. Maybe it was being renovated, he thought as he peered through the gates: there were building contractor containers immediately outside, although there was little evidence of anything happening on the pier itself. Still, he couldn't see much, his view obscured by the concrete wall flanking the gates. A great wave of disappointment built up in him. Maybe she'd given him the wrong address deliberately, trying to dishearten him and make him give up the chase. His neck twitched in an involuntary spasm that made him shake his head; no, she wouldn't have done that, she seemed too kind on the phone.

There were security notices up on the barbed wire of the fence: trespassers would be prosecuted, the area was under surveillance. That was that, then, there would be nothing ahead. He pressed his face to the gate, clasping the cold wire mesh and leaning on it, looking through to the decayed pier, feeling crushed, rotted, as derelict as the greenish planks, slick with mould, only to feel the gate give, and then swing forwards with a yawning shriek.

At first, he was so surprised that he let go, and the gate swung back towards him. He'd assumed it would be locked, and hadn't even bothered to make sure. But it wasn't. He pushed it again experimentally, and when it swung away once more he moved in.

His heart leapt when he saw another small line of houses on the far side of the wall. They were wooden, the planks of their walls faded from the combined effects of sun and salt water, but they looked as ruined as the rest of the pier, unlived in, the windows frosted with salt rime, the roofs sagging under the weight of years. The door of the first house looked like it had melded with the frame, and the handle had entirely rusted into position. But the number was still recognisable: 76.

He walked slowly down past the next house, aware that he should watch his step here, convinced he could feel the entire structure rocking beneath him in the wind, but feeling a mixture of exultation and panic as he came to the final house. Number 78. It looked better kept than the others; the door seemed to have been opened recently. He looked up, and thought he saw a movement at the window; but the light reflecting off the water made him unsure.

He looked around, half-expecting guard dogs to run from wherever the vaunted security was based, but there was nothing, only the distant sounds of the wind and the sea and the groan of the planks underfoot. He knocked on the door, and waited for a reply. Still there was nothing, and he stepped back again to peer up. This time he was sure he saw some movement above him, and he returned to the door to knock again, harder. To his surprise, the door creaked open.

Gingerly, testing the ground with his foot, afraid of stepping on a rotting plank and plunging to the beach below or, worse, ending on the seaweed-slimed rocks, he stepped inside. The first thing he noticed was that the salty sea smell was less strong here, just one note in the musty air, and subsumed by something else; the unmistakable smell of perfume. As his eyes adjusted to the gloom, he could make out a flight of stairs ahead of him, and a corridor leading into darkness to its side.

'Hello?' he called out, silently cursing himself for a

fool. There could be nothing for him here; at least he hadn't boasted to anyone else about this errand, but he coloured as he realised that his contact in LA might have tricked him, lured him here, taking one of his most prized possessions into the bargain, and that his humiliation would soon be all over the internet, making him a laughing stock in the community he prized so highly. He turned, his cheeks burning, and was about to step out of the house again when he heard a reply.

'Hello?' It was the voice he'd spoken to, low and warmer in the flesh. He stopped. He hadn't expected a reply. 'Is that Steven?'

His heart pounded violently in his chest, and he had to pause before replying, croakily, 'Yes.'

The voice lilted down the stairs to him. 'Come upstairs; I'm on the first floor.'

Where he'd reddened with anger just moments before, he knew he was pale now, and felt sick. Still, this was what he'd come for and, as he stepped towards the stairs, his shoes crunching on the sand feathered over the wooden floor, some of his former excitement returned.

He climbed the steps slowly, mechanically feeling the camera in his shoulder bag and looking down to see his shoes leaving prints in the dust lying thickly on the stairs. Nobody had come this way for a while, that much was clear. Perhaps there was another exit? No, it was more likely that she was convalescing from a long illness. She was old, she might not be mobile; perhaps she had a helper, someone who came to do her shopping for her, someone who kept her company, told her stories.

His heart in his mouth, he stood before the door at the end of the stairs and knocked, his arm leaden.

'Come on in, it's open,' called out the voice.

Steve pushed the door open and stepped inside. Immediately his apprehension faded, as he found himself in a treasure trove of cheesecake paraphernalia. The room was lit garishly by hoops of naked bulbs around several mirrors, and he stood in the entrance, blinking after emerging from the gloom. His eyes took in the framed photographs on the walls, almost all of Lisette herself; the movie poster that took up the best part of one wall, for *Moon's Milk*, a burlesque film she'd starred in, her one Hollywood feature, which Steve knew back to front: he even had the same poster himself at home. And on a clothes rail running along the wall to his left he saw some of the outfits she'd worn in the photo shoots. He'd had no idea such things existed, and he moved forwards to touch them, amazed, when his fingers made contact with the leather, the satin, the silk, that they were in such good condition.

But even as he felt them, the history soaking up through his fingertips and leaving him light headed, he realised he'd already seen her, sitting in front of a mirror and make-up table at the far end of the room. And what he saw he refused to accept.

The figure with the long black hair, sitting in a chair before the mirror, dressed in a laced black corset, a basque and a short skirt, could not be Lisette. She was even wearing stockings and suspenders, for Christ's sake, that he could see glittering in the light over her crossed legs: in her seventies, and wearing stockings and suspenders, heels too. There was no way this woman was much over thirty. She was gazing at him through the mirror, but he couldn't look directly at her reflection, trying to tell himself that it was all a joke; he had been tricked. Then he looked into her eyes, and his defences melted. He'd have known that look anywhere: it *was* her, there was no mistaking it.

'Lisette?' His voice was faint.

She turned then, and stood. 'Hello, Steven.'

Everything about her was exactly the same: her

figure, her clothes, her hair. She even wore the same coquettish expression as he had above his desk: his favourite photograph of her. For a second he thought he might be dreaming, then he realised what had happened. It was her daughter – granddaughter, even. It was the only reasonable explanation.

'Are you – ' he began tentatively '– Lisette's daughter?'

She laughed, and took a step towards him. He, in turn, stepped back. 'It's me, Steven.'

'It can't be.' His voice faltered, then he continued, bolder. 'But you've done a damn fine job of it. I thought I was the leading authority on your mother – or is it your grandmother?' He eyed her quizzically, but she just returned his gaze, an amused expression on her face. 'But I suppose you had better access than me. Still, why haven't you shown yourself until now? You could make a fortune out there, looking like that. You're her spitting image.' A sudden rush of ideas occurred to him. 'I could be your agent.' And lover, he thought, mentally undressing her.

She smiled at him, and Steve recognised the expression of amused disdain adults use when humouring children; then she turned and sat back down in the chair in front of her dressing table, picked up a hairbrush and began to brush her hair.

'My glory days are over, Steven. Would you mind –?' She beckoned to him with the hairbrush, her eyes on his through the mirror, and it took him a second to work out what she wanted.

He stepped up behind her and took the hairbrush from her hand then began to run it through her locks, marvelling at her hair's glossy smoothness. She seemed flawless; no hairs came out when he pulled the hairbrush away. There was a tightness in his chest.

'You're so . . . beautiful,' he whispered.

She smiled, and half-turned in her seat to look up at him. 'That's what Irving and John used to say.' She turned back, to let him carry on.

All the nervous tension Steve had felt in anticipation of this meeting suddenly welled up at this reference to his heroes, and he stiffened in annoyance. So she was going to carry on with this charade, was she? Steve stopped brushing her hair and patted it down, his sudden flare of anger translating into an equally sudden resolve. If she was going to use him as part of her cute game, he could do the same. He'd come too far to leave empty handed.

'Irving and John, eh, Lisette? Why don't you model for me the way you did for them?'

She turned her head and startled him with a knowing wink. 'You don't waste any time, do you? But I love to model, you must know that by now. What did you say on the phone? You're my biggest fan?' She laughed again, and for some reason the sound made Steve shiver. 'So how do you want me?'

More baffled than ever by the rapid change in tone, and not a little flustered by her easy acquiescence, Steve ran the possibilities through his mind. If this was a set-up, a joke with him as the fall guy, he'd make damn sure he got as much as he could out of the situation: she had winked at him, after all, with something undeniably lascivious in her expression. If it wasn't a set-up, and Lisette's daughter had taken on her mother's mantle, it was a situation that could make both of them rich, with new photosets, magazine appearances, guest spots at fetish parties ... Steve's confidence grew as he realised that, whatever happened, he was sure to leave here a happy man.

He backed away, retrieved his camera from his shoulder bag and asked her to turn her chair around.

She did so and instantly struck a pose, crossing her legs, squeezing her shoulders together to enhance her cleavage as she swung to one side and pouted over one shoulder at him.

'Good, very good,' he murmured.

The banks of wall lights meant he could see everything; even as he froze each moment, he knew these pictures would turn out beautifully. She threw herself into pose after pose, effortlessly repeating sequences he knew by heart but always giving them an extra twist, something new not only for the camera but for him too, he was sure, flashing glimpses of the inviting shadows between her thighs, the satin of her knickers occasionally catching the light, or licking her lips suggestively as she ran her fingers along her thighs or over her basque.

'Lisette –' he began, his voice hoarse as he dropped the camera and tried surreptitiously to adjust his crotch, increasingly excited by her poses.

She giggled, and he doubted the movement had escaped her. 'I know what you're going to ask me, Steven. You boys always come to this around now.'

What boys? 'What's that?'

'You want to tie me up, don't you?'

Steve, taken by surprise, coughed non-committally.

'It's OK,' she said, grinning. 'It wouldn't be a proper photo shoot without some bondage, would it? There's some rope over there.' She waved to a battered-looking leather trunk under one of the racks of clothes.

Steve walked over, slightly uncomfortably, and bent down to open the trunk. He wasn't quite able to suppress a gasp of shock as he opened it. There were coils of rope there, as she'd said, of varying lengths and thicknesses; but there were other things too, whips and masks, clamps and knives, and tangles of straps at whose use he couldn't even guess, and beneath them all the grotesquely modelled veins of a number of oversized rubber cocks.

After gingerly removing a bundle of white ropes, he closed the trunk lid and advanced towards Lisette, his heart racing and his mouth dry. She by contrast looked relaxed, amused by his evident shock, and he felt another wave of discomfort that she – on the verge of being tied up, no less – managed to maintain the upper hand.

'See anything you like?' she asked in a teasing tone.

'We could try some of it out later,' he replied, bravado masking his uncertainty.

She laughed, and drew her wrists together behind the chair. 'I'm ready when you are.'

He looped a length of rope tightly around her wrists by way of reply, then passed the two ends through the back of the chair. Lisette shifted to one side, smiling curiously at him, as he pulled the ropes up between her legs and bunched her skirt tightly around her thighs.

'Aaah,' she called out in a discomfort Steven was tempted to ignore until her next request. 'Pull the skirt up, I don't want it tight there.'

Steven paused and gazed into her eyes. The mocking tone had gone now, he was pleased to see, replaced by a heavy-lidded excitement. He nodded, and pulled at the back of the skirt so that it rode up, exposing first the tops of her stockings and the soft white skin of her thighs, then her black satin knickers, a darker patch of dampness showing towards the middle. Taking her at her word, he pulled on the ropes until they bit into the knickers, squeezing the pouch of her sex then, as she squirmed and gasped, slipping into the crease, pulling the satin fabric with them and exposing lines of tight black curls to either side.

Spurred by the exposure, he worked quickly, drawing the ropes up over her torso and criss-crossing them across her chest so that her breasts, their curve already enhanced by the basque, were bunched between the shiny white lines. He completed the cross around the back of her neck, then stepped back to survey the job. He'd expected outrage, or some kind of struggle, from her, and she did tug on the ropes, lifting her head and hands back, but only, it seemed, to tighten the ropes cutting into her crotch.

'Now that you've got me all tied up, what are you going to do to me?' she asked.

Steve stared at her again, scarcely able to believe her response to his actions, and still half-convinced that cameras were following his every move. Fuck it, if he was being filmed, he'd give them a show to remember.

'I'm going to make you suck my cock,' he said hoarsely.

Surely the game was up now; surely this girl would ask him to stop, and whoever was in on this with her would emerge from the shadows, hands raised to ward him off.

But nobody came. There was just him and her, and as he gazed into her eyes she licked her lips in provocative response to his suggestion. He needed no further encouragement, and advanced until the crotch of his jeans was level with her face. Far from struggling or begging to be freed, the girl was scissoring her legs back and forth, working the tight rope into the crease of her panties, as she gazed at the bulge between Steve's legs. The unmistakable aroma of female arousal wafted up to him.

Bunching up her luxuriant hair in one hand, he unzipped himself with the other, letting his cock spring out into her face. 'All right, you've asked for this, whoever you are.' But the menace in his tone was undone by the sight of her craning her head forwards, evidently desperate for the taste of his cock in her mouth.

Holding her in place with the hand in her hair, he smeared the angry purple bulb of his cockhead over her face, smudging her lipstick and leaving thin trails of spittle from where she'd already managed to lick the shaft. As she enveloped the head with her thick lips, making little squeals of excitement that tightened his balls, her eyes gazing up into his, he was struck by the sudden conviction that this *was* Lisette, the object of his obsession, sprung as though fully formed from the darkest recesses of his mind. His rational mind told him it was impossible, but as his cock sank into the warm mouth and she began to suck, hollowing her cheeks and running her tongue over the shaft, the rest of him knew this was no fake.

Giving a strangled cry, he wrenched at her basque, tearing the joins and letting the soft white flesh of her breasts spill out, the pink nipples already hard. As he shoved her head up and down on his cock with one hand, he tugged and clawed at her nipples with the other, leaving angry red marks that died slowly on the tender skin, then leant forwards to bite into the giving mounds, all control gone now, as she purred then gasped at his sudden frenzy of passion.

Her legs were moving faster now, pressed tightly together as she squirmed on the seat, pulling the rope deep into her crease. He locked eyes with her as he thrust his cock into her mouth, slowing now to allow her to play her tongue over his engorged glans, slide it over the shaft then hollow her cheeks and shake her head back and forth, clearly relishing the taste.

He pulled away and pushed his balls towards her, and she gave a little mew of excitement before licking enthusiastically at the tight sac. Encouraged by his deep groan as he rubbed the shaft over her cheeks, she sucked at his balls, trying to fit as much of them as possible into her mouth, tonguing them hard and fast, until her legs locked, her body shook, a tremor that seemed to begin in her feet and rise like a wave all the way to her head, and she gazed deep into Steve's eyes, her mouth momentarily free and gasping as she rocked against her bonds.

The sight tipped Steve over the edge, and he clenched the fingers of one hand hard around her hair while moving the other to caress her neck as she still shuddered from her orgasm, the realisation of his fantasy complete as he stuffed his cock all the way into her mouth, her lips flared around its base, feeling her throat contract under his fingers as she gagged and milked the spunk from his heavy balls, his back arching as he emptied his life into her.

Drained, he released her and stumbled back. Unsteady on his feet, he giggled as an ankle gave under him, barely able to keep his balance. The room went dark and still. As he crumpled to his knees, his vision slowly fading, the figure on the chair before him raised her arms impossibly high behind her head, the grotesque movement matched by a horrible creaking, then lowered them forwards and on to her lap, a sly smile on her spunk-smeared lips.

'My biggest fan, Steve? That's what the others said too. Don't worry, you'll have time to work it out among yourselves. All the time in the world.'

The deep, throaty laugh that followed was the last thing Steve heard before the darkness swallowed him up.

The sun had gone down by the time Steve awoke. He didn't know where he was at first, only that his head was splitting. His first thought was that he must have missed the last bus back to Bristol; then he wondered where Lisette was; and then he realised he wasn't in her room. Not the room he'd been in previously, anyway. A waning moon shining through a cracked cobwebbed window was enough to show him that. No, he seemed to be sitting in some kind of storeroom now, and as his eyes adjusted to the gloom he could see what looked like chairs, facing him and extending in rows to either side.

'Lisette?' he called out, but the sound was a mere croak. Water, he thought blindly. I must have water. He willed his body to stand, and tottered up, impossibly weak, but his legs gave way beneath him, and as his momentum carried him forwards he reached out in front of him, his mouth open in a silent scream.

As his hands fell on the dry thing in the chair opposite, he heard it make a sound, the dry moan of autumn leaves rustling in the wind, and this time as he flinched back his legs held, enough for him to stumble back into the shaft of moonlight and look at the stringy cobwebs hanging from his hands from where he'd fallen, and the dessicated wrinkled parchment that had been his skin wrapped over the brittle dry bone that had been his arm.

WICKED WORDS ANTHOLOGIES –

THE BEST IN WOMEN'S EROTIC WRITING FROM THE UK AND USA

Really do live up to their title of 'wicked' – Forum

Deliciously sexy and explicitly erotic, *Wicked Words* collections are guaranteed to excite. This immensely popular series is perfect for those who enjoy lust-filled, wildly indulgent sexy stories. The series is a showcase of writing by women at the cutting edge of the genre, pushing the boundaries of unashamed, explicit writing.

The first ten *Wicked Words* collections are now available in eye-catching illustrative covers and, since 2005, we have been publishing themed collections beginning with *Sex in the Office*. If you never got the chance to buy all the books when they were first published, you can now complete your collection and be the envy of your friends! Look out for the colourful covers – guaranteed to stand out from everything else on the erotica shelves – or alternatively order from us direct on our website at www.black-lace-books.com

Full of action and attitude, humour and hedonism, they are a wonderful contribution to any erotic book collection. Each book contains 15–20 stories. Here's a sampler of what's on offer:

More Wicked Words

ISBN 978 0 352 33487 9
£6.99

- Tasha's in lust with a celebrity chef – it's his temper that drives her wild.
- Reverend Billy Washburn needs salvation from Sister Julie – a teenage temptress who's set him on fire.
- Pearl doesn't want to get married; she just wants sex and blueberry smoothies on her LA poolside patio.

Wicked Words 3

ISBN 978 0 352 33522 7
£6.99

- The seductive dentist – Nick's encounter with sexy Dr May turns into a pretty unorthodox check-up.
- The gender-playing journalist – Kat lusts after male strangers whilst cruising as a gay man.
- The submissive PA – Mandy's new job fulfils her fantasies and reveals her boss's fetish for all things leather.

Wicked Words 4

ISBN 978 0 352 33603 3
£6.99

- Alexia has always fantasised about being Marilyn Monroe. One day a surprise package arrives with a sexy courier.
- Bridget is tired of being a chef. Maybe a little experimentation with a colleague is all she needs to get back her love of food.
- A mysterious woman prowls the back streets of New York, seeking pleasure from the sleaziest corners of the city.

Wicked Words 5

ISBN 978 0 352 33642 2
£6.99

- Connor the tax auditor gets a shocking surprise when he investigates a client's expenses claim for strap-on sex toys.
- Kate the sexy museum curator allows a buff young graduate to make a thorough excavation of her hidden treasures.
- Melanie the interior designer and porn fan swaps blokes with her best mate and gets up to nasty fun with the builders.

Wicked Words 6

ISBN 978 0 352 33690 3
£6.99

- Maxine gets turned on selling exquisite lingerie to gentlemen customers.
- Jules is stripped naked and covered in cream when she becomes the birthday cake for her brother's best mate's thirtieth.
- Elle wears handcuffs for an indecent liaison with a stranger in a motel room.

Wicked Words 7

ISBN 978 0 352 33743 6
£6.99

- An artist's model wants to be more than just painted, and things get pretty steamy in the studio.
- A bride-to-be pays a clandestine visit to the bathroom with her future father-in-law, and gets much more than she bargained for.
- An uptight MP has his mind (and something else!) blown by a charming young woman of devious intentions.

Wicked Words 8

ISBN 978 0 352 33787 0
£6.99

- Adam the young supermarket assistant cannot believe his luck when a saucy female customer needs his help.
- Lauren's first night at a fetish club brings out the sexy show-off in her when she is required to wear an outrageously daring rubber outfit.
- Cat's fantasies about hunky construction workers come true when they start work opposite her Santa Monica beach house.

Wicked Words 9

ISBN 978 0 352 33860 0

- Sarah gets a surprise when she and her husband go dogging in the local car park.
- The Wytchfinder interrogates a pagan wild woman and finds himself aroused to bursting point.
- Miss Charmond's charm school relies on old-fashioned discipline to keep wayward girls in line.

Wicked Words 10 – The Best of Wicked Words

ISBN 978 0 352 33893 8

- An editor's choice of the best, most original stories of the past five years.

Sex in the Office

ISBN 978 0 352 33944 7

- A lady boss with a foot fetish
- A security guard who's a CCTV voyeur
- An office cleaner with a crush on the MD

Explores the forbidden – and sometimes blatant – lusts that abound in the workplace where characters get up to something they shouldn't, with someone they shouldn't – someone who works in the office.

Sex on Holiday

ISBN 978 0 352 33961 4

- Spanking in Prague
- Domination in Switzerland
- Sexy salsa in Cuba

Holidays always bring a certain frisson. There's a naughty holiday fling to suit every taste in this X-rated collection. With a rich sensuality and an eye on the exotic, this makes the perfect beach read!

Sex at the Sports Club

ISBN 978 0 352 33991 8

- A young cricketer is seduced by his mate's mum
- A couple swap partners on the golf course
- An athletic female polo player sorts out the opposition

Everyone loves a good sport – especially if he has fantastic thighs and a great bod! Whether in the showers after a rugby match, or proving his all at the tennis court, there's something about a man working his body to the limit that really gets a girl going. In this latest themed collection we explore the sexual tensions that go on at various sports clubs.

Sex in Uniform

ISBN 978 0 352 34002 3

- A tourist meets a mysterious usherette in a Parisian cinema
- A nun seduces an unusual confirmation from a priest
- A chauffeur sees it all via the rear-view mirror

Once again, our writers new and old have risen to the challenge and produced so many steamy and memorable stories for fans of men and women in uniform. Polished buttons and peaked caps will never look the same again.

Sex in the Kitchen

ISBN 978 0 352 34018 4

- Dusty's got a sweet tooth and the pastry chef is making her mouth water
- Honey's crazy enough about Jamie to be prepared and served as his main course
- Milly is a wine buyer who gets a big surprise in a French cellar

Whether it's a fiery chef cooking up a storm in a Michelin-starred restaurant or the minimal calm of sushi for two, there's nothing like the promise of fine feasting to get in the mood for love. From lavish banquets to a packed lunch at a motorway service station, this Wicked Words collection guarantees to serve up a good portion!

Sex on the Move

ISBN 978 0 352 34034 4

- Nadia Kasparova sees the earth move from a space station while investigating sex at zero gravity
- Candy likes leather pants, big powerful bikes, miles of open road and the men who ride them
- Penny and Clair run a limousine business guaranteed to STRETCH the expectations of anyone lucky enough to sit in the back

Being on the move can be an escape from convention, the eyes of those we know, and from ourselves. There are few experiences as liberating as travelling. So whether it's planes, trains and automobiles, ships or even a space station, you can count on the Wicked Words authors to capture the exhilaration, freedom and passion of modern women on the move. Original tales of lust and abandon guaranteed to surprise and thrill!

Sex and Music

ISBN 978 0 352 34061 0

- Tess sings in key with the pianist-masseur who can play such beautiful music, up and down her body
- Alison will go to any length to be taught violin with a maestro, and the discipline is all part of the pleasure
- Chrissy's a fast disco girl who wants to try it slow and easy with the blues

From the primal sexual scream of heavy metal to the delicate brush of a maestro's fingers on the pale neck of his pupil, the latest themed collection from Wicked Words plays on ten and delivers at full volume. Whether it's in the front row of a stadium, or during intimate lessons in a private study, the passion is as much about the performance as the performer. And you can trust Black Lace's authors to produce the most thrilling scenarios and kinks to expose this electric connection between sex and music.

Sex and Shopping

ISBN 978 0 352 34076 4

- Francesca exchanges the man in her life after an encounter in the men's changing rooms
- Juliet gets a ladder in her stockings, but meeting the mysterious stranger who replaces them hits a few snags
- Adele creates an internet shopping experience with a twist: her new online business launches with only one item for sale: herself

Who says shopping is a sex-substitute? Wicked Words discovers it's just about the best time to make all kinds of deals and special purchases. Transactions of the sensual variety that keep the tills and senses ringing long after the stores have closed. Whether you're shopping for shoes, jeans, a corset, or the guy that delivers it to your door, *Sex and Shopping* is a must-have item.

Sex in Public

ISBN 978 0 352 34089 4

Sex in the great outdoors – there's nothing quite like it! Whether taking a few leisurely hours in the countryside or a frantic five minutes on a city street, *Sex in Public* explores the height of female misbehaviour in public. Impetuous passion, frenzied intensity, reckless daring, unlikely settings, the thrill of almost getting caught to the thrill of deliberately getting caught, this is edge-of-the-seat reading. There are no end to the varieties, the locations, the positions and the limits of *Sex in Public*!

Black Lace has never been naughtier. Our short stories are kinkier and more daring than ever before; this new collection of fantasy fiction will make you blush, flush, squirm and dream.

Sex with Strangers

ISBN 978 0 352 34105 1

One of the most popular, darkest, dangerous and edgy fantasies around, and it never goes out of fashion: sex with the stranger. So is it the thrill of instant gratification? Or being absolved of all that comes with familiarity? Or is it the ecstasy of pure abandon? The mystery of the unknown? Or the novelty of something new? Let's find out, because the writers in this collection have gone deep and wide to capture the suspense, the anticipation, the drama and the adventure that comes with sex and the stranger.